Born of Deception

Born of

DECEPTION

TERI BROWN

Balzer + Bray
An Imprint of HarperCollins*Publishers*

Balzer + Bray is an imprint of HarperCollins Publishers.

Born of Deception

 For information address HarperCollins Children's Books, a division of HarperCollins Publishers,

10 East 53rd Street, New York, NY 10022.

www.epicreads.com

Library of Congress Cataloging-in-Publication Data

Brown, Teri J.

Born of deception / Teri Brown. — First edition.

pages cm

Sequel to: Born of illusion.

Summary: Moving to London in the 1920s to join a prestigious European vaudeville tour and reunite with her boyfriend, Cole, budding illusionist Anna must harness her special powers and navigate the underworld of magic before her murderous enemies catch up with her.

ISBN 978-0-06-218757-4 (hardback)

[1. Psychic ability—Fiction. 2. Magicians—Fiction. 3. Secret societies—Fiction. 4. Love—Fiction. 5. Europe—History—1918–1945—Fiction.] I. Title.

PZ7.B81797Bm 2014 2013047770

[Fic]—dc23 CIP

AC

Typography by Ray Shappell

14 15 16 17 18 LP/RRDH 10 9 8 7 6 5 4 3 2 1

First Edition

As always, this book is for my husband, Alan L. Brown. After twenty-five years, you're still the one.

ONE

A circle of children surround me, their bright faces turned upward, as if eagerly awaiting the cascading lights of a fireworks show. They're not, of course. The stuffy, proper salon of the *Rex* would never allow something as gaudy as fireworks to invade its gilded interior. The impromptu magic show I'm performing is probably as garish a display as the ship has ever seen.

"What's up your sleeve today, miss?" The little boy's British accent reminds me of Cole, and I smile.

I'd been heading to the upper deck to catch my first glimpse of England when I was waylaid by a mob of beribboned, curly-headed girls and freckle-faced little boys in short pants. It had begun the first day aboard ship, when I'd shown a sobbing child a simple magic trick to help her harried mother. From that moment on, I'd been like the Pied Piper of Hamelin, followed by children wherever I went. They seemed to communicate by some unseen network of signals because they would appear out of nowhere, demanding tricks. I didn't mind. Performing simple tricks for children is a joy.

The parents adore me only marginally less than their children for keeping their tots so occupied.

"Do another!" demands a little dumpling of a girl, as imperious as Marie Antoinette.

I hesitate, wanting nothing more than to reach the deck of the ship so I can look out toward the land where Cole will be waiting. Racking my brain for something that will appease them, I feel around in the pocket of my winter coat until I locate a rubber hair band. I widen my eyes at them theatrically. "Would you like to see a hair band jump?"

The children clamor their assent and I kneel to their level while their parents look on indulgently.

"Watch carefully," I instruct.

I slide the band around the base of my pinky and ring fingers. With my other hand, I insert the tips of my pinky, ring, index, and middle fingers into it as well, until all four fingers on the first hand are resting inside . . . from the children's vantage point it looks exactly the same. When I straighten my fingers, the band appears to jump from the last two fingers to the first two.

They clap, delighted, and my heart warms as I perform the trick several more times. I show them how it's done and bid them to go practice so they can amaze their friends back home. The children disperse as they run to their parents, begging for hair bands, and I slip away, pleased by the success of my diversionary tactics.

Once on deck, a shiver runs through me, as much from anticipation as from the cold. For the last six days, I've been stuck aboard this aging though still beautiful ocean liner, battling an onslaught of emotions as bright and varied as circus juggling pins. The steady rumble and throb of the ship's steam engines is louder on deck and the sound of the crew working behind me adds to my exhilaration.

The RMS *Rex* had once been considered equaled in beauty only by the *Titanic*, whose sinking I'd foreseen in a vision, days before it actually happened . . . not a memory that makes for particularly restful nights aboard ship. And exhaustion hasn't helped the nerves that have plagued me for the past week.

Brimming with exhilaration and anxiety, I bounce from foot to foot as I spot the bleak British shoreline. It's been two months since Cole and I have seen one another. Two months since I've felt the physical connection that draws us to each other whenever we're in close proximity.

And two months since I'd felt the telepathic link that we have together as fellow psychics, or Sensitives, as he calls us.

We'd exchanged letters, of course, sometimes two a week, and I imagined them passing one another, quite literally, as two ships that pass in the night. But it's hard to keep a strong bond that way and at times it felt as if our connection had grown as thin as the paper we wrote on. Cole has a difficult enough time expressing his feelings in person, let alone writing them down. There were times his rather stilted language made me feel as if I were his favorite sister instead of the girl he loved and had kissed breathless on more than one occasion. I need to look into his dark eyes and fall into their velvety warmth. I need to feel the psychic link that makes Cole different from anyone else.

The cold January wind gusts off the ocean and I'm coated with a fine spray of icy salt water. Only a few passengers have braved the frigid weather to look for the the entrance to the River Thames. Maybe like me, they're novices at luxurious ocean travel and don't want to miss a single experience. This isn't my first crossing, but considering the fact that the last time I was traveling in my mother's womb, everything is new to me.

I draw a deep breath of the frigid, salty air into my lungs, shoring up my resolve. Cole isn't the only thing waiting for me in England. I'm starting a whole new life, one away from my mother and her husband, Jacques. A life where I'll be performing my magic onstage in some of the most famous theaters in Europe. I pray that my new boss, Louie Larkin, a man famous for having a nose for talent, will like me.

A young man joins me at the rail. I give him a curious glance, my attention caught by the trilby hat set at a jaunty angle on his head. He turns and my breath catches. I'm only a few feet away from the most handsome man I have ever seen. He looks to be in his early twenties, with eyes so blue they could make the sky jealous. The slow smile he bestows on me lights up his face.

"It's quite a sight, isn't it?" he says in a western drawl as leisurely as his smile.

My mouth shuts with a snap and I nod, unable to speak. Then I nearly jump out of my skin as the ship's horn blows a one-hour warning until landing. His eyes crinkle with amusement. "Excuse me," I mumble, and flee, the iciness of my cheeks melting from the heat of humiliation.

When will I stop being so awkward around handsome young men? I wonder as I hurry to my cabin. My first meeting with Cole had been equally uncomfortable, only worse because I had never encountered another Sensitive before. The invisible charge that occurred when we shook hands was alarming, to say the least. Of course, as someone who'd mostly been raised on vaudeville circuits, boys as handsome as Cole and the stranger on deck are a rarity for me. Growing up, most of the men I knew well were considered circus freaks or oddities by normal folks. No wonder I'm so clumsy.

I finish packing my things and the porters soon come by to take my luggage. I fret as they wheel away the gleaming wooden trunk with the curved top that nearly reaches my waist. It's the one I keep my magic props in and a million times more important than the one containing my clothes. I'm sure I could find decent props in London, but it would take too much time and I already have much to do before formal rehearsals start. Deep in the ship's belly, the levitation table and the iron maiden that Mr. Darby, my dear old neighbor, had made just for me will be taken directly to the theater.

I pull my cloche further down on my head and wrap a scarf around my neck. I hate meeting Cole looking like an Eskimo, but better an Eskimo than an ice block. I gather up my beaded handbag and a small satchel, and then, taking a deep breath, follow the rest of the passengers to the lower deck where we'll be disembarking.

I tiptoe and squint, trying to spot Cole in the crowd of wildly waving people below the ship, but all I can see are a sea of black bowlers dotted by the occasional bright cloche. Even though I don't see him, my heart speeds up, knowing he's there. I had paid extra attention to my appearance that morning, using more than my usual amount of face powder, rouge, and kohl. I bite my lip and wonder if he will greet me with a kiss or if he'll retreat into reserved shyness as he often does when his emotions get the better of him.

My breath hitches. *I hope he kisses me.*

It takes the better part of an hour for the sailors to finish mooring the *Rex*, and my toes and cheeks are numb by the time they're done. Seasoned travelers, having waited for this moment in the warmth of the salon, join us as we make our long, slow way toward the gangway.

I finally step down onto solid ground and the world tilts just a bit. A sailor reaches out to catch my arm. "Easy now," he says.

I smile absently, my eyes scanning the crowds waiting to receive us. Wisps of fog settle in, obscuring my view, and I follow the rest of the throng, hoping Cole will be able to find me. London is overwhelming in a way New York never was, and I'm not sure why. It's not as if they don't speak English, and yet all around me I hear a hodgepodge of languages, of which English is only one. Cranes tower overhead, waiting to unload the ship's cargo, and the scent of tar, salt, and fish is heavy in the air. I stop, unsure of which way to go. Suddenly someone is by my side.

"If you're looking for your party, miss, they may be waiting for you near the entrance of the quay."

I turn and find myself staring into the blue, blue eyes of the young man I so stupidly ran from earlier. I clear my throat. "I'm not sure where that is," I say, hoping to redeem myself and show him that I'm not entirely ridiculous. "This is my first time in London."

He gives me another slow smile. "Mine, too. I asked someone where to get a taxicab and he told me how to get to the street. It's right this way." He points with his head, as both of his hands are holding cases.

He navigates the crowd as I fall in behind him. It strikes me that I probably shouldn't be following a total stranger in such a foreign place, but there's something about his open face that invites trust. I'm just about to see if I can feel his emotions, one of my psychic abilities, when I hear my name.

"Anna!"

I stop and my savior is swallowed up instantly in the crowd, but I forget that as I am suddenly enveloped in a warm hug that thrills me to the tips of my toes. *Cole!*

He holds me close for a moment and so many impressions flood my senses I can barely stand upright: the scratchiness of his wool overcoat against my cheek, the sound of my own heart beating in my ears, the warmth and depth of his love, and the excitement of his emotions as our unique psychic link is made. For years I thought I was alone in my abilities and at times I thought they would drive me mad. Then I met Cole and something fundamental inside me shifted.

I was no longer alone.

Now he's here. His head is bent close to mine and I lift my face to stare into his dark, licorice-colored eyes. They glow at me with that special light they sometimes get, and I tilt my head back, sure he's going to kiss me. Instead, he pulls back to look at me. My heart dips in disappointment even though I know he has never liked being overtly affectionate in public.

"I thought I would never find you in this crowd," he says.

I remember the man who had tried to help me and look around to thank him, but he's nowhere to be found. Then I have eyes for no one but Cole. I had forgotten how tall he is and how the intelligent planes of his face give him the look of a distinguished professor to match his accent.

"London is so big!"

"No bigger than New York," he teases, and my happiness bubbles over like a glass of New Year's Eve champagne. Cole turns to a young Indian man who stepped up next to him. The man is dressed in a suit and overcoat like Cole, but instead of sporting a bowler, there's a white turban clipped together in the front with a gold pin. I look from him to Cole, confused.

"Anna, I would like you to meet Pratik Dahrma, a friend of mine. Pratik, this is my—" he hesitates only for a moment "—girl, Anna Van Housen. I've told you about her."

The young Indian man gives a shy smile, showing teeth as glistening white as the turban on his head. "You have mentioned her much more than a time or two, my friend." Pratik bows to me. "He has spoken of little else for the past week."

Red stains Cole's cheeks and warmth spreads over me. "It's nice to meet you." I hold my hand out, but Pratik just looks at it blankly before comprehension dawns and he awkwardly reaches out to shake it.

I feel it the moment our hands touch—that electric sensation I felt when I first met Cole. We both release our hands in a hurry, and I glance at Cole, my breath quickening. He nods, confirming what I already knew. Pratik is a Sensitive.

Pratik appears less than surprised, so obviously he knows about me. I'm not sure how I feel about Cole telling a total stranger a secret I've guarded so protectively my entire life. It feels just as odd as him bringing someone else to our reunion. What was he thinking?

He must sense my disappointment because he takes my satchel and tucks his arm into mine. "Pratik and I had a meeting this morning. He still gets lost in the city, so I told him I would drop him off at his flat. I did clarify that we needed to come here first. Nothing could make me late to meet you."

I perceive the apology in his voice and in the connection

running between us. In my head, I always envision it as a silver cord joining us and transmitting our emotions. Cole's abilities are different from mine—his are limited to detecting the presence of other Sensitives and making their abilities stronger. But those differences don't seem to affect our ability to communicate on a deeper level than just words. It's one of the reasons why our relationship is so infinitely precious to me. I give him a reassuring nod. "Of course, I'm eager to meet your friends."

We begin walking away from the ship and I look across him at Pratik. "Are you new to London, too, Mr. Dahrma?"

"Please call me Pratik," he says. "And, yes. I have only been here in the city for a short time. Mr. Gamel found me in Bombay."

He says it like I should know who Mr. Gamel is. I look at Cole, perplexed.

"She doesn't know anyone in the Society yet," he tells Pratik.

Pratik tilts his head in apology. "I am sorry. Cole has spoken of you so often, I forget that there is much you do not know. You will like Mr. Gamel. He is a strange man but a good one."

"Mr. Gamel is the new board president," Cole says, his voice suddenly tight. "Pratik has a far more charitable view of him than I do."

"You would too, if he saved you as he saved me," Pratik says simply.

I wonder what he means as we hurry off to claim my

trunks. By the time we pack everything up, the moment to ask Pratik about it has passed and before long we're riding in Cole's luxurious motorcar. Being pressed so close to Cole's side leaves me breathless with that buttery warmth his nearness always generates. It seems odd to be feeling this way with a complete stranger by my side, and an uncomfortable silence falls over us.

"I think you will like the Society, Anna," Pratik says. "Everyone has been good to me."

For the first time, I notice hesitation in his manner and I get a strong sense of vulnerability emanating from him. This is a young man who has been deeply hurt by someone or something. As someone who is also distrustful of strangers, that feeling puts me at ease.

"I hope so. I'm a little nervous, actually," I tell him.

"It is always good to be cautious. Even now that I have been a member for several months, I am still wary. But then that is my nature. It is your nature too, isn't it?"

Though his words are a question, the look in his eyes is certain, and I wonder suddenly exactly what his abilities are. For all I know, he could be reading my mind as we speak.

I lower my eyes for a moment and then nod. I get the feeling that this man values honesty and transparency above all else. "My mother and I were involved in activities that were less than legitimate. Caution was always valued."

He nods. "I grew up on the streets of Bombay. My parents left me at the door of an orphanage when I was three. I hated it there and ran away. It was so overcrowded no one bothered to look. I stole for my supper, so being mistrustful was a way of life."

He relates these facts in the calmest voice imaginable, and my heart goes out to him. "You seem very forthright now," I tell him.

He gives me a slight smile. "Because I know you are someone I can trust," he says simply. "Mr. Gamel is teaching me how to control my abilities."

We pull up and park in front of a brick building before I can ask him what those abilities are.

Pratik opens the door to the motorcar and climbs out.

"It was very nice to meet you, Anna. I will see you at the Society." He bows his head and, after a little wave, disappears into the building.

"He seems very sad," I murmur, watching him go.

"He is, but he's getting better. Mr. Gamel found him in an asylum in Bombay. Can you imagine having your abilities and being completely alone?"

I turn back to Cole, whose dark eyes are pensive. My mother couldn't nurture a houseplant, but at least she didn't abandon me at an orphanage. "What are his abilities?"

Cole shakes his head. "It's hard to explain. He can see the essence or spirit of different people. That's about as close as I can come to understanding it. But not everyone's and not all the time. He says they're like colored smoke or fog around people's heads. The different colors of smoke mean different things."

I frown. "And I thought my abilities were odd."

Cole laughs. "Enough about Pratik. Come here." His arm snakes around me and pulls me close. "I have been waiting for this since the moment I saw you," he whispers. Then his mouth comes down on mine and I can hardly think or breathe because my heart is so very full of Cole. As the kiss deepens and my lips part, our psychic connection is so open and clear, it's as if we are sharing the same soul. It's like melting into ribbons of chocolate—decadent, lovely, and infinitely sweet. He breaks away and chuckles. "I cannot believe how much I missed you."

I sit back and smile as he pulls away from the curb. I forgive him for bringing someone to our reunion and for not kissing me the moment he saw me. And as I remember how very far I've come from cheating people out of money at my mother's command and worrying about where our next meal was going to come from, I feel as if I'm about to burst. I'm in London with Cole and will soon be performing my magic onstage.

It is an absolutely perfect moment.

And the perfect moments continue. After settling me in the shabby hotel that will be my home while in the city, Cole and I spend the rest of the afternoon driving around London so I can get acclimated. I gape out my window as we pass iconic sights such as Buckingham Palace, Westminster Abbey, and Big Ben.

"Aren't we going to stop anywhere?" I ask, my nose pressed to the glass.

"Too many tourists," Cole sniffs.

I slap him playfully on the arm. "I am a tourist!"

"Another time. I want to show you something special." He grins at me.

The streets are packed with both people and motorcars, and it's odd to see Cole driving so confidently through the chaos. Though he's always been self-assured, there had been something tentative about the way he approached New York and you never forgot he was living in a foreign city. Here in London, a city that feels so alien to me, he's more comfortable than I've ever seen him. He's at home and I'm the stranger.

The thought unsettles me and I fall silent until Cole parks on a small cobbled street that seems as remote from big city London as a medieval village. "Where are we?" I ask as he opens my door.

"Wanstead. It's still in London, but on the River Roding. We're on Nightingale Lane, to be precise."

That tells me little, but I love the name. "Nightingale Lane," I murmur, relishing the sound. Would New York have a little street tucked away that looks as if it were straight out of Shakespeare? I wouldn't think so. The thin winter sun is lowering on the horizon, casting a chilly, enchanted air over the gables and leaded windows predominant in this ancient neighborhood. I follow Cole across uneven cobblestones into a building on the corner. A wooden sign hanging over the door reads *Mob's Hole* in fancy script.

I suck in a delighted breath as my eyes adjust to the dim interior. We're in a large and spacious pub with heavy wooden tables and low, dark timbers on the ceiling. An enormous stone fireplace in one corner looks as if it were made for large cast-iron pots of simmering stew, while I imagine the long bar against the opposite wall has seen thousands of pints slide across its age-polished top. The gleaming wood stairs to the left of the front door even have dips in the middle of each tread from the countless steps of countless weary travelers. The scents of age, grease, and burning wood lie as heavy in the room as the smoke curling off the pipes of the old men playing chess in the corner.

"It's not much," Cole says as we take a seat near the crackling fire, "but they have the best chips in London."

I detect the concern in his voice. "It's wonderful," I assure him.

He gives me a relieved smile. "I love this place. I was worried that maybe you would have rather gone to some fancy club to dance or something."

I shake my head. "This is perfect. I'd rather you showed me places that are important to you."

Cole looks down, tracing a knot on the table with his fingers. "It's been so long since I've seen you. I planned to bring you here, but when I saw you standing on the dock, looking so lovely and American modern, I started doubting myself."

Tenderness fills my heart. Why had I been so worried? Cole's reserve is how he masks his painful shyness around most women. Only with me does he let down his guard. I reach out and touch his fingers.

He looks up and his sudden smile softens the dignified

planes of his face. “I’m so happy you’re here,” he says softly before the waitress reaches our table.

He says it again before kissing me good night outside my hotel. I nod in assent, but as I make my way up to my room I realize that happy doesn’t even come close to describing how I feel.

Blissful. I feel blissful.

TWO

The next morning, I walk into the dilapidated theater that will be the troupe's home base for the next several months. It's small and, if the number of days it's available for rehearsal is any indication, only marginally successful, which makes it perfect for our needs. We can store our props here even when we're not using it.

The floors of the theater are its original wood and have long lost their luster. They squeak as I tiptoe down the aisle and sit on one of the stained brown seats. A dozen or so people are gathered in knots in front of the stage, no doubt introducing themselves, though if the level of camaraderie is any indication, many of them already know one another.

I feel awkward joining them—most of them are older and have more experience than I do. I'd received a list of participating acts when I signed my contract, and I study the people before me, wondering who is in which act. Some of them are easy. . . . I've seen pictures of Jeanne Hart, the redheaded songstress. She's our headliner and well regarded worldwide. I guess that the three men with similar features are the Woodruff brothers, who are both classical musicians and blackface performers. I'm not sure who the rest are, but I know I'll have them sorted out before too long. We'll be spending a lot of time together the next couple of months. I'm so engrossed in watching the others that I don't notice that someone is next to me until he sits down. I startle and look up into the familiar deep cerulean blue of the most amazing eyes I have ever seen. It's the man from the ship.

I look around, wildly wondering if he followed me and if someone would help if he were to accost me.

He holds out his hand. "I thought you looked familiar when I saw you on the ship. I was going to say something but I didn't get a chance and then you were busy with your friends. My name is Bronco Billy. I do rope tricks."

I shake his hand uncertainly and blush, remembering my hasty retreat yesterday on deck. Then I frown. "You said I looked familiar? Have we met?"

He shook his head. "No, but I saw you and your mom perform once. Your levitation trick brought the house down."

He went to that show?

I'd only performed the trick once, the night I stole the show away from my mother. A shiver crawls up my back, remembering the horrible experience that occurred afterward.

What are the odds that he would have been to that show? "I'm glad you enjoyed it," I told him. I swallow and try to think of something to say. Bronco Billy is probably the handsomest man I have ever met and as much time as I spent out west, I've never seen a cowboy like him before. His hair is the color of sunshine, which makes the unearthly blue of his eyes even more intense. His nose is straight, his chin and jaw are strong and manly, and his lips are full. He speaks with a light drawl that, when combined with the open friendliness of his face, makes him seem even more trustworthy. I sense nothing from him but sociable curiosity.

His eyes crinkle up at the corners and I stare, my heart skipping wildly in my chest. I swallow. My heart shouldn't be behaving this way for anyone but Cole. Of course, any heart might be confused when faced with such male beauty.

"I did enjoy it," he says. "You were pretty as a picture and twice as talented."

"Talented as a picture?" I ask.

He laughs. "You know what I meant. How do you like London?"

My eyes narrow. "Hey! Where did your drawl go?"

He grins and his cheeks redden a bit. "I have a confession: I'm not really a cowboy. I only use the drawl during my act or when I'm nervous. I was actually raised in Philadelphia."

Part of me wants to ask why he was nervous about sitting next to me, but I'm more curious about how he developed a cowboy act in Philadelphia. "How did you become a cowboy?" I ask.

"Like I said, I was raised in the city, but I used to devour all those penny books about the West. All I wanted in the world was to be a cowboy. I was the only kid in school who carried a lariat everywhere he went. Of course, by the time I was old enough to run away west, the need for cowboys was drastically reduced. I worked on a couple of ranches, but the pay was poor, the living conditions abysmal, and the work was boring, so I used to do rope and gun tricks to entertain the other fellows."

I want to ask him more, but just then Louie, the show director, spots us and hurries over to where we're sitting. "Billy, can you help the Woodruffs move some props backstage?"

With a tip of his cowboy hat, Billy ambles off, his boots scuffing along the floor.

Louie resembles a penguin with his short, stubby body and his short, stubby hands tucked into his lapels. An unlit cigar is attached permanently to his lips and he chews on it constantly. I've met him several times in New York, but I've never seen him actually light it—I wonder if it's the same one or if he trades them out on occasion.

I stand, bracing myself, and he gives me an exuberant hug. Though I have a natural distrust of managers, it's hard not to respond to Louie Larkin's larger-than-life persona.

"How you doing, doll? You all right? You ready for the dummy runs?"

Louie speaks rapidly in a show-business lingo that would confuse a normal person. Luckily, with years of experience, I'm not a normal person and know he's asking if I'm ready for a series of rehearsals before we begin playing in front of an audience.

Before I can answer, he continues. "I'm moving you up on the bill, Anna Banana. How do you like them apples? We've had a cancellation on the tour. Mama Belinsky of the Belinsky family acrobatic ensemble is having another baby. Who'd have thought it?" He asks the question as if genuinely outraged and then continues without waiting for an answer. "I'm putting you third from the top with only the Woodruffs and Jeanne above you. I've only seen your act once, but I have a feeling you're gonna be a little moneymaker, a real show stealer." He looks up. "Russell! Hold up."

He pats my arm and leaves me blinking, having said his piece.

I'm being moved up on the bill already? I clasp my hands together tightly to keep from clapping and jumping up and down like a child. He must really think I have potential to move me up this quickly. He hasn't even seen me perform in front of a live audience!

I sit back down as everyone prepares for the meeting, marveling at my good fortune. After being raised on the road and never knowing if we were going to be flush or broke at any given moment or if my mother was going to be taken to jail for our fake séances, this kind of success is hard to relate to.

Performing magic has always been my salvation. No matter what's happening in my real life, the moment I step out onstage everything falls away except the connection between me and the audience. Even when I performed with my mother, I looked forward to the moment when I could entertain and awe the people watching me. There's nothing like it on earth. Now that I have my own act, I'll be able to stretch myself as a magician and performer, trying illusions my mother would never allow for fear of being upstaged.

Bronco Billy saunters back out from behind the curtain and resumes his seat next to me. Filled with happiness, I give him and everyone else a brilliant smile. He stares a moment and then smiles back.

The happiness stays with me all morning and by the time Cole comes to the hotel to collect me for our afternoon together, I'm downright giddy. The only fly in my ointment is our appointment to meet with the board members of the Society for Psychical Research for tea, but I've been firmly pushing that out of my mind all morning.

It's overcast but not raining, so we decide to walk. The tickling in my toes almost sends me tap-dancing across the cobbled streets and sidewalks, but Cole's steadying hand on my elbow keeps me to a ladylike pace, though my attempt at modesty is somewhat marred by the excited swivel of my head as we reach Shaftsbury Avenue and pass theater after theater.

If the troupe is a hit in other major European cities, I just might be performing my magic in one of these beautiful, ancient theaters. Theaters so old that they make anything we have to offer in the States look gauche.

Of course, the old theater we're currently practicing in

is a long way from Leicester Square and the Strand. Not so much in geography—we've only been walking for about twenty minutes—but in glitz and shine, it's like comparing the great Houdini to his lesser known brother, the just-all-right Hardeen.

Or would that be my just-all-right *uncle* Hardeen? I reflect for a moment on my complex relationship with Harry Houdini, who is either my father or my mentor and the man who gave me this incredible opportunity. My mother says he's my father, but I learned early to suspect every word that comes out of her exquisitely painted bow-shaped mouth. On the other hand, he's taken a greater than normal interest in my career and if my instincts are right, the great Houdini is as much of a psychic as I am, which means I may have gotten my Sensitivity from him.

Unable to contain myself, I skip a bit as I walk: The thrill of having an entire ocean between my mother and me is liberating. Of course, when Mother sails to France next month with Jacques, she'll only be a hop, skip, and a boat from me, but I have weeks before I have to worry about that.

Cole smiles down at my exuberance, his rich eyes filled with warmth. My heart joins my feet in its tap dance. Having Cole by my side is like cotton candy clouds of almost perfect happiness surrounding everything I do.

"I take it you're not nervous," he says.

"About what?" For a moment I'm confused, but then his words sink in like a dart, bursting my happy bubble. My psychic abilities, the same ones I've spent a lifetime hiding from my ambitious mother so she wouldn't turn me into a circus sideshow, the same ones that almost got my mother and me killed, are going be trotted out and examined by total strangers this afternoon. "Well, I wasn't until you brought it up."

My steps slow. *This is what I want*, I remind myself. Those members of the Society with psychical talents, other Sensitives like Cole and me, can help teach me how to control my abilities.

It's the other members—the scientists who study them—who worry me.

We stop altogether and I stare at our reflection in a shop window. I adjust the belt of my wraparound coat against the wind blowing off the Thames. The top of my cherry-red cloche barely comes up to Cole's shoulder and his bowler hat gives him even more inches over me. I stand on my tiptoes and he laughs.

"You shouldn't worry so much. No one is going to make you do anything you don't want to do. Not while I'm around." He slips an arm about my shoulders and I nestle closer, basking in the safety and warmth he gives me. As always, an almost electrical current flows between us, like a flexible silver line connecting us.

I smile back at him, trying to banish my worry. We're like a perfect, harmonic match.

"I want you to meet someone," Cole said suddenly, interrupting my thoughts. "I think she'll be able to alleviate your concern about the Society. Or at least give you the information you'll need to know."

She?

My mind flicks back to the letter with the curlicue handwriting I'd pickpocketed several months before. Not one of my finer moments, but even though it hadn't been a love letter, it had still been written by a female. The mysterious "L."

"Who?" My voice comes out more surly than I'd intended.

"Her name is Leandra. I've known her for ages. I think you'll like her."

Reluctantly, I follow along, feeling ill at ease and not at all sure I want to meet Leandra, who he's *known for ages.* We take the subway, or what Londoners call the tube, to Camden Town and walk about four blocks to a small brick house in a row of small brick houses. I've been silent most of the way here, and even though he must know I'm cross, he refuses to ask why. Or perhaps he simply hasn't noticed. My jealousy feels more and more childish as time passes.

"I hope she knows we're coming," I say, breaking the silence. I may not know a lot about British etiquette, but I do know that impromptu visits are frowned upon.

"Oh, she's probably been expecting us from the moment you arrived." Cole breezes through a small iron gate and up the steps. I follow halfheartedly. By the time I reach him he's already rung the bell.

A gray-haired woman takes our coats and ushers us down a narrow hallway. Then we make a quick right into a sun-soaked sitting room. I blink at the girl sitting on the couch.

Her golden head is bent over an embroidery hoop and even from here I can see a line of concentration between her eyes. Then she looks up, and she's so pretty and fresh, my heart sinks. Her dress is cornflower blue with a crisp white collar and her bobbed hair falls in soft waves to her jawline. It's only when she rises from the sofa with her hand outstretched that I realize she's several years older than Cole and I.

"I'm so glad to finally meet you! I've been looking forward to this."

I take her hand and feel an immediate reaction. Not as intense as the electricity I feel with Cole but rather a tingling warmth like I'd felt with Pratik. *She's a Sensitive*, I think with some surprise. Then I chastise myself for my stupidity. Of course she is. Cole said she would alleviate my concerns over meeting the Society's board members. I'm not sure I'll ever get over the novelty of meeting other people with psychic abilities.

"Nice to meet you," I murmur. "I'm Anna Van Housen."

"Leandra. Leandra Wright. Please sit down." She turns to Cole and gives him hug, which, to my surprise, he returns warmly. What happened to his shyness around women?

She tilts her face up, a lovely smile curving her lips. "What have you been doing with yourself? It's been a week since I've seen you! The boys are going to be livid at missing you, but they spend all day in school now. I miss them dreadfully."

Leandra's lilting English accent and gay mannerisms definitely belong to the curlicue penmanship, and from the look of adoration on her face it seems as if she holds Cole in very high regard indeed.

She turns away from him and snatches up my hand. I follow her to the sofa. Through her touch I feel her excitement and curiosity over meeting me, but there's also something else, a block of some kind. I frown, puzzled. The only blocks I have ever felt are intended to hide emotions from me. I can feel Leandra's emotions with no problem.

What is she blocking, then?

She drops my hand as we sit and faces me, her clear green eyes surveying me with interest.

"Anna was exhausted last night," Cole says. "I drove her around London for a bit and then we got a bite to eat."

I frown. Why didn't he tell her that he wanted to take me someplace special for our first night together in months?

"Did you take her to Mob's Hole?" She turns to me. "I love it there. We used to go all the time before I had the boys. Aren't the chips divine?"

Disappointment tightens my throat. For some reason I thought Mob's Hole was a special place Cole wanted to share just with me. The thought of him tucked away in the corner of that cozy old place with Leandra hurts. Of course, I knew he had friends; London is his home, after all. But did she have to be so pretty and vivacious? I murmur that the chips were indeed divine.

If she notices my reserve, she gives no sign but continues on as if afraid to stop talking. "Cole tells me you're a magician! How utterly marvelous. When shall you perform?

I would love to attend. Oh, wait. Can you stay for tea? We might as well get that started if you can."

"Actually that's why we came by," Cole says, sitting forward. "Anna is meeting some of the board members for tea this afternoon and is a bit apprehensive."

Leandra's mouth flattens. "I knew she was a smart girl."

"Leandra!" Cole exclaims. "You're supposed to help, not hinder."

She shakes her head. "It's rather a mess right now. The only reason I'm still involved is to help new Sensitives, though that is getting more and more difficult under the rules of the new board president." She turns to me. "Sensitives are not allowed to vote on Society policy. Some of the scientists believe we shouldn't be trained to control our abilities. They want to put us all in a lab."

"Oh, you're exaggerating. Not all of them. Some are pretty decent chaps." He waves a hand at Leandra. "I know, I know. There are some pretty deep divisions within the Society. But I still think we do more good than ill and we need to keep pushing for equal say in policy."

"Maybe," Leandra concedes. "But it's difficult to be nice to anyone with all the new rules."

I clear my throat. "That's the second time you've mentioned that. What kind of rules?" Somehow I am not reassured.

"New recruits aren't being trained right away. That's a concession to the scientists who believe that any kind of training will skew the results of their precious tests. Now, with young Sensitives such as yourself, it doesn't matter so much. But many older Sensitives are in pretty poor mental shape. They have no idea what is going on and feel completely alone. Or they try to tell someone about their experiences and end up in asylums. Can you imagine hearing other people's thoughts all the time and not being able to turn it off?" Leandra shudders. "Plus, interaction between the Sensitives is being highly discouraged."

"What?" Cole's eyebrows rise in alarm. "Our strength lies in sharing our knowledge."

"They don't want our knowledge shared, and they definitely don't want us strong," Leandra says flatly. "They proved that when they elected Darius Gamel to serve as president."

"I don't like Darius Gamel any more than you do, but he did make a break with Dr. Boyle before they kicked him out of the Society. They were never shown to have any connection other than simple friendship."

I startle at the name, a shiver going down my spine. Dr. Franklin Boyle is the reason my mother was kidnapped and I almost drowned in the Hudson River. The new president of the board is a *friend* of his?

Cole gives me a quick sympathetic glance and I glare. He wants me to meet these people?

"Isn't that enough?" Leandra snaps, then, as if sensing my mood, she reaches out and takes my hand. "I don't mean to scare you. I'm just angry. The organization does have a worthy intent—it's just gotten a bit sidetracked."

Like before, her emotions are clear and open and I sense only concern. Everything she says is truth, but then, as if a dam has broken, I feel a roar of anger washing over me like a storm surge.

She's not just angry, she's furious.

Leandra snatches her hand away and looks abashed. "Cole hasn't told me about your abilities, but I take it mind reading is one of them? That's what that felt like, anyway."

It feels strange to talk openly about my gifts. I've kept them hidden for so long, the sudden exposure is disturbing. "Actually, no. I can't read minds. I sense emotions."

"Oh," Leandra says softly. For a moment her forehead wrinkles and her eyes look brooding. Then she brightens. "I bet that comes in very handy. I've never heard of anyone else with that ability. And the board members won't be expecting that one at all. You would be able to get a good read on everyone."

"You're not asking her to spy?" Cole asks, his voice incredulous.

"Oh, don't be such a goody-goody," Leandra says, and I hide a smile. "I didn't mean that exactly, only that it would be useful. You don't know how much things have changed. You've been gone for months."

She turns back to me. "It's completely up to you, my dear. If you get any impressions and wish to share them, Harrison and I would be most appreciative. Harrison is my husband and a detective with Scotland Yard."

Her voice is proud, and I glance at Cole. "Is that where

you got the idea of being a detective?"

"Harrison is quite the fellow," Cole admits. "I'd be proud to be like him."

Does he want to be like him because Harrison is a wonderful guy or because Cole is trying to win Leandra's approval?

Leandra flushes with pleasure at the compliment to her husband, and I'm suddenly ashamed of my jealous thoughts. What's wrong with me? She's obviously devoted to her family.

She turns to me. "What are your other abilities, if you don't mind my asking?"

I try not to mind but I do. It still feels so personal. "Why don't you tell me what yours are?" I counter.

Leandra flashes a wry grin. "Touché. I dream."

I blink. "Excuse me?"

Her lips curl upward, but I sense the shadows behind the smile. "I dream other people's dreams. Or nightmares."

I sit back, flabbergasted. What would that be like? Seeing visions of the future is bad enough, but to see the nightmares of others? "That must be awful," I manage.

She shrugs. "I'm used to it."

Cole stands. "I hate to cut this short, but we need to be at Claridge's by four."

Leandra walks us to the door and this time I don't even have to touch her to feel her worry.

"Well, good luck. I'm sure it's going to be fine." Her voice is comforting, but I'm not in the least comforted.

What if I'm making the biggest mistake of my life?

★ ★ ★

I stop Cole just outside the hotel, my heart pounding. "What are they going to want to know about me? How much do I have to tell them?" Talking about my life has never been easy. What if they ask who my father is?

Cole squeezes my hand, understanding my reticence. "Don't be so worried. You don't have to tell them anything you don't want to. Sensitives are secretive people. Like you, they've learned there are things it isn't wise to talk about. Besides, the board members aren't really that interested in you or your background, just your abilities."

I swallow. "Somehow I don't find that reassuring," I tell him as he holds the door open for me.

Claridge's is prim, privileged, and pompous enough to make my tacky American self squirm in discomfort. Cole told me the owners just refurbished it, but somehow it looks as if it's been exactly the same for the past one hundred years. Perhaps it's the dignified, stiffly starched maître d' who welcomes us, or the matching waiters serving tea to the dozens of well-heeled patrons sitting at tiny tables. The creamy plaster ceiling with its swirls and whorls is a work of art designed to intimidate, and the high arches and columns surrounding the room are awe inspiring. Everything serves to remind me that I'm a long, long way from New York, where most restaurants are designed to entertain as well as feed. I'm so daunted I almost forget to worry about meeting the board members.

Almost.

I feel the men's eyes upon me as I approach the table on the heels of a waiter so disapproving he could be my mother in disguise. Why are there are only two board members? One, a large redheaded man, I quickly measure as friendly. It's the other who sends a shiver of apprehension up my spine. His eyes are small and dark, like raisins that have sat in the sun too long, and his mouth is a thin flat line. The anxiety whirling in my stomach grows as I realize they sat Cole and me at opposite ends of the white linen-covered table.

Neither of the board members offers to shake my hand as we're introduced, and I'm frustrated by my inability to get a read on what they're feeling. Though Cole taught me how to sense people's feelings without touching them, my control is still erratic and it is difficult to do with more than one person anyway. Is their reluctance to shake my hand intentional or just some odd British custom? I sit, feeling terribly underdressed in my simple yellow sheath. I wanted to wear something sunny to combat the gloomy London winter, but sitting among the other patrons all dressed in dark dignified colors, I feel as conspicuous as a canary among ravens.

"Thank you so much for meeting with us, Miss Van Housen," the man with the raisin eyes says.

I redden. I had been so intimidated that I'd glossed right over the introductions and have no idea which board member is which. "Thank you," I say. "I'm sorry, I'm hopeless with names?" I raise my voice at the end, hoping he will get the hint and he does, reintroducing everyone. This time I listen carefully.

"This is Julian Casperson," he says, smoothly indicating the other man. "I am Darius Gamel, president of the board. My apologies for having such a small contingent to welcome you. Julian is a researcher as well as a board member and the two of us are the only ones employed by the Society full-time. The other board members and researchers had previous engagements."

I smile, shooting him a look from under my lashes. Somehow I had envisioned Dr. Franklin Boyle's friend having the same charm as he did, but whereas Dr. Boyle looked like an English squire, Mr. Gamel, with his pale skin and long face, looks more like a cadaver.

The image brings to mind Walter, the only dead person I've ever met. My mother and I had been doing fake séances for years, but all that changed when Cole attended one—because of his heightening effect on my abilities, the séance became very, very real. I was possessed by a young soldier who had been in the Great War. Walter had died of dysentery, yet *he* looked healthier than Mr. Gamel.

I bite my lower lip and bring my focus back to the conversation. My nerves are getting the better of me. I shoot a worried glance at Cole, but he's looking at Mr. Casperson as if trying to figure something out. I try to put out a strand, or ribbon, as Cole had instructed when teaching me how to feel someone's emotions without touching them, but I can't concentrate.

The waiter standing to the right of our table suddenly springs into action and fills the delicate white cups with tea.

"I hope you don't mind, but we've already ordered," Mr. Gamel says. "I wanted to make sure we have plenty of time to get to know you. Did Colin tell you how the process works?"

His voice is friendly enough, with a formality that most Englishmen seem to have. That same formality had been a bit off-putting when I had first met Cole, but once I got used to it I rather liked it. It makes him seem solid and mature. I look at Cole across the table, only to find him staring back at me, puzzled. I realize they're waiting for me to answer.

"Oh. I'm sorry. No, he didn't clarify . . ." My voice trails off and I swallow, but Mr. Gamel just smiles, his thin lips stretching over sharp little teeth.

"Then allow me. This is just a friendly get-together, as you Americans call it. There is no obligation on either side. Because the interview, if you will, is taking place in public, we will, of course, be very circumspect in what we say. If, after meeting us today, you are still interested in learning more, it will be at a more private venue."

I frown. "How circumspect do we have to be? How am I supposed to know if I want to learn more if I learn nothing to begin with?"

Mr. Casperson smiles. "Ah. I see Miss Van Housen has the celebrated American candor. I like it. We Scots are also rather direct. Ask away. The Society for Psychical Research is a public organization. For the most part." He gives me a jolly wink and I'm not sure whether to smile or be offended.

My mind blanks. I know I have questions that need to be

asked, important ones. But I can't seem to think of a single one.

I'm saved as the waiter lays out silver platters of tiny tea sandwiches, scones, and clotted cream. Mr. Gamel holds the tray of sandwiches out to me and I take several.

As I spread my scone with jam and serve myself a generous dollop of the cream, my mind races, trying to think of a question, any question. In spite of my hunger, everything tastes like sand. Desperately, I take a swallow of tea and it burns my tongue. A question pops into my head and I cling to it. "How many Sensitives are there in the Society?"

A volley of glances ricochets around the table and I frown. Simple question, simple answer.

Suddenly I feel Cole sending me a lifeline across the table. It's like a silver strand reaching in my direction just like we've been practicing. He thinks if I can visualize what I'm sensing that I will have better control over it. We used to have to work at it, but even after two months apart, our connection is clear. I don't really understand it, but I'm grateful for his help. I reach out with my mind and grab the strand.

The effect is immediate. I start to calm as soon as I feel his presence. My anxiety fades and my mind sharpens. Relieved, I turn back to observe the men sitting at the table. All are regarding me with some measure of discomfort.

"That's a rather difficult question to answer," Mr. Gamel says.

"I don't see how. Don't you track your Sensitives?"

"Of course!" Mr. Casperson says. "They're a very important part of our research."

I ignore that, concentrating instead on Mr. Gamel's face. Though I used to be able to feel the emotions of others only through touch, proximity to Cole has heightened my abilities. Oddly, though, everything feels off right now, as if a telephone operator had somehow mixed up the wires. Mr. Gamel is hiding something. Or is it coming from Mr. Casperson? I look from one to the other, panic blooming in my chest. I've always relied on my abilities to assess whatever situation I've found myself in. Not being able to use them is rather like missing a limb.

"The number is fluid," Mr. Gamel cuts in smoothly. "Sensitives are free to come and go as they please, and recently that number has fluctuated quite a bit."

"Why do you think that is?" Cole asks, with a look at me.

Mr. Gamel shrugs his bony shoulders. "Who knows?" He turns to me. "As Cole is aware, Sensitives are not always reliable. It's hard to tell what motivates them to go or stay."

Yet another volley of glances sets my suspicions to soaring.

Cole gives a thin smile. "Perhaps Sensitives wouldn't be so willing to leave if they were treated as if they had value. We're not rats in a laboratory."

"No one thinks of you like that, my dear boy." Mr. Casperson jumps into the conversation.

"I would like to think no one thinks of anyone like that, but that's not what I've been hearing." Cole's disquiet reaches me, but his voice is matter-of-fact and I marvel at his control.

Mr. Gamel nods. "I know some Sensitives are unhappy

with some of the new rules we have put into place, but in all honesty, we are only trying to do what is best for both the Sensitives and the scientists. Without the research, we don't know how to best assist Sensitives in their quest to control their abilities. Without the scientists, the research that helps Sensitives would not happen. Of course, without Sensitives, there is nothing to research. The recent changes in policy reflect our desire to balance everyone's needs." Mr. Gamel looks to me. "Miss Van Housen, as Colin is aware, many Sensitives come to us broken and without hope. Not many are as lucky as you have been, to reach adulthood with all your mental faculties intact. We have given hope to many Sensitives and have recently retained a psychiatrist to help us in our endeavor. On the other hand, we need to be able to conduct our research as well. So, you see our dilemma?"

He shrugs as if hopelessly caught between altruism and furthering mankind's knowledge. He feels sincere, but Cole's dark eyes show his misgivings.

I've had enough. I don't know what is going on, but I just want to get out of here.

I stand, even though there's food still left on my plate. Mr. Gamel looks up at me, surprised. "I would like to meet with you again at the Society, but right now I have another appointment."

The men stand and Mr. Casperson knocks over a chair in his haste. "But we haven't had a chance to talk about your abilities," he says, righting his chair.

I smile. "Just as you have things you wish to be discreet

about, I do as well. Thank you very much for seeing me. Good day, gentlemen."

Cole follows me out of the hotel and down the street. Darkness is falling and the lamps on the motorcars cast strange shadows on London's buildings, until I finally lean against a brick wall and take several deep breaths.

"What happened in there?" Cole asks, concern written across his handsome face. He looks like a professor with his forehead furrowed and a frown creasing his lips, and my own mouth curls in spite of my unease. I slip my hand into his and he smiles back, though the worry lingers in his eyes.

"I'm not sure. I was nervous. I couldn't think." That isn't exactly how it felt, but as I can't really describe the odd sensations I was having, I leave it at that.

"Do you feel better now?" he asks anxiously. "Let's get you back to the hotel." He hails a taxicab and climbs in next to me.

He's so attentive; the odd confused feeling I had fades as we get farther and farther from the restaurant. "Are any of those men Sensitives?" I ask. That's the only explanation that makes sense considering how quickly I'm recovering. Of course, the only person who has ever altered my abilities is Cole, but then, I've never really been around other Sensitives. I don't know how my abilities would react.

Cole shakes his head. "No. I knew them all before I went to the States. I would have been able to tell. What did you think of them? Did you sense anything?"

I shrug. "I was too busy being a nervous wreck to get a clear read on anyone."

He nods. "That's what I thought might happen." He's silent for a moment. "Do you have rehearsal now?"

"Not until this evening."

The taxi stops in front of my hotel and Cole leaps out to open my door. I exit and shiver as a gust of cold wind hits me. He reaches down and pecks my cheek. Returning to his country seems to have increased his shyness. I wish he would just take me in his arms to reassure me, but he only pats my arm distractedly.

"I'll call the hotel tomorrow and leave a message once they get back to me. You get some rest before your rehearsal, all right?"

I nod and watch as his motorcar chugs off. My nerves are as unsettled as the weather, and for the very first time I almost wish my mother were here. Then I shiver, knowing how uneasy I must be feeling to wish such a thing. Superstitiously, I take it back, knocking quickly on the wooden doorjamb of the hotel door before entering.

Mother is the last thing I need right now.

THREE

I try resting as Cole suggested, but I'm as jumpy and out of sorts as if ants are running up and down my spine. From Leandra's strange undercurrent of rage to my condition at tea, I'm feeling harassed and exposed. Not that my abilities don't usually leave me feeling uncomfortable. The capacity to see catastrophic events before they happen and to talk to the dead aren't exactly conducive to a serene existence. But things just feel different now that people know about me. I feel . . . unsafe. As someone who grew up craving safety above all else, the sensation is disturbing.

Impatiently, I scoot off my narrow bed and run a comb through my hair. The old mirror over the bureau is pitted and makes my face look wavy. Only the blue-green eyes staring back at me seem familiar.

The hotel is more of a boardinghouse than a hotel, minus the bad boardinghouse food, which is fine with me. But it's still small and dilapidated and the walls are probably more paint than wood.

I riffle through the chipped wardrobe for something to wear to rehearsal. Because I do so many sleight-of-hand tricks, I usually wear some kind of oriental-inspired dress with loose sleeves. I change into a China blue silk and settle a black gigolo hat with a blue feather on my head. My call isn't until tonight, but I might as well go to rehearsal early. I'm not accomplishing anything and I'm too twitchy to stay here alone.

Snatching up my wool coat from the back of the faded print chair where I'd tossed it earlier, I head out the door and down the stairs. I generally avoid the elevator, which creaks alarmingly as it makes its slow, torturous way up and down the building. At least the hotel is clean, I think, crossing through the run-down lobby. During our traveling years, my mother and I stayed in hotels and boardinghouses so bad that even the rats had left in a mass exodus.

The best thing about the hotel is that it's a half block from our theater, so it takes me no time at all to get there. Tiptoeing out to the front, I slip into a seat to watch the other acts. The Little Sisters are performing and I watch their rapid interplay. I have to hand it to Martin Beck, the famous manager who put together the troupe—he certainly knows talent. Sally and Sandy soon have me laughing with their physical pratfalls and quick exchange of jokes. The act is even more hilarious once you realize that Sally is actually Sal, a brother dressed as a sister. So convincing is his costume and mincing voice that only those in the front row would wonder if he were male or female.

Louie claps his hands and the "sisters" come down the stairs. After a brief conference, he slaps Sally on the back and yells for the next act to come out.

I watch until it's my turn to go on. I'm nervous the way I always am before a performance. Even though this is just a rehearsal, a lot is riding on it. I know that Louie is watching from somewhere in the back of the auditorium, judging whether or not he made the right decision to move me up on the bill.

Once backstage, I check my props. The hinge on the dove's cage stuck last time I used it and I want to make sure the stagehand lubricated it correctly. Everything I use has to be in perfect working order. I'd hate for the hoop trick to fail because one of the hoops is bent and they won't link together properly. Or for an escape trick to flop because the door squeaked.

Once my props are checked, I run through my act. I've mixed older tried-and-true tricks, like my disappearing doves and connecting rings, with new ones such as the dollar-in-a-lemon trick, where I borrow a bill from an audience member and make it appear in a lemon. The tricks increase in both difficulty and pizazz until my grand finale—the levitating table. The assistant, a woman Louie hired before I arrived, wheels my iron maiden out onto the stage.

"Stop!"

Louie's voice reaches me from the back of the auditorium, and I pause, swallowing hard. *What did I do wrong?*

He walks up to the edge of the stage. "Beautiful, doll, but

let's switch the iron maiden escape with the levitation trick. The effect is more stunning." His cigar wags up and down as he speaks, but his eyes are narrowed, considering. His comical looks hide a shrewd mind.

But still . . . the levitation trick is my closing illusion as it's so visually stunning. "Why would you want the escape trick to be last? I think the levitation trick leaves a better impression."

"I'm looking to try something different, sweetheart. Let's turn the iron maiden bit into an escape-gone-wrong trick to make it look as if you've failed."

I raise my eyebrows. For this trick, my hands are cuffed and I'm placed in a modified iron maiden—a box shaped like an upright human body with a hinged section that swings outward. The front of the box was supposedly painted to look like me, but the face is so ugly, I prefer not to think about it. The interior of the box is lined with wicked metal spikes. Once inside, my ankles are cuffed, then my assistant closes the box and secures it with metal bands placed through the hinges. She encircles the box with a red curtain that only parts at the front. To escape, I have to remove the cuffs from my hands (easy), grip one of the spikes at the hinge side of the cover, and lift upward a fraction of an inch. Slowly, the ratchet pin on the hinge comes loose, and it's just a matter of opening the box at the side using the padlocks as hinges. After getting the box open, I remove the cuffs from my ankles and replace the pins by pushing them through the hinges from the bottom. Then voilà! The box is secure and ready for an audience member to inspect.

"I don't understand. What do you mean you want it to look as if I've failed?"

A slow smile plays about his lips. "Blood."

I swallow. "Blood?" My stomach churns as I recall the last time I saw blood. It had been pooling around a dead man at the going-away party Cynthia had thrown me. The time before that, it had been from a bullet wound in my own shoulder. I don't have the best memories of blood.

"Yeah. Fake blood. Once you're in the box, you can squeeze some blood on the floor and let it ooze out. Then you come out with bloody hands, looking as if you barely made it. It would be a sensation!"

I tilt my head, thinking. It's very good, my aversion to blood notwithstanding. And he's right, I couldn't do the levitation illusion afterward if I'm supposed to be hurt. So I give him a nod. "I'll do the escape trick last."

He beams. "Perfect. We'll practice it that way tomorrow. You can take off. Go have fun. It's London, you're young!"

He turns away, already engrossed in another of the myriad production problems that always plague a show. As both director and producer, Louie's hands are full.

My assistant, Mollie, and I put away my things. I'm half tempted to ask if she wants to have supper with me, but I know she has a little girl she needs to get home to, so I say good-bye and head back to my hotel. I figure I'll just grab something to eat at the café next door and call it an early night. I don't like eating by myself, but Cole had said he would see me in the morning. He's probably eating with his mother, and I can't begrudge him time with his family. But still, after a day like today, I'd rather not be alone. Plus, I'd forgotten to tell him my good news about moving up on the bill. Of course, not being in show business, he probably wouldn't understand, and I would have to explain it to him, which would take most of the fun out of it. Maybe it's better that he can't have dinner tonight.

I pick up a newspaper and read reviews of various shows while I dine on a simple meal of shepherd's pie and tea. I spot Sal and Bronco Billy pass by the window in their street clothes and wonder what they're doing. Probably going out to have fun.

Feeling sorry for myself, I pay my bill with unfamiliar notes, hoping I've tipped the waitress enough. The weather has turned, and a steady rain wets my face along with a few tears as I make my lonely way back to the hotel. I almost wish my mother was here. No. Scratch that. I wish Cynthia were here. Cynthia Gaylord came to one of my mother's séances and we ended up best friends, even though she's married and a few years older than I am. As a famous gangster's niece, she carries a loaded gun on her at all times and I carry a balisong knife in my handbag. We united over our weaponry and have been best friends ever since.

She promised to come and see me as soon as the show runs in London, but we have about a week of rehearsals and then we leave to perform in Hungary, Poland, and Czechoslovakia. Though London is our home base, we won't be formally playing here until March.

The cold, drizzly weather does little to lift my spirits and I pick up my pace, wanting to get back to the relative warmth of my room, even if all I'll be doing is reading a book and heading to bed. Once there, I listen to the rain beating on my window and wonder why I feel so sorry for myself. All in all, it wasn't a bad day. I'm just tired. Things will look better in the morning.

My night is restless and it seems only moments before I'm awakened by a knock on the door. "You have messages," a sunny voice calls.

Disoriented, I sit up in bed and scrub my hand over my face. I must have lain awake for hours before sleep finally found me. I gather the envelopes the messenger left on the doorstep and go through them. One is from Louie with my call time today and another is from Cole.

Anna,
Something came up and I won't be able to make it until this evening. If you aren't at the hotel, I'll come to the theater. Would you like to go to dinner at Frascati's?
Cole

My shoulders slump. I notice that he didn't tell me exactly what had come up and I could be his sister for all the affection the note contains.

After spending last evening alone, I definitely don't feel like being by myself again. Frustrated, I open the third message and stare at the letterhead. *Society for Psychical Research.* Under the letterhead is the address and Mr. Gamel's title in formal script.

Dear Miss Van Housen,
It was a pleasure meeting you yesterday. If you are interested in touring our facility and learning more about us, I will be in the office from two to five this afternoon. I hope to see you then. I think you would make a valuable contribution to our research and our knowledge of psychical phenomena.
Sincerely,
Darius Gamel

My pulse speeds up. He's officially going to invite me to join the Society. Do I want to join? After a lifetime of feeling alone with my strangeness, the thought of a community of others like myself is both appealing and terrifying.

I snatch a deck of cards off the bedside table and shuffle them, a nervous habit I've had for years. On one hand, I'm skeptical of sharing my abilities with people who see me as a lab rat. On the other hand, I long to meet others like myself who have struggled with the same fears and doubts.

I set down the cards and plop down on the bed. What a time for Cole to be preoccupied. All my instincts tell me to politely reschedule the meeting for a time when Cole can join me, but perversely part of me wants to go anyway. He has his own life. Why should I have to wait for him to make time for me?

Undecided, I wash and dress and run to a little café down the street for breakfast. My call is at eleven today, so I don't linger.

Bronco Billy is just leaving as I get to the theater. He gives me his slow, easy smile. My mouth goes dry and I blink.

"Be careful—Louie is in a foul mood today," he says in passing.

I want to ask him what happened but instead just stare like an idiot.

Men shouldn't be allowed to be that beautiful.

I can hear Louie yelling at Jeanne all the way to the side door. I tiptoe down the hallway, ignoring the stomach-turning stench of sweat, mildew, and greasepaint. The backstage of almost every theater I've ever been in smells the same way, though in the West, you can swap out the mildew for cow manure.

Poking my head around the frayed velvet curtain I see our lovely songbird, the soprano Jeanne Hart, calmly watching Louie work himself up into a swivet. His anger pulses out from him in waves and his mouth is practically foaming around his cigar.

"You can't just do that, Jeanne! You can't pick and choose what shows you will and won't do!"

I can't see Jeanne's face from where I'm standing, but there's no mistaking the amusement in her voice. "I can do whatever I like, darling. Check my contract. The one you signed. What do you think 'theater approval' means?"

Jeanne Hart is beautiful in a sultry, sensuous way. Her hair is a burnished red, her mouth is too wide, and her heavy-lidded green eyes are slightly tilted at the corners. No matter the weather, she dresses in a way that shows off her lovely polished arms and makes the most of her ample breasts. But you forget her seductive looks the moment she sings—the purity of her voice is heartbreaking.

"It doesn't bloody well mean you get to pick and choose where you'll sing and where you won't," Louie blusters.

"But it does. Check with your lawyer and next time be more careful what you sign. Now, do you want me to start from the top?"

"No, I don't want you to start at the top!" he screams. "I want you to get your sneaking upper-class behind off the stage! You're fired!"

Jeanne turns and saunters off the stage, her lovely well-shaped head held high. When she reaches me, she gives my arm a reassuring pat. "Don't look so stricken. He can't fire me, I'm his wife."

My mouth falls open. *The stunning Jeanne Hart is married to Louie the penguin?* The clicking of her heels grows fainter as she walks down the hall to her dressing room. Pressing my lips together, I walk downstage. Louie had taken a seat in the front and is mopping his forehead with a red handkerchief.

"Do the escape-gone-wrong routine," he snaps when he spots me. I nod at my assistant, who has just appeared upstage. We run through it several times and each time it's easier. I want to ask Louie where the fake blood is going to be hidden, but don't want to irritate him further. I'm not sure his heart can take any more vexation.

"Do you want me to practice the whole routine?" I ask after I'm done.

He shakes his head, looking calmer. At least his face isn't as red. "No, you can take a break until dress rehearsal on Thursday. You're happy with third billing, aren't you?" he asks before I exit the stage.

I nod. Second billing is a throwaway spot. Usually, the audience is restless by then and just wants to see the main attraction. Third spot from the end and top billing are the best spots in the lineup. I've been at the top of the bill before, but that was when I was with my mother, not just Anna the Magician.

"Good." He waves a hand, his quick mind already leaping to the next problem at hand.

I give my assistant a thumbs-up, and she waves and disappears through the door. The stagehand is taking away the iron maiden as I leave. "Thanks!" I mouth as the comedian, Bruce Horner, starts his routine.

I hurry to my hotel room to get ready for my appointment. Doubt niggles in my stomach as I change into a plain skirt and blouse and run a brush through my hair. I know I should wait for Cole, but curiosity and my determination to be independent win out.

Before heading to my appointment at the Society, I order fish and chips from a stall. The man behind the counter fries them in a vat of bubbling oil and shakes salt over the whole thing before serving them to me in a cone of newspaper. Like a Londoner, I eat them right in the street under a store awning, giggling as vinegar and oil run out down my hands. The man kindly gives me a damp towel to clean myself up with and after doing so, I hail a cab.

I stare out the window, watching drizzle saturate the city. London feels different from New York. It's not really less busy and the clothing is similar, though you're much more likely to run into a woman still clinging to the longer skirts of another era here. But the city is older than anything we have in America, and it's not unusual to find entire blocks filled with buildings constructed during the medieval era. In New York, most Gothic architecture is simply a clever reproduction. Another difference is in the inhabitants. People on the streets of London tend to be far more polite than in New York, but much less friendly, if that makes any sense.

I rest my forehead against the cool window, trying to calm myself. My decision to attend the meeting without Cole seems more and more foolhardy the closer I get to the Society. After all, there are people here who neither Cole nor Leandra trust. But then I get angry with myself. It's not as though anyone in the Society can force me to do anything against my will. I'm seventeen now and working and living on my own. Surely I'm old enough to make my own decisions.

My attention is caught by a familiar-looking man crossing the street in front of me. I stare puzzled for a moment before recognition comes with heart-stopping realization.

Dr. Boyle.

Dr. Boyle wanted Cole to join his demented plan to attain wealth and power so badly he was willing to do anything—including extortion, blackmail, and kidnapping—to accomplish it. The scar from the gunshot wound I obtained last fall in that evil man's quest still aches.

Frantically, I slide to the other side of the seat, trying to see if that is indeed who it was. I didn't get a good look at him, but the man did have the same ruddy English squire looks that Dr. Boyle has. I stare at the man's retreating back as my taxicab drives in the opposite direction. My heart slows. I might have been mistaken. I probably was. I am, after all, in England. There are probably lots of men who look like country squires here.

The motorcar stops in front of a tall, nondescript brick building and I hand the driver some pound notes, hoping I'm not being taken advantage of. I can't seem to figure out the money exchange to save my life and I'm going through much more money than I thought I would.

I hesitate in front of the building. If I wanted to change my mind, now is the time. I look up, and for a moment I think I see a pale face staring down at me but then it disappears. I shiver. I take a deep breath, firm my chin, and march to the front door. There's no sign hanging out front to indicate if this is the right place or not, but the number matches, so this must be it. I'm just wondering whether I should knock or go on in when the door is flung open.

A young woman about my age stands in the doorway and I stare as if mesmerized. I've worked in theaters all my life, so beautiful women are nothing new to me, but I've never seen anyone as arresting as the girl before me. Her hair is caught back with a silver ribbon and hangs in glossy black ringlets down her back. For the first time I regret my own bobbed locks. Her skin glows like a pink rose dusted with cinnamon and the fringe of her lashes cast shadows on her cheekbones. But it's her eyes that grab my attention and hold it: They're large and so dark you can barely tell the pupil from the iris.

"You must be Anna! Come in. The powers that be are expecting you."

I hesitate in the doorway and lift my lips in a tentative smile. The girl's own smile is friendly and open.

She stands aside to let me in and I find myself in a formally appointed reception room with a matched set of overstuffed red chairs and several large potted palms. A small French desk sits next to a door ornately carved with symbols. "My name is Calypso Ruiz. Mr. Gamel and the others are occupied, but I can take you upstairs."

I shift uncomfortably. "Oh. Perhaps now isn't a good time? I can come back later, if that would be better."

She shakes her head, causing her curls to riot. "Don't be

silly. I've been looking forward to meeting you! Would you like the grand tour?"

She gives me an enchanting smile and I shake off my jitters. My bad experiences in New York left me jumpy and suspicious.

Actually, that's not true. My whole life has left me jumpy and suspicious.

Returning the smile, I nod.

She waves her arm at the door. "After you."

I walk ahead and my eyes widen. The wood on the door is dark, probably mahogany, and covered with exquisitely detailed carvings. They almost look like cryptograms interlaced with grape vines and ivy. "This is beautiful. Do you know what the symbols mean?"

She shrugs. "Not sure. I know it's old. Maybe Gamel would know. He knows everything."

She gives me a wink and I grin, liking her more and more.

"Actually, Mr. Price would be the one to ask. He had the door installed."

"I haven't met Mr. Price yet."

Calypso makes a face. "You will. He's one of the researchers and he's said to be brilliant, though he's a bit terrifying if you ask me."

I want to ask her why he's scary, but can feel her impatience, so I turn the knob and walk through. She follows me and I'm surprised when she leaves the inner door open. Surely they wouldn't want just anyone off the street to come in, would they?

I shut it myself and then follow her down a long hall. She's wearing a plain cotton blouse and a red-and-yellow flowered skirt that swirls around her calves as she walks. She chatters away in a musical accent I can't place. It's definitely not English, nor is it European like Cole's. It's more exotic and makes me think of tropical breezes and white sandy beaches.

"The Society has been in this building for about a year. This floor is mainly offices, where the scientists compile their data and Sensitives are vetted. Some of the experiments are down here, too." She turns to me, a frown marring her lovely features. "Have you been tested yet?" I shake my head and her frown deepens. "That's odd. Usually Sensitives are tested before they're given the tour. They must be very sure about your abilities."

Calypso doesn't show me the offices but instead leads me to a stairwell at the end of the hallway. "We spend most of our time up here."

"How long have you been a part of the Society?" I ask.

"Four months." She stops and turns to me. Because she's two steps ahead, she towers over me, though on level ground we're about the same height. "I've been waiting for someone my age to join up. I don't have many friends here."

She dimples into a disarming smile that I would find immediately suspect, if she weren't so open and friendly. My duplicitous mother is the most charismatic woman God ever placed on the earth, so I'm not only immune to charm, I'm suspicious of it. But there's something so immediately likable about Calypso that I find myself responding.

Like the hallway below, the walls are done in a cream plaster with intricate molding at the ceiling. At the top of the stairs, a door opens up to a wide room with a dark parquet floor, several leather club chairs, a comfortable leather couch, and shelves with rows of books. An arched doorway on the other side of the room opens into a packed meeting room. A knot of people near the bookshelves appear to be having an intense, whispered conversation, while louder voices issue from the adjoining room.

The overall feeling is tense and, though I can't pick up just one emotion in a room full of them, the common thread I feel is fear. Suddenly, I wish Cole were here with me instead of off doing whatever it was he had deemed more important. Of course, I didn't let him know I was coming, so I really can't fault him. But now I desperately wish I had waited.

Because something feels very, very wrong.

FOUR

A rather round young man spots us and hurries over. He stops and eyes me, suspicion written all over his pale freckled face. "Who is this?"

"Anna," Calypso says simply, not introducing us.

"Anna Van Housen," I amend, holding out my hand. He looks at it for a moment before shaking his head.

"I'm sorry. I don't do that."

My hand drops to my side.

"My name is Jared Taylor."

Jared looks to be in his early to mid-twenties, and everything about him, from his pale red hair to his pale eyelashes over pale blue eyes, is nondescript. I wonder what his abilities are that he doesn't shake hands. Having tried to avoid touch for most of my life, I sympathize with whatever it is.

He clears his throat, trying to cover an awkward moment. "It's nice to meet you, Anna. I'm sorry you aren't getting much of a welcome. We have a bit of a situation here." He glances into the meeting room.

"What's going on?" I ask. I don't mean to pry, but the emotions swirling around the room have my nerves on edge.

Jared glances again at the open door. "I'm not sure . . ."

"Oh please, she's practically one of us," Calypso says. She turns to me. "A Sensitive went missing today. He was taken from his home. Or Mr. Gamel's home, I should say."

Apprehension mushrooms in my stomach. "Pratik?" I whisper.

Calypso nods, her forehead wrinkling. "You know Pratik?"

I nod. "He came with Cole to pick me up from the ship. What happened?"

"Apparently Pratik didn't feel well this morning and stayed home. When Gamel returned home for lunch, he found the door open and his house in disarray."

"Calypso!" Mr. Gamel walks into the room, catching her words. "I've warned you to be more circumspect about what you say."

Instead of looking chastened, Calypso merely shrugs. "I haven't the time for your cloak-and-dagger mentality, Mr. Gamel."

"Our cloak-and-dagger mentality may be more important than ever," Mr. Gamel snaps.

I frown as agitation comes off him in frazzled waves. "Why do you say that, Mr. Gamel?"

He turns to me with a little bow of his head. "My apologies, Miss Van Housen. When I sent that message this morning, I had no idea what the day would hold."

"I don't see why not. This is the second Sensitive who has gone missing in a matter of weeks," Calypso breaks in.

"Enough!" Mr. Gamel thunders.

Unfazed by his anger, Calypso raises her eyebrows at me. "Welcome to the family, Anna. Don't mind Mr. Gamel. He's not nearly as gruff as he sounds."

Mr. Gamel ignores her. "There is nothing to indicate foul play with Jonathon Velasquez. He merely moved on, just as he always has."

"But with poor Pratik . . . ," she says.

"Leave it alone, Calypso," Mr. Casperson orders, coming up behind Gamel.

Strangely enough, she does, and Mr. Gamel continues more quietly, "This is an unfortunate incident, but there is nothing to tie his abduction with his abilities. No one is targeting Sensitives."

I detect the worry under his words. No matter what he says, Mr. Gamel is very concerned.

"Unfortunately, we cannot offer the welcome we had originally intended, but I'm sure Calypso will take care of you. I must speak to the authorities. As Pratik's sponsor they will want to interview me."

He gives another bow and exits, leaving me with Calypso, Jared, and Mr. Casperson. One of the women standing by the bookshelves joins us and Mr. Casperson introduces us. I learned my lesson and don't try to shake hands, instead offering a European nod of the head in greeting.

"Anna Van Housen, Jared's twin, Jenny Taylor."

Jenny is as slender as her brother is chubby, but shares the same strawberry blonde hair and freckled skin.

I'm curious about their abilities and yet dread the moment when we'll discuss them. I've never been good at sharing bits and pieces of myself.

"How many Sensitives are there?" I ask.

"You mean how many are in our happy little family?" Calypso smiles.

Mr. Casperson frowns, his blue eyes disapproving. "There used to be ten, but several moved away and others have distanced themselves from the Society. So I guess that leaves six?"

Jenny nods. "For now."

Mr. Casperson glances at his pocket watch. "My apologies, but I really must be going. I have an appointment for dinner. Good day."

He nods, and soon I can hear his quick staccato steps descending the staircase.

"Don't you all have places to be?" A man's voice booms out across the room and I jump.

The tall man walking toward us has large features, a massive head, and sharp, knowing eyes. He spots me and I see surprise flicker across his face before it settles back into annoyance. He holds out his hand without hesitation and I know that this is a man who is afraid of very little.

"I apologize for my rudeness. I am Mr. Harry Price, one of the researchers. You must be Anna Van Housen. I've been looking forward to our meeting, but I hardly think today is the day for socializing." He casts a stern eye over the Sensitives. "Perhaps it would be best if you came back in a few days."

Jared and Jenny nod at me, snatch up their coats, and leave.

I notice that no one said a word to Mr. Price.

Calypso tilts her chin and glares at Mr. Price before defiantly tossing her head. "Come on, Anna. Let's go grab some dinner."

She tucks her arm into mine and I let her lead me out the door and down the stairs. By the time we reach the street, she's giggling like a child.

"I'm sorry, but the look on his face was priceless. The scientists and board members have started discouraging our friendships, but I think that's just ridiculous, don't you? Who do they think they are, telling us who we can and can't talk to?"

The emotions conveyed from her touch are dizzying. They go from simple glee to resentment to anger in a flash, and as soon as we reach the carved door I pull my arm from hers in relief.

"When did they start discouraging socialization among the Sensitives?" I ask.

She waits until I open the door and sails through like a young queen, then surprisingly, opens the outside door and holds it for me.

"It started in just the last couple of months," she says, and then changes the subject. Her thoughts are apparently as variable as her feelings. "So, do you want to go to dinner or do you have someplace you need to be?" she asks matter-of-factly.

I shake my head. "I'm meeting someone for dinner, but perhaps some other time?"

"I'd like that. We have so much to talk about. I'll see you in a couple of days?"

Her smile lights up her face and eyes and I return it. As she heads down the street with a merry wave, my heart warms in spite of the chill. London seems a bit less lonely. Maybe being a member of the Society is going to be better than I hoped.

Unlike Claridge's decor, which is so proper as to be uncomfortable, the opulence of Frascati's has an overdone American feel that puts me at ease. We enter through yellow revolving doors and are escorted to our seats past a vestibule with a plush red carpet, bright brocade settees, and gilt chandeliers. The dining area itself is decorated in gold and silver and surrounds a banjo-shaped dance floor. An orchestra is warming up on the other side of the room, and there are so many fresh flower arrangements that it smells like a summer garden in the middle of winter.

"When are you going to tell me what's wrong?" Cole asks as soon as we're seated.

He had picked me up at the hotel in his shiny motorcar, and while I should have felt like the luckiest girl in the world sitting against the luxurious leather seat, I had a hard time relaxing. I know I have to tell him about the visit to the Society and ask him if he knows about Pratik, but I also know he's going to be angry and upset, so I put it off. "Sometimes I forget you can feel what I feel. It hardly seems fair."

He lifts an eyebrow and his lips curl at the corners. My heart skips a beat. Most of the time I'm used to how good-looking he is, but sometimes it sneaks up on me.

"You can feel what I feel too, so it's hardly an advantage. It's only a disadvantage when we try to hide things."

His accent is more pronounced, which means he's tired, and I'm instantly contrite. I hadn't even asked him what had come up to make him miss our day together. "You first," I tell him. "What happened today? Is everything all right?"

He nods. "It is now. My mother became horribly ill this morning with extreme stomach pain. I had to call for the doctor."

"I'm so sorry." I put my hand over his on the table. "How is she now?"

"She's fine. The doctor couldn't find anything wrong and gave her something to help with the pain. She fell asleep for a few hours and when she woke up, she was perfectly fine. I was going to cancel this evening, but she insisted I come out. My grandmother is with her, so it will be all right."

I sense his worry and squeeze his hand. "I'm sure she's fine."

He nods. "She'd like you to come for tea this Sunday. I told her you were going to be going on tour soon and she and my grandmother would like to meet you before you go."

I swallow and put my hands in my lap. Tea with Cole's mother and grandmother? I know Cole comes from old English money. How can I, a poor American in show business, measure up to that? "That sounds lovely."

He laughs as if sensing my thoughts. "Stop fretting. They're going to love you. Now, tell me what is bothering you besides facing two dowagers over tea?"

I stare at the menu, avoiding his eyes. "What does *déjeuner* mean?"

"A midday meal, or lunch. I didn't know you couldn't speak French."

A surge of annoyance mixed with embarrassment sweeps over me and my cheeks heat. How upper-class English of him to assume that everyone had learned French. "I didn't go to school," I tell him, my words clipped.

"I'm sorry. You're so well read I forget that you're self-educated. Now what's wrong besides your boyfriend's thoughtlessness?"

"Monsieur, mademoiselle, have you decided?"

I turn to the waiter with relief, but know I'm only putting off the inevitable.

After we give our order, I turn to find Cole regarding me gravely. I sigh. "I got a message from Mr. Gamel this morning. He wanted to meet with me."

Cole nods. "I figured he would. When?"

"This afternoon." I glance up at him and his face is still.

Taking a deep breath I continue, "I actually met some of the other Sensitives."

Cole studies one of the giant potted palms decorating the restaurant. His brow furrows and he finally turns to me. "I wish you would have waited. I really want to be with you whenever you go there."

I try for a light laugh but end up barking like a seal. "Honestly, if I am going to be a member, I'll have to go on my own occasionally. If you think it's dangerous, I don't have to be a member."

Cole shakes his head, impatient. "But you wanted to connect with other Sensitives. It's what you've wanted since the first time I told you there were others like us."

For a moment I think back to that conversation, how relieved I'd been to learn that I wasn't crazy, that other people had strange abilities like mine. I'd spent so much of my life hiding my abilities, to know there were others . . . I nod. "I did. I do. I just didn't know it would be so complicated."

His dark eyes soften, looking like black velvet in the light. "I'm sorry. But under the circumstances . . ." He shrugs. "I'm just not sure I trust everyone on the board. That doesn't mean I don't think the Society is worth it. That it's not worth fighting for. Sensitives need protection and help. If you could have seen Pratik when he first got here . . ."

"Pratik!"

Cole brows rise. "What?"

"At the Society today. That's why Mr. Gamel couldn't meet with me. Pratik is missing."

Our food arrives and we fall silent until the waiter leaves.

Cole turns to me, his face white. "I think you had better start at the beginning."

I recount my afternoon as he stirs his soup round and round with his spoon. "Do you think Dr. Boyle could be behind the abduction?"

Cole holds up a finger. "First things first. We don't even know if it's an abduction. Pratik's a nice fellow but very quiet. He's had a rough time and always seems to have a lot going on up here." Cole taps his finger against his forehead. "It's entirely possible that Pratik had some sort of an episode and ran off."

"Mr. Gamel didn't seem to think so. He called the authorities."

"He probably called on Harrison to investigate. He wouldn't go to the other police. At least not right away." Cole absentmindedly spoons consommé into his mouth.

I stare. "Why wouldn't he go to the police? I know the existence of Sensitives is very hush-hush, but does that mean that something could happen to one of us and no one would care?"

Cole looks around the room and frowns. "Not so loud. Of course, people would care. Harrison is a detective with Scotland Yard. He is someone we trust—and a darn good investigator."

I lean back in my rich leather chair and cross my arms. I really, really do not like being hushed. And what *we* is he talking about? Is he aligning himself with the scientists?

The board? I thought it was *us* against *them*. I can't help but feel like London is different and we're different in it. Our synchronicity seems off in this city that is his home but is as foreign to me as a new costume.

The waiter comes to take our food; though I haven't touched mine, he replaces it with a plate of terrine with chutney and tiny triangles of toast. I want to tell him to take it away, that I'm not hungry, but don't want to completely ruin the evening.

Disturbed, I reach out psychically to try to get a sense of Cole's emotions. Something far different from the warm connection I usually feel from him zings down the line. I frown, concentrating. The hairs along my arms rise as an unfamiliar, almost predatory feeling insinuates itself between us. It's as if there's an intruder on our wavelength. Cole stiffens and I know he feels it too. I freeze as his eyes search the patrons, busy eating all around us.

"What are you feeling?" I ask Cole, still not moving.

His forehead furrows. "I'm not sure. It feels like a Sensitive, but it's no one I know and it's really soft . . ."—his voice trails off for a moment and when he continues, his voice is so low I barely hear him—"almost like a caress."

Suddenly annoyed, I break our connection. "That's not how it felt to me," I tell him crossly.

He startles. "Pardon?"

I shake my head, not sure what he meant or what I meant or what it was I even felt. The feeling fades and I hope it was just an anomaly.

We eat in silence for a few minutes even though my stomach is rolling.

The waiter takes our terrine and brings us poached sole in hollandaise sauce. My heart sinks. This is supposed to be a special evening for us and here we are practically arguing.

Cole clears his throat. "I'm sorry. I didn't mean to sound bossy. I just worry. I nearly lost you once, I couldn't stand to go through that again and if Pratik's disappearance does turn out to be an abduction, it could mean a reappearance of Dr. Boyle. So please be careful."

I clear my throat. "Speaking of Dr. Boyle . . ."

His head rises abruptly.

"I thought I saw someone who looked like him today on my way to the Society. It was only for a moment, so I can't be sure."

He shakes his head. "Harrison has people all over the country looking for him. We would know if he was in England." I must look worried because his face softens and he reaches out to touch my hand. "I'll have Harrison check again, all right? I don't want you to be worried."

I melt. I have no defenses against someone who is so very handsome and so very sincere and who cares about me so very much. But I can't help but feel that coming to London has somehow changed our relationship, and not necessarily for the better.

FIVE

I spend another restless night tossing and turning. Cole had kissed me good-bye last night after our dinner, but I could feel his preoccupation. I know he wanted to run by Leandra and Harrison's to find out if there had been any developments in Pratik's disappearance, but even though I understood, it still hurt.

The last thing I expect when I finally arise and go to hunt up a late breakfast is Calypso waiting for me in the lobby.

"How did you know where I live?" I ask. I'm actually thankful for her impromptu appearance. Calypso is just the distraction I need.

She grins. "I told you—we're like a family. Everybody knows everything."

We head out into the strangely balmy January day. So different from the day I arrived. I ask her if winter in London is always so unpredictable and she shakes her head. "Nope. It's usually just cold rain, but every once in a while we get a break. Let's take advantage of it!"

She takes me to Bond Street to window-shop, which Calypso says is more fun than actually buying anything. That's a relief, since I shouldn't really spend money anyway. Yes, my mother could now be considered wealthy due to her marriage to Jacques and their successful theatrical management business, but the less money I have to take from them, the more independent of her I am.

Calypso stops at a newsstand. "Oooh! A new issue of *Punch*! I just love *Punch*, don't you? We can read it over lunch."

Tucking her arm into mine, she carries on as if we've known one another for years. Something about her cheerful attitude reminds me of Cynthia, though the emotional sensations I get from them are very different. Cynthia's feelings are always simple, direct. Calypso's are as varied as the wind, always moving from one direction to another. Though her mercurial personality is a part of her charm, I wonder if it won't get a bit exhausting.

As much as I want to feel the same way about Calypso as she seems to feel about me, I just don't make friends that quickly. Cynthia was an exception. I'd spent my life skirting the outside of polite society. Girls who worked in circuses, helped their mother set up fake séances designed to cheat people out of money, and escaped from handcuffs for fun weren't invited to birthday parties given by nice children. Making friends with girls my own age isn't one of my talents. Cynthia and I became friends simply because nothing gets in the way of what Cynthia wants and for some reason, she wanted me.

So while I'm grateful for Calypso's ardent offer of friendship, it's a challenge for me to be as open as she is. It's just not in me. However, I'm determined to try. I could use a friend in London and at the Society. Aside from Cole, that is.

"Have you heard anything about Pratik?" I ask.

She shakes her head. "No. That's all everyone is talking about right now and my stomach can't take any more worry."

For a moment I sense her anxiety and then her mood changes as she sees something in a shop window. She drags me over. "We're going in," she informs me.

"I thought the whole point of window-shopping was to not go in," I protest, but she just laughs, her extraordinary black eyes sparkling.

The inside is done in black and white and minimally decorated—one of those shops where everything screams French and expensive. The kind my mother always wanted to shop at but couldn't until recently. But the hats are simply lovely. A black felt knockabout with a rolled brim and tangerine and turquoise decorative beading captures my rapt attention.

"It's beautiful! Try it on," Calypso urges.

"Oh, I don't know." I'm not in love with clothes like my mother is. The deprivation and uncertainty of my early years made stashing money under my mattress more desirable than spending it on dresses. But there are times like this, when I see something that takes my breath away and I understand why some women spend so much money on glad rags.

Calypso takes the hat off the stand. "It's perfect for you."

Knockabout hats are sportier than cloches and for a moment I get a vision of wearing it out driving in Cole's motorcar. I feel myself weaken.

A slim-skirted salesgirl in a rose-colored sweater and a wrist full of bangles joins us. "It would go beautifully with your dark hair and blue eyes. You should try it on."

I take a deep breath. "I'll do it."

We move in front of a mirror and I remove my black cloche with the silk flower on the side. Calypso places the knockabout on my head and then adjusts it.

"Ouch!" I jerk away as my hair is pulled.

"I'm sorry! My ring got tangled in your hair."

I stare at her for a moment in the mirror. Her eyes are full of apology. "It's all right," I tell her even though my scalp still tingles.

Then I look in the mirror and forget about the incident because the hat is perfect, perfect, perfect and I know I have to have it. "How much?" I ask.

"Fifteen guineas."

I struggle to convert the amount to dollars in my head so I can put it in context. It sounds like an awful lot to me. I turn to Calypso for help, but she's watching the salesgirl, a look of concentration on her face.

"That's too much money," Calypso tells her, a small smile

playing about her delicately pink lips.

The woman smiles back, her manner pleasant. "We're a one-price store. No bargaining."

Still Calypso stares, her black eyes almost opaque. "No. It's too much money."

I take off the hat, staring from one to the other. What's going on? A tingle brushes across my arms like a prickly caress, and the salesgirl nods sadly. "It is too expensive," she agrees.

"My friend will pay seven guineas," Calypso says. The number is half what the salesgirl had named.

"No, it's fine . . . ," I start to say, but Calypso holds up her hand and gives me a sly wink. I fall silent, suddenly suspicious.

"Seven guineas is fine," the salesgirl says. She looks at me, her face still pleasant. "Would you like that in a box?"

Calypso turns to me, her eyes lit with excitement. I feel it shooting off her like sparks. "Oh, wear it out and put your old one in the box. You look smashing!"

I swallow and hand the woman my cloche. I follow as she takes it to the counter at the front of the store and pulls out a sleek black hatbox.

"That will be seven guineas," she says, putting the hatbox into a bag for me.

Wordlessly, I hand her my money. Calypso is looking at some extravagantly beaded bandeaux near the entrance to the store. I keep one eye on her. She senses my stare and gives me a bandit's smile.

After paying and taking my bag, Calypso and I walk out the door. "What was that?" I demand the second the door closes behind us.

To her credit she doesn't try to pretend that she doesn't know what I'm talking about. Instead she shrugs and gives me another cheeky grin. "I influenced her."

"Excuse me?" I'm no innocent. I've seen mesmerism in action, but that woman hadn't been in a trance.

"I'll tell you over lunch," she yells over the loud motor of a truck passing by. "I'm starving!" Calypso takes my arm and darts out into the street, pulling me along in her wake. She expertly dodges the cars bearing down on us and ignores the blaring horns. By the time we reach the other side my heart is racing.

I yank my arm out of hers and she laughs at me. "What? Are you chicken?"

I toss my head but can't help but grin at her. She reminds me more and more of Cynthia by the minute. What is it about me that attracts such reckless people? "No. I'm cautious."

"Same thing, if you ask me." She pulls a door open and we enter a small, elegant little teahouse. The scent of meat pies and freshly baked scones makes my mouth water, but I remain resolute. She is going to tell me what she meant by influencing that salesgirl. We remove our coats at the table, and I notice she's wearing a brightly patterned yellow and orange silk shift. The colors highlight her exotic beauty, making her skin glow. Again her hair is tied back from her face with a ribbon and it cascades in a shining mass down her back. Even though I'm wearing a modish Chanel-style suit, I feel frumpy next to Calypso's fresh, girlish grace.

After we order, Calypso pours the tea into our delicately painted teacups. I stare at her without touching my cup until she gets the message.

"Oh, fine," she says with an exaggerated sigh, looking like a scolded child. "We've never spoken about our abilities, so how would you know? I can influence people. Not all the time, and not with everyone, but often enough to make it a true ability. It's like putting them in a trance or something."

She looks away and I open myself up to her but sense no deceit.

"How old are you?" I ask suddenly.

Her brows arch, surprised by the question. "Almost seventeen."

Just a bit younger than I am. "How long have you known about your ability?"

Her fingers trace the rim of her cup for a long moment. "I guess I've always been able to do it. My mother was easy. She would tell me I couldn't have another tart and I would wish for another one with all my heart and then she would change her mind. I didn't understand what I had done. I thought my wishes just came true a lot and considered myself lucky. I guess I was about seven when I began to experiment with it."

"And you say it doesn't work all the time?" My abilities are hit-and-miss as well, though under Cole's tutelage they're becoming more consistent.

She shakes her head. "No. It confused me for a long time

until I realized that my abilities won't work on anyone with a high level of spirituality or on other Sensitives." She must have seen my confusion because she laughs. "I was sent to a Catholic boarding school when my parents became estranged. Wishing didn't work on ninety percent of the nuns."

I smile and feel the tension I've felt since the millinery shop draining away. There's nothing sinister about her abilities. Calypso is rather like a kitten: playful and affectionate but never letting you forget about the claws. Considering my mother and my gun-toting best friend, would I even like someone without claws?

"What's really frightening is the ten percent of nuns that your abilities did work on!" I say. "What was wrong with them?"

She giggles. "I know. What were nonspiritual nuns doing teaching school?"

"Who knows? And, Calypso?" I look her straight in the eye and her face stills. "Next time don't influence someone to give me a cheaper price. I'd rather just pay for my hats."

Her shoulders slump, but then she brightens. "Let's talk about you now. What are your abilities?"

I hesitate.

"Oh, come on. I told you mine."

"I can channel the dead." I give her what I consider the least of my talents. My habit of self-protection is too strong to allow me to offer complete disclosure.

Calypso's eyes glitter with excitement. "What a fantastic ability! How often do you do it? Is it hard? I would love to be able to talk to the dead! Can you imagine talking to

Aristotle? Or Catherine La Voisin, or Morgan le Fay!"

"Isn't Morgan le Fay just a story?" I ask, trying to remember my Tennyson.

"Oh, no. She's real. My father once said we were related to her."

"I always assumed the Arthur stories were just legends."

Calypso shakes her head. "Don't let any red-blooded Englishmen hear you say that."

"So you're English, then?" I ask.

"Half English. My father was born here, but my mother is originally from Trinidad and moved to Greece as a child."

I nod. That explains the accent.

"Why are we talking about me again? I want to know about you. Who have you talked to?"

For a minute I'm confused, until I realize she's talking about dead people. I shake my head, not wanting to tell her that I've only done it once. "It's not that simple. And I don't know how to control it either."

A waitress serves our meat pies and we dig in. I'm half hoping that's the end of the questions, but it's not.

"So you're like me. Is that why you want to be a member of the Society? To learn control?"

"Partly. Though I've learned a lot of control working with Cole."

"Cole is wonderful, isn't he? I've only met him briefly since he's been back, but he is so nice. And handsome! Are you two close, then?"

It's a normal reaction, but my insides knot up in a tangle

of jealousy. Mortified, I glance down at my half-eaten meat pie, my hunger dissipating as I remember the tension at dinner last night. Cole had sent me a note this morning telling me he was tied up with preuniversity testing and family obligations but would meet me tomorrow night at the theater. I realize Calypso is still waiting for an answer and I give what I hope is a happy smile. "Yes, actually, we are."

Her brows rise, but she doesn't comment on my hesitation and instead asks me about my magic act. The conversation moves from that to her life as a child in Greece and by the time we're finished with our meal, I feel like I've made a friend.

She confirms this feeling with her next words. "It's like we've known one another forever. Are you doing anything this evening?"

I shake my head, thinking of Cole's note. "I'm on my own."

"Then come to a costume party with me tonight. It will be so much more fun if you come!"

I bite my lip.

"Please? You don't have to dress up if you don't want to."

I nod. I might as well. "All right. Count me in."

She bounces in her seat. "Wonderful! My friend Cecil and I will pick you up."

I smile at her enthusiasm, excitement rising in my chest. Well, maybe a night without Cole won't be so bad. He has his own life apart from me, after all. There is no reason why I can't have a life of my own, as well.

★★★

The car that parks out in front of the hotel is low and sleek. Calypso waves from the back as excited as a child in a parade. She's dressed like a Gypsy—which, considering her coloring, she actually could be—and, indeed, doesn't look like she's in a costume at all. I spent the afternoon putting together my own getup. I had the rather unoriginal idea of going as a magician, so I borrowed a top hat from Sandy and a black evening jacket from Louie, who gave it to me with some trepidation. "You be careful. I feel responsible for you, and these Brit bashes make New York parties look tame."

I told him that I'd be careful and didn't mention the crazy scavenger hunt Cynthia had thrown as my good-bye party.

I'd added a rose from the hotel lobby as a boutonniere and fashioned a wand from a wooden hanger. Handcuffs hang from my wrists like bracelets.

As I crawl in the back with Calypso, she introduces me to her friend, a young man who is dressed as a queen. "Anna Van Housen, this is Cecil Beaton, or should I say Queen Elizabeth? Cecil, this is Anna Van Housen, or should I say Harry Houdini?"

I gasp as if I'd been kicked in the stomach, but somehow make the right noises as I squeeze in next to them.

Calypso chatters to Cecil, blissfully unaware of the panic her words had caused. I forced myself to breathe. She couldn't possibly know that Houdini might be my father, could she?

When she turns to me and hands me a flask, I don't even hesitate and take a long drink that burns as it hits my stomach. I choke, my eyes watering as I hand it back to her, but the relaxation I feel is immediate.

"Calypso tells me you're an actual magician, Miss Van Housen. Perhaps you will treat us to a demonstration this evening?" Cecil asks in a high, reedy voice.

"Not Miss Van Housen! Harry! That's what I'm going to call you tonight, poppet."

Then she reaches over and gives my shoulder a friendly little nip. I jump, and she and Cecil laugh.

The party is being given in some sort of private room at Grey's Club. Or rooms, I should say, as a large dance floor branches off into several hallways with smaller, even more private rooms. It's the first time I've been in one of London's clubs, the kind that New York can only aspire to. Grey's Club was established exclusively for men and only allows women at private parties such as this one. I look around, trying to catch a glimpse of the famous snobbery behind the gay trappings of the party, but can only see the stunning colors.

The walls of the spacious room are covered with draperies of blue Indian silk, and giant urns of fresh flowers abound. One of the fake potted palms already has empty bottles stuck on its branches, a harbinger of the debauchery to come. On the shining parquet dance floor, couples in various costumes swing around and around as a band plays American jazz in one corner.

Dazzled, I spot Romeo doing the Charleston with Little Miss Muffet, Marie Antoinette dancing with Captain Hook, and a man wearing only a diaper swaying with a woman dressed as Mozart.

"Here!" Calypso snatches a couple of drinks off a tray being carried by a waiter in a tuxedo.

I take a cautious sip, pleased with the fruity taste. Then I remember, there's no prohibition in England so the booze is much, much better than most of the rotgut we get back home.

"Elizabeth! Come meet my friend."

A pretty, rather thin young woman dressed as a toddler joins us. She and Calypso press their cheeks together before turning to me. "Elizabeth Ponsonby, this is Anna Van Housen. She's an American magician. For real, not just tonight."

Elizabeth raises eyebrows that have been penciled in darkly above pleasant, rather vacuous blue eyes. "So nice to meet you. You must perform for us at some point. Your handcuffs are deevie! I love them. My poor parents would have kittens if I started wearing handcuffs." She puffs off her long cigarette holder and blows the smoke into a cloud above her head.

I shake my cuffs at her. "The important thing is to always have the key, or learn how to pick them open. Otherwise they could be dangerous."

Elizabeth laughs, her eyes already moving past us, her demeanor restless. This is clearly a woman who doesn't stay in one place long. "Oh, there's Babe! Excuse me, will you? And don't forget, I want a magical demonstration before the night is over."

With a twitch of her skinny shoulders she's gone and

Calypso is once again scanning the crowd. Suddenly her eyes narrow and I feel her jittery irritation. "What is he doing here?" she mutters. "I'll be right back," she says, and takes off across the room, her full knee-length red-and-gold skirt swishing furiously.

I try to spot who she is after, but only see a black-haired young man dressed as a rajah disappearing through a door with Calypso hot on his heels.

Abandoned, I sip my drink and tap my toes. I love to dance, though rarely get the opportunity. Cole doesn't seem like the dancing type, so I've never brought it up.

"Anna! What are you doing here?"

I jump at the sound of my name. Whirling around, I stare into Bronco Billy's handsome face. He's wearing his full cowboy getup and has a petite, blond, medieval princess on one arm and a languid brunette angel on the other. "I'm pretending to be a magician," I tell him, unaccountably irritated by his companions. "What are you doing here?"

The grin he flashes is saucy and shows the deep dimples at the corners of his mouth. "Pretending to be a cowboy. Would you like to dance?"

I blink. "Aren't you going to introduce me to your friends?"

He looks from side to side as if surprised to discover the girls still clinging to his arms. "Oh, I don't know their names. Sorry, ladies, this here is Anna and we're going to dance now. See you later? Here, have a drink. Looks like you can use one."

He takes the glass from my hand and passes it to the

medieval princess before pulling me out on the dance floor.

"Thank God you were here," he says swinging me into his arms. "I thought I was never going to get rid of them."

"Where did you meet them?" I ask, glancing over his shoulder to where the girls are staring at us, their faces sour.

"On the street. Now, before you lecture, I was just moseying on back to the hotel after practice and they yelled out of a cab that they would give me a ride to the party. Apparently, they thought I was on my way here. I figured why not, but after getting into the car I realized they were the kind of girls I wouldn't easily rid myself of."

"Do you have a lot of trouble with that?" Part of me is curious; another part is strangely jealous, which is horrible considering that I'm in love with Cole. *It's only because he's so handsome*, I comfort myself. *Any girl would feel the same way.*

He glances at me sideways as if he knows what I'm thinking and tilts me into a fast dip. I squeal and he laughs. The music quickens and Bronco Billy matches his steps. "Not that often," he says. "But often enough to make it annoying. City girls love a cowboy."

I change the subject, not wanting to hear any more about city girls. "Where did you learn to dance, Bronco Billy? Philadelphia?"

He nods. "And for the love of God, don't call me Bronco Billy. That's my stage name. Billy is fine."

I smile in assent, and give up conversation to concentrate. I need all my wits and breath to keep up with him. I look up, only to find his eyes are looking directly into mine and he gives me that magical smile that would make any girl's toes curl.

"You know how I got here," he says. "How did you end up at this shindig?"

The music moves into a slow dance song and he pulls me close. For a moment I can't breathe and then I shake my head. *Get ahold of yourself.* Even though I'm inexperienced, I'm not a child. I grew up on the road, the daughter of a modern woman who took lovers for pleasure as well as the meals or lodging they occasionally provided.

"A friend invited me." I concentrate on my steps and stare over his shoulder.

"Where is he?" Bronco Billy asks, looking around.

"*She* disappeared soon after we got here." I must have sounded worried because his arm tightens.

"Don't worry, I'll make sure you get back to the hotel all right."

I raise an eyebrow. "Do you know the way home?"

"Not exactly, but just how big could London be anyway?" He grins and I smile. The dance floor is so crowded we can hardly move, and he leads me out of the crowd and to an unoccupied corner.

"Boy, these Brits know how to throw a party, don't they?" He stares out into the throng of people, interest written all over his handsome face. A young man dressed as Henry VIII is trying to down an entire bottle of champagne in the center of an appreciative crowd.

My eyes widen as I recognize one of the revelers. "They

aren't all British." I nod toward a lovely young woman dressed as an Indian maiden. "I think that's Zelda Fitzgerald." I wildly look around for her famous husband.

"'There is a moment—Oh, just before the first kiss, a whispered word—something that makes it worthwhile.'"

My head jerks up to see the expression on Billy's face. He's looking out into the dancers, but his eyes are far away. He notices my surprise and gives me a bashful, aw-shucks-ma'am look. "I'm sorry. I loved that book."

"*This Side of Paradise* is one of my favorites," I tell him.

He nods. "I kept a little pocket version in my saddle pouch. I used to read when I was lonely. Sometimes I felt as if books were the only friends I had."

I know that feeling so exactly that my throat swells. We share a glance of complete understanding and then I look away, uncomfortable by the intimacy of the moment.

"Stay here," he says, and disappears. I'm grateful for the chance to recover and by the time he returns, two drinks in his hands, I've shoved the feeling out of my head.

"I hope you don't mind these are nonalcoholic. I'm not really a big drinker."

"I'm not either," I assure him. He gives me a wide smile and my heart skips a beat. *Stop that.*

Just then Calypso joins me, her pretty face looking drawn. "Are you ready to leave?" she asks. "I don't feel so good."

"Oh." I glance at Bronco Billy, who stares at Calypso as if she were a strange bird that just landed on the pommel of his saddle. "Yes, I'm ready."

"I can take you home if you like," Bronco Billy says.

Calypso glances at him as if just noticing his presence. I quickly introduce them and then answer his question, "That's all right. You stay and have fun. Thank you for the dances."

His presence is confusing, and the last thing I need in my life is more confusion. I hurriedly follow Calypso out the door and we get into the car we arrived in.

"Cecil said his driver will take us to wherever we want to go. He'll probably be at the party all night."

I almost ask why she wanted to leave so early, but my head is suddenly aching and I have a strange buzzing in my ears. I press my head against the window to cool it. Perhaps the booze wasn't as high quality as I thought it was.

I push Calypso's disappearance at the party out of my mind. Let her have her intrigue. I'll stick to my magic. That's what I came to London for. I didn't come for Cole or cowboys with hair the color of sunshine, the Society, or even to get away from my mother, though that is surely a bonus. I came to perform my magic, and that's what I'm going to do.

SIX

The unseasonal warmth of the past few days is gone as Cole and I drive to his house for tea with his mother and grandmother. The sky is dark with clouds producing a relentless downpour of drenching rain.

I've paired my new knockabout with a rust-colored wool coat my mother insisted on giving me when I left. The deep fur collar keeps my neck warm as well as giving me some much needed confidence. But in spite of my new hat and smashing coat, my stomach is churning from the anxious emotions coming off Cole. I want to ask him what's wrong, but if he's worried about me meeting his family, I don't want to know it. I'm nervous enough as it is.

When Cole cuts the engine of the car, we're in front of a large Queen Anne–style residence with a facade so formal and imposing that the swarm of butterflies in my stomach takes flight.

As I sit in the motorcar, waiting for Cole to open my door, I stare at the rows of sash windows set flush against the brickwork and the sweeping stone steps leading to a carved marble doorcase. Large white stone quoins on the corners of the house contrast with the cold gray of the brick.

This is a house to be reckoned with. A house that makes me squirm in embarrassment at my American accent, my circus upbringing, and my criminal past. This house wouldn't understand that I did what I had to do in order to ensure the survival of my mother and myself.

The people inside probably won't either.

I step out of the motorcar and am gratified that Cole takes my arm so I won't make a fool of myself and run in the other direction. As if sensing my misgivings, Cole gives my arm a squeeze.

"They aren't ogres, you know. My grandmother is a bit old-fashioned, but that's just her way. My mother is going to love you."

My stomach tightens. Meaning that his grandmother won't.

The door opens as we come up the steps and I'm face-to-face with his mother. I'd half expected a stiff disapproving butler to open the door, not this welcoming, gray-haired woman who looks at me with Cole's eyes. "You must be Anna. Cole has told me so much about you."

She offers her hand and I keep hold of Cole's arm as I reach out to greet her. His control increases my own and I feel nothing but the warmth of her hand.

If she's not happy to see me with her son, I definitely don't want to know it.

"I'm delighted to meet you, Mrs. Archer."

"Please, call me Muriel."

Other than the dark eyes, Cole's mother looks nothing like him and I wonder if he got his intelligent good looks from his father. Muriel's long face is saved from being horse-like by the firmness of her chin and the fullness of her lips. Her hair is an iron gray that will never turn silver and her hands and feet are large. She's an impressive woman who stops just short of being imposing by the kindness of her face and the warmth of her smile.

"Let us go into the sitting room, shall we? Robert has just laid a cozy fire so we will be much more comfortable in there than the dining room."

I smile as Cole and I follow her down a large hall with a high ceiling and elaborate plasterwork. She and Cole have more in common than their eyes. They also have a measured way of speaking that is quintessentially British.

"Where is Grandmother?" Cole asks when we enter the empty room.

"Oh, I'm sure she'll be down directly," Muriel says, waving her hand vaguely.

My stomach lurches. I hope so. What would I do if she decided to show her disapproval by refusing to have tea with an upstart, no-name American? What would Cole do?

I take a seat on an overstuffed blue sofa. The sitting room is less formal than I expected, but still more formal than is common in the States. The walls are a delicate robin's-egg blue, which contrasts beautifully with the dark parquet floor and the white marble fireplace. Stiff wingback chairs sit next to slender, polished tables that one should never set a cup on. On the other hand, the rugs on the floor look deliciously soft, and fuzzy throws are flung casually over the chairs.

Muriel sits on the chair opposite the sofa and Cole takes a seat very close to me. We're not touching, but I can still feel his calming influence. "Robert will bring us our tea in a moment." She turns to me. "Cole tells me you're quite well traveled."

I stifle a laugh. Well, yes, if you call moving from one flea-infested boardinghouse to another all across small-town America well traveled. It wasn't always bad, of course. When we were flush, we might stay in a fancy hotel for a week or two, but it never lasted long. "I've seen quite a bit of the States, but I've never been to Europe before, so this is exciting."

She gives me a gracious smile and I have a suspicion she knows more than she's letting on about my past. "I hear you're a talented magician. How did that come about? Most girls your age aspire to be office girls in the city or perhaps actresses in the picture shows."

Her voice is perplexed and a bit wary and I understand. Muriel Archer isn't making any judgments. Yet. But she is concerned that her son is so taken with someone with such an odd profession.

I'm not offended. I'd feel the same way.

I try to figure out how to explain my love of magic in a positive way. I swallow and settle on the truth. At least part of the truth.

"My mother was a magician's assistant when she lived in Hungary, so I guess a love and appreciation for magic is in my blood."

"Lord have mercy, she's a Hungarian magician!" I startle at the fervent words uttered behind my back.

Turning my head, I track the stately progress of an elderly woman dressed head to toe in black. The rustle of her old-fashioned taffeta heralds her progress as does the tappity-tap of her gold-handled cane. Her hair is piled on her head in a mass of silver curls and a choker of pearls gleams around her neck.

"Now, Mother," Muriel clucks as the dowager takes the seat next to her.

I'm struck dumb as her sharp blue eyes appraise me. My knees feel suddenly painfully bare even though they're covered by silk stockings, and I resist the urge to yank down my skirt.

"It's wonderful to see you, Cole," the old woman says. "I don't see you nearly enough, but I understand. The young do gad about so. Now sit up, dear. There's a boy."

I feel Cole straighten next to me. He clears his throat. "You're looking well, Grandmother. May I present Miss Anna Van Housen?"

My lips curve in a tentative smile.

His grandmother sniffs. "If you must."

The smile slips off my face, but Cole continues as if his grandmother hadn't spoken. "Anna, this is my grandmother. And please don't fret. Her bark is far worse than her bite."

The woman leans forward onto the cane. "My bite is precisely as bad as my bark."

I believe it.

An ancient butler, who I assume is Robert, comes in with a tinkling tea cart. It's loaded with enough tiny little finger foods to satiate an entire army of Lilliputians. He carefully lifts a silver tray from the cart and places it on the table in front of us.

"Perhaps our guest would like to pour the tea?" Cole's grandmother interjects, a gleam in her pale blue eyes.

I swallow hard. Then, to let her know I'm not that easily intimidated, I curl my lips up ever so slightly at the corners. "Oh, you don't want me pouring. I would hate to spill it." I don't add, *all over you* but I don't have to, my meaning is clear.

Shades of my mother.

"I'll pour," Muriel says hastily.

A heavy silence descends as Cole's mother pours the tea and little plates of food are passed. A slight buzzing starts in my ears and I shake my head, wondering if I'm getting sick.

Cole's grandmother clears her throat. "So as an entertainer, do you perform onstage with men?"

I almost choke on a crumpet. I lift my eyes to meet hers. She stares back at me, malice written in the creases and lines of her face. I know in an instant that this is no grumpy old woman who can be won over. To her I will never be more than gutter trash her grandson picked up—and American gutter trash to boot.

"Grandmother," Cole exclaims, but I lay a hand on his arm to let him know that it's all right.

"I usually performed with my mother, but occasionally I performed with a sword swallower named Swineguard. He was like a father to me, actually." I pick up a clean butter knife and twirl it. It flashes in and out of my fingers before I calmly dip it into the butter to spread on my crumpet.

There's a long silence before Cole says cheerfully, "Did I forget to tell you? Anna worked in a circus too!"

Cole's grandmother's mouth purses. "How curious."

In spite of my bravado, my face flushes. I hate being judged for things I had no control over. The buzzing in my ears increases and I give everyone a vague smile. What *is* that?

I turn to his mother, who is glancing from me to her mother-in-law with the horrified look of someone who's found herself in a drama not of her making. I take pity.

"What a lovely tea, Muriel," I tell her even though my head feels so fuzzy, I can barely swallow a bite.

"Thank you, dear. Cole tells me you're going on tour soon?"

"Merciful heavens," his grandmother murmurs.

Everyone ignores her. The buzzing in my ears is like a symphony of honeybees getting ready to take flight, and everything tastes like paper. Desperately, I take a swallow of tea, only to burn my tongue. I shake my head to clear it and Cole gives me an odd look. "Yes, we'll be gone for three weeks and giving ten performances. This is a minirun to work the kinks out of the show."

"Where are you going?" Muriel asks.

His grandmother snorts to let us know exactly where she thinks I'm going.

My mind is curiously blank and I look at Cole in near panic. I don't want to get sick in front of his mother and grandmother. I suddenly feel his presence, comforting me, and the answer pops into my mind. "Budapest, Warsaw, and Prague are the big cities, and I think there are a couple of smaller venues, as well. We'll be doing several shows at each, tweaking our performances until we get them just right. Then we'll come back here for a couple of weeks before we go to France."

"How exciting!" Muriel says.

It *is* exciting. Entertaining people with my magic—feeling their excitement, watching their amazement—is what I love doing best in the world. So why don't I feel more excited? Perhaps because I'm sitting with people who believe that performers are one small step above Gypsies and thieves.

Even though the buzzing has abated, my head still feels as if I'm trying to think through a bowl of aspic. Cole senses that something is amiss and shifts the conversation to the university and what he'll be studying.

"I don't understand why you want to be a detective," his grandmother sniffs. "Why waste a fine legal education on that when you can go into the civil service like your father? That's what I would like to know. Being a detective is so common."

Cole and his mother continue talking as if they hadn't heard and the rest of the tea goes just like that. His grandmother throws in comments so spiteful that I want to blow up at her, while the other two both behave as if it's normal. Perhaps it is, but by the time we finish our tea, my temples are throbbing and I'm more than ready to leave.

Cole's mother is effusive in her good-byes, no doubt trying to make up for her mother-in-law's poor behavior. His grandmother picks up a book and begins reading to avoid saying good-bye to me, so I leave it be and hurry out the door.

As we walk back to the motorcar Cole says, "They liked you."

I stop, a surprised laugh escaping before I can choke it back. "Cole, that was *awful*!"

He smiles. "Oh come on. It wasn't that bad. My grandmother can be a bit gruff, but . . ."

"You're joking, right? She was absolutely nasty to me."

He opens the door for me and then shuts it. Hard.

He can't be serious.

"Were we even in the same room?" I wonder when he climbs in.

"I think you're overreacting just a bit. She's basically harmless . . ."

"She's as harmless as a piranha. What about the things she was saying to you?"

"What things? Oh, you mean about being a detective? That's just the way she is. She's had a harder life than you would think. My grandfather died when my father was very young and she raised the children by herself. She was devastated when my father died in the war."

I press my forehead against the cold window. Yes, it must have been so hard raising three children by herself in that rich house with all those servants.

He places his hand on my shoulder and I turn my head to look at him. "My grandmother will warm up to you, and my mother already loves you. I can tell."

He gives me such a reassuring smile that I can't help but smile back. He starts the car and pulls away from the curb and I study his strong profile in the waning light. His Homburg is tilted ever so slightly on his head and the sharp clever planes of his face are filled with character. But in reality he was raised by nannies and tutors and in boarding school and privilege. Yes, he lost his father and was stranded deep within enemy territory while at school during the Great War, but as horrible as that was, he has never gone without food or shelter. I've done without both. Right now, the chasm between us feels insurmountable.

The next morning, I pull out the slip of paper Calypso gave me the day of our outing and telephone her at her boardinghouse. Luckily, she's free and we arrange to meet after my rehearsal. I don't want to spend the day alone, worrying about the stiffness that seems to have sprung up between Cole and me. I already spent a fitful night worrying about the strange episode I had at his house, which he neglected to ask me about. Then I lay in bed and worried why he hadn't asked me about it. He knew something was wrong. Had I offended him, speaking that way about his grandmother? Then I worried about that, too. There seemed to be no end of the things to worry about, so I decided some lighthearted fun with a friend is just what I need.

Anything is better than moping about the hotel waiting for Cole to get in touch with me.

Calypso is in the lobby when I get back from the theater and greets me with a kiss on the cheek. "I'm so glad you rang me up," she says, her dark eyes pensive. "I'm worried about Pratik and don't want to be by myself."

"I didn't want to be by myself today either, so I guess it was meant to be. Has anything else happened?" I ask.

She shakes her head. "No. I just started thinking about his disappearance and then I couldn't stop. I hardly slept at all."

I tilt my head. Her normally lively spirit is considerably dimmer and dark circles lie heavy under her eyes. She looks as exhausted as I feel and I link my arm with hers. "You know what my best friend once said? That there is nothing that ails one that can't be made considerably better by a piece of delectable chocolate cake. Do you know of a handy bakery?"

She gives me a smile. "I knew you would make me feel better. There's one over by where I live that may have just what we're looking for."

Both of us are still dressed for the cold, in wool coats and dark hats, so we simply turn around and head back out. We take the tube to St. Charles stop and I'm amazed at how clean it seems to be compared with New York's subway. When we emerge, the rain has picked up and we huddle under her large black umbrella watching the water cascade down its sides.

"We'll have to get you your very own umbrella," she says. "It's practically a rite of passage, you know."

"Yours is plenty big!" I tell her, marveling at its size.

"I have an extra one just like it in my room. We'll go get it after our cake." She leads me swiftly down a narrow street flanked by three- and four-story buildings, so close together they almost blot out the sky. These gracious old structures would be architectural wonders anywhere else in the world, but the people here live, fight, give birth, and die in them as if they aren't anything unusual. I have no time for lollygagging, though, as the street is busy with motorists, and I'm delighted to see a double-decker bus splashing toward us. Calypso waits until it goes by and then once again we risk life and limb by darting across the thoroughfare, dodging traffic. She ignores the number of horns honking at us and steps up onto the sidewalk as if that's a normal occurrence. Perhaps it is.

She takes me through a narrow door with panes of glass so old they look wavy, and I'm immediately assailed by the warm, yeasty scent of fresh bread. She shuts her umbrella and points me in the direction of one of the empty, chipped café tables in front of the shop. "Go sit and I will order us the best hot chocolate and chocolate cake you have ever tasted."

I sit at one of the small tables in front of a large bay window that is so steamy from the heat of the ovens in the back that it's impossible to see through. The bakery is warm and cozy and just perfect for a gray, drizzly afternoon. I slip my coat off my shoulders and take the cup Calypso offers. The chocolate is hot and comforting and I bless the person who made it.

By the time she returns with the cake, I am already feeling much better. She sets the slice between us and hands me a fork. Her hair is plaited loosely in the back with a ribbon, and dark waves frame her face. She still looks tired, but less worried.

I take a sip of my hot chocolate and close my eyes for a moment, enjoying the creaminess.

She laughs. "I told you it was good. Try the cake."

I take a forkful of cake and then nod as a velvety sweetness spreads through my mouth. "You were right. It's delicious." We smile at one another and I feel a discernible lightening of the emotions between us.

I'm suddenly curious about this girl who is fast starting to fill the void created after saying good-bye to Cynthia. "I take it you don't have family here?"

The drop in her mood is so sudden, I look up from the cake, startled.

Her mouth twists. "I do but we're estranged. My mother is in the States."

Her expression is closed, and I know I shouldn't pry but

am compelled to ask, "And your father?"

"My father is here in London, but we don't speak." Her smile is grim. "I take after him in many ways and he can't accept the fact that I may be as talented or more talented than he is."

My eyes widen. "Is he a Sensitive?"

She snorts. "No. He's an *in*sensitive."

"Is that why you stay in a boardinghouse?" I'm curious about her life. She's younger than I am but seems both childish and ageless at the same time.

She nods. "The Society rents rooms for us in a house not too far from their old office. It's a nice place and it's ever so much better than staying with my father in the mausoleum."

She gives an exaggerated shudder.

I frown. "Do all the Sensitives live there? At the boardinghouse?"

She nods.

"Then why was Pratik staying with Mr. Gamel?"

She presses her lips together. "I'm not exactly sure. He didn't make friends easily."

She stands and puts on her coat. "Are you finished?"

I nod reluctantly. The thought of going out into the rain doesn't hold much appeal, but impatience is shooting off her in little sparks. So I crawl into my coat before heading back out into the drizzle.

I follow her through a maze of narrow streets, and traffic becomes scarce. Black umbrellas bob along the sidewalks like a funereal march of mushrooms. The rain has lessened, but one can hear the dripping as if the world is so saturated that it will never dry out. Foreboding runs down my spine, as if someone just walked over my grave.

"Here we are!"

She pulls me up a short walk to a gray stone Georgian building that rises four stories from the street. Black wrought iron decorative bars cover the lower windows, giving it the look of a prison. The black paint on the front door is chipped and the stone steps are pitted. The house itself is flanked by two other row homes done in the same style, but better cared for, giving this one the look of a poor and bitter relation.

Suddenly a feeling of apprehension rushes over me and I stop at the threshold, my limbs sluggish and heavy.

Calypso turns to me. "What's wrong?"

My tension eases at the sound of her voice. Silly. I'm being silly.

I follow her into the house, chiding myself. *I just need to get used to the ancient atmosphere of London*, I tell myself. Of course, it seems creepy considering how old everything is. And the fog and the wet aren't helping.

The foyer leads to a wide hallway, with arched doors on either side. "There's the dining room in there, but most of us don't eat here much." She lowers her voice. "The cook is horrible. That's the lounge."

Calypso pauses and I poke my head in. Deep leather couches, rows of bookcases, and a large fireplace give the room a cozy feel except for the chill that permeates the entire house. "It would be nice with a fire," I tell her, and she nods.

"The landlady refuses to pay for either a good cook or any heat that she doesn't have to. Jared once left a glass of water on the window ledge as an experiment and it was frozen solid the next morning."

I shiver. It's hard to imagine what her father's house is like if this place is better.

"My room is upstairs but let's go get the umbrella first before I forget it. It's down in the cellar . . ."

Just then a faint scream comes from deeper within the house. Both Calypso and I freeze.

"Did you hear that?" she asks.

My stomach churns and my legs twitch as if they are going to run me out of the house on their own. Before I can answer, another scream sounds and this time it doesn't stop.

Calypso whirls around and runs toward the source of the sound, and in spite of legs that want to collapse underneath me, I follow. At the end of the hall she turns in to the kitchen, where an older woman in a long apron stares transfixed at an open door across the room. When she sees Calypso, she points at the door.

We approach cautiously. The screams take on an eerie, keening quality, and my whole body trembles at the sound. It takes every bit of self-control I have to follow Calypso down those rickety steps. As we descend, the dank smell of an ancient basement assaults my nostrils. Fear and a strange sense of suppressed excitement ripple through the air, though I can't tell if the emotions belong to Calypso or the terrified woman we find still screaming at the bottom. It's a young woman with dark blond hair. Her face is dead white and her blue eyes are wide with horror. An upturned basket of laundry lies at her feet. I follow her terrified gaze and my stomach lurches at the sight that greets me.

Pratik.

Calypso skids to a stop and her hand goes over her mouth. The woman jumps when she sees us and then, as if released, turns and races up the stairs. I stand frozen, staring.

Pratik is sitting up against an old-fashioned washing machine with his hands lying in his lap, palms upward. Something round and dark like a beetle gleams against one palm, but I can't tell what it is. His vacant eyes are staring at something horrifying that only he can see and his dark skin is sallow and sunken, as if his essence has been drained. Even from a distance I can tell that his clothes are mussed, as if they had been thrown on hastily. His white turban is nowhere in evidence.

"Is he dead?" Calypso whispers.

I try to speak but no sound comes out. I swallow hard and try again. "Yes." I know he's dead without even taking a closer look.

She turns to me then, her eyes glowing coals in a face so white I can see the tracings of veins under her skin. "Can you feel him?" she asks suddenly. "Is his ghost here?"

A thread of curiosity runs through the horror in her voice. I shake my head, suddenly sick to my stomach. "No.

It doesn't work like that."

She nods as if confirming a suspicion, then turns back to the body. "We need to call Mr. Gamel right away."

"What?" I can't keep the incredulousness from my voice. "Don't we need to call the police?"

She shakes her head. "No. Mr. Gamel first."

She brushes past me and goes back up the stairs.

I swallow convulsively and grip the stair rail for support. Just a few days ago, that young man was talking to me. I remember the sadness of his smile and wonder if I'll ever forget the vulnerable look in his eyes.

I can't help but take one more glance at his body before I follow Calypso up the steps. His eyes aren't vulnerable now.

Only haunted.

SEVEN

There's no place left to sit at the table, so people line the walls of the small room of the Society's headquarters. Cole stands next to me, his hand firmly in mine, as if he wants everyone to know I am under his protection. The connection between us is so tangible and heartfelt; I can feel the depth of his emotions for me. They're as warm and comforting as a soft blanket wrapped about my shoulders. Is it love? Sometimes I know it is. Other times I'm unsure. Cole isn't comfortable talking about his feelings and I'm too self-conscious to bring it up on my own.

We're standing with the other Sensitives—Rose, the young woman who found Pratik's body; Jared; and Jenny. Calypso hasn't arrived yet. The board members are at the table, while the rest of the scientists stand at the other side of the table. The tension in the room is so strong my stomach is roiling. Rose is tense and pale after her ordeal. She had gone down to the basement to do her washing and had instead found Pratik. She told me in no uncertain terms that she would tell her story before the Society and then she was done.

After the inquisition by the police yesterday, not to mention having to sleep in the same house where she had found her friend's body, I don't blame her.

Leandra sweeps into the room in a chic black afternoon dress with gold embroidery at the neckline and a layered skirt. She's wearing a black felt helmet hat and her shining blond hair is worn with dashing spit curls on her cheeks. The murmuring in the room pauses for a moment before resuming. She gives me a warm hug. Her concern washes over me, but I still feel that sense of buried darkness. It's very close to the surface today, like molten lava moving just beneath the earth's crust. I wonder what would happen if it blew?

"How are you doing?" she asks. "We wanted to come with you last night, but with the bobbies already there, we had to wait until the Yard was informed officially. There would have been too many questions had Harrison just arrived out of the blue. He was there all night."

I nod. The landlady had called the law before Calypso could call Mr. Gamel. It's not as if anyone could stop her without raising suspicion. I had been there for several hours, answering questions as well.

Leandra turns to the man who had followed her in. "This is my husband, Harrison. Harrison, this is Cole's Anna."

I flush at that and as we shake hands he gives me a smile. He doesn't look like a detective, but then I've never met anyone from Scotland Yard before. He's not as tall as Cole but almost, with light brown hair and eyes that are as blue as mine. His face glows with a quiet kindness and upon seeing the obvious affection between him and Leandra, I'm a bit abashed by my jealousy of Leandra and Cole. "It's nice to meet you," I murmur.

"I see the room is as divided as usual," Leandra says, looking around.

"The more things change, the more they stay the same," Harrison says.

"So do you know why the meeting has been called other than the obvious?" Cole asks.

"There are certain details which make this impossible to sweep under the rug," Harrison says under his breath as Mr. Gamel calls the meeting to order.

"I'm sure you've all heard the rumors so I wanted to gather everyone together in order to set the story straight and answer any questions you might have."

"Any questions?" Leandra challenges.

Mr. Gamel smiles in her direction, but I notice he doesn't meet her eyes. "So nice to see you, Leandra. Your fine wit has been missed." He turns back to the other board members without answering her. "I am very sorry to have to tell you that a former member of our Society has indeed been found dead under suspicious circumstances. While this is unfortunate, we still do not have enough facts to say with impunity that this has anything to do with us."

"I beg to differ," Harrison says before stepping forward, but Mr. Gamel holds up a finger.

"Please let me finish and then we will open the meeting up for comments."

"Why don't you let him speak?" Jenny says. "Isn't he our investigator on the case?"

"I will let him speak. I simply wish to finish my statement, so our official position is clear."

"How can you have an official position without even consulting us?" Leandra demands.

Mr. Gamel produces a gavel out of nowhere and pounds on the table. "This is exactly what I had hoped to avoid. Our official position is that we will continue with business as usual, but while we are certain Pratik wasn't killed because of his Sensitivity, we would like to assure our Sensitives of their value by having them all move here. We have a large, fully equipped flat on the upper floor and we would like to open it up to all of you, for your own safety, of course."

There is an immediate uproar among the Sensitives, and Mr. Gamel pounds on the table to no avail. Suddenly the door slams and most of us jump.

Calypso looks around, her dark eyes alight. "What did I miss?"

No one speaks for a moment. She's wearing a simple beige dress made of lace with a handkerchief hemline. Silver hoops glisten in her ears and her hair is piled in a messy knot on top of her head. She stands like a Gypsy princess, gazing upon the rest of us as if we were her subjects. I have to hand it to her: She knows how to make an entrance. Her presence is arresting.

"They want to lock us up in the attic," Jared says.

Bedlam breaks out again, and Calypso shrugs and comes over to where I'm standing. "This is crazy! Don't you think this is crazy?" she demands, leaning in to kiss my cheek. She notices Leandra and Harrison. "Oh, hello."

I can tell by the tone of her voice she doesn't much like Leandra, though the glance she gives Harrison says she doesn't mind him at all. I almost smile. Even in the middle of a crisis, Calypso finds time to flirt with a handsome man right under his wife's nose. I can see Cynthia doing the same thing.

Leandra quivers and gives Calypso a contemptuous once-over before turning back to the argument.

If Calypso notices Leandra's dismissal of her, she gives no sign because her eyes have locked onto Cole next to me. "Cole! Thank you so much for coming over last night. Your presence was such a comfort." She puts out her hand not to shake but in a way that strongly suggests that he kiss it. To my surprise he lets go of my hand and does exactly that.

"So glad I could be of service," he says, his cheeks flushing.

My urge to smile fades as Calypso gazes up at him, looking like an exotic rose. Cole stares back at her as if entranced. I feel no power coming off her as I did in the hat shop, but then, as beautiful as she is, she probably doesn't have to use her powers of suggestion to attract men. Besides, didn't she tell me she couldn't influence Sensitives?

I press my lips together in annoyance.

"Anna and I were so grateful for your presence."

The sound of my name seems to startle him and he drops her hand.

"Order! Order!" More gavel pounding. Once the room is

quiet, Mr. Gamel stands. "Of course, we're not holding anyone prisoner. I just wanted to offer our protection to anyone who doesn't feel safe."

"If Jonathon's disappearance and Pratik's death aren't linked and you think it has nothing to do with us, why are you offering your protection?" Jenny asks.

Mr. Gamel shuts his eyes for a minute and I note the dark circles under them. He probably didn't get much sleep last night either. "I have said it before and I will say it again. Jonathon left of his own accord. Pratik's death is a tragedy and I have every confidence that Scotland Yard will soon find the perpetrator of that horrible crime."

"How can you say that Pratik's Sensitivity or his affiliation with the Society was not a factor in his murder?" Cole asks. His tone is reasonable, but I can sense his suppressed anger. I take his hand again, remembering that he and Pratik were friends.

Mr. Gamel clears his throat. "I'm just saying that a connection has not been established—"

"What would it take for a connection to be established?" Leandra asks, her voice incredulous. "He was taken from your home under suspicious circumstances and found in the basement of a boardinghouse where several Sensitives live. It's foolhardy to think there isn't a connection."

"I am offering protection to anyone who wishes to take advantage of it." Mr. Gamel is losing his patience and I wonder why he is fighting so hard against a connection between Pratik's murder and the Society. Like Leandra, I think this is obvious.

"And why should we trust you to protect us?" Leandra continues. "You don't even allow us the privilege of sitting in on board meetings that concern us."

"The main thing is that you are all valuable and the work shouldn't be interrupted," Mr. Price says. "We should keep to as normal a routine as possible."

"God forbid the work be interrupted," Jared says.

Jenny agrees. "It's not their lives that are in danger."

Julian Casperson rises. "At this point, I think it would be imprudent to jump to conclusions. We have offered the apartment only for those who don't feel safe. Harrison? What is your opinion on all this?"

The room quiets and I note that even the board members and the scientist look at Harrison with respect.

"The details of the murder, which I'll not repeat here, are disturbing. This looks to be a ritualistic murder of some sort of religious cult, either satanic or otherwise."

I close my eyes for a moment, light-headed, and Cole squeezes my hand. My mind goes back to the afternoon before and I remember the dark, round item in Pratik's hand.

"Blimey, are you saying poor Pratik was sacrificed?" Mr. Casperson asks.

Harrison shakes his head. "There simply isn't enough evidence to know."

"Do you have any suspects?" Mr. Price drums his fingers lightly on the table, but his sharp dark eyes are everywhere.

"I can't comment on that. Cole and I will be looking into this on our own, but as a detective with Scotland Yard, I am unable to comment on the actual investigation. However

I can say that under these circumstances, everyone here should be careful. We have no proof the two incidents are linked, but I think it would be foolish to assume they aren't until we can track Jonathon down."

Jared frowns. "So you think we should move in here?"

"It's not up to me to decide that. It's up to each individual. But I'm moving Leandra and the children out of town until we can find out more."

I glance at Leandra. From the flat set of her mouth she is none too happy about this news.

Mr. Gamel takes advantage of the lull in conversation to reassert his authority. "So you see, it is up to each of you, but if you do not choose to move to the safety of the apartment, please do not move around the city by yourself too much. Even though I am sure this will be cleared up very soon, I want you all to be vigilant."

Mr. Price frowns. "I have all the faith in our friend here," he interjects with a nod toward Harrison, "but perhaps we should bring in an expert in satanic cults to assess the situation?"

"Who did you have in mind?" Mr. Casperson asks.

"Aleister Crowley?" Harrison asks.

"Aleister Crowley's brand of black magic is not welcome here," Mr. Price thunders, and I startle.

Calypso jumps at the tone of Mr. Price's voice and she hugs herself nervously, watching the interchange.

Mr. Gamel waves a hand. "I agree that Mr. Crowley's presence would only further complicate matters. Surely we have enough people with that sort of expertise that we don't need to bring in anyone else. And, like I said, I believe this whole matter will be cleared up very soon."

How could a ritualistic murder be cleared up? I wonder as people break into tense groups. I glance at my fellow Sensitives. Their concern is palpable.

I turn to Leandra, whose green eyes are flashing. "I wouldn't move in here," she tells the others. "Honestly, do you trust these people? And, moreover, if someone is targeting Sensitives, do you really all want to be in the same place?"

She has a point.

Rose shakes her head, a nervous tic in her cheek working. "I'm done," she announces. "I don't want any part of this. I'm better at controlling my ability now and I'd rather take my chances on the outside. My fiancé has always wanted me to leave and now seems like the perfect time. I just came to tell the board my story. I don't owe anyone, even poor Pratik, anything more than that."

Leandra gives her a hug. "I would leave too, except I want to be here for new people like Anna." She nods at me and I smile, though if truth be told, I'm not even sure I want to be here.

I look again to where Cole, Jared, and Harrison are being held in thrall by Calypso and I wonder why I hadn't noticed Cole letting go of my hand again. My stomach clenching, I say good-bye and join him.

He startles and blushes scarlet when I put my hand on his arm. I know how reserved he is around women and I can tell

Calypso makes him uncomfortable.

The question is, is it because she's a woman or is it because he finds her attractive?

Calypso watches us, a smile on her lips. Is she trying to capture Cole's attention or is this just a part of her nature? I open myself up and am immediately assaulted by so many emotions my mind spins.

I clutch Cole's arm. The fear in the room is tangible, and I feel white-hot anger as well as dread and panic. I turn my head this way and that, my gorge rising. It's too much. I try to close myself off, shut myself down, but the waves of emotion are relentless. Cole keeps talking to Calypso and doesn't seem to notice my distress. The room dims and a red curtain rises behind my eyes.

Why doesn't Cole notice?

"Anna!"

I hear Leandra's voice as if it were coming from far away and my knees buckle. Cole catches me before I fall and a chair appears from out of nowhere. I sink into it, grateful for the support. Suddenly someone is touching my face. The fingertips, cool, comforting, move gently across my cheeks and eyelids, and linger on my temples. My heart rate slows and the curtain recedes.

I open my eyes and find myself staring into Jenny's pale, freckled face. Her eyes are only inches away from mine and it's her cool hands against my forehead. "Are you all right now?" she asks, her voice as refreshing and soothing as a mountain stream.

I nod.

Her hands drop to her sides and red colors her pallid complexion.

"You're a healer!" I exclaim.

She shakes her head. "Not really. I just have an ability to make people feel better. I can't heal illnesses or diseases, just help comfort those who suffer from them." She looks down at her hands as if embarrassed.

Now *that's* a useful ability in an ailing world.

"Thank you," I whisper.

She smiles.

Slowly, I realize that everyone in the room is staring. Concern fills Cole's dark eyes as he bends over me, and I resist the urge to push him away. I was in trouble and he didn't notice because he was too taken with Calypso to see what was right in front of him until I had practically collapsed on the floor.

"I'm fine," I tell him, my words coming out more tersely than I had intended. I glance around at the room full of people and soften my tone. "I'm fine, really."

"It's no wonder you collapsed, poor thing, considering." Leandra's warm hand is on my shoulder.

Calypso, too, is by my side. "Are you sure you're all right?" she asks, worry written all over her lovely features.

I nod.

"Are you going to move into the Society?" Calypso asks.

I shake my head. "No. I'm leaving tomorrow for a few weeks on the road."

Cole has his hand on my back and he shakes his head

as well. "I'm not either. It isn't convenient and I am going to be doing a lot of investigating with Harrison. Finding Jonathon and figuring out who killed Pratik are our top priorities."

A thought chills my blood. "But won't that put you in danger?"

"Don't worry, Anna. We're not going to take any risks," Harrison says. "Now if you will excuse me, I'm going to talk to Gamel before we leave. Will you be all right?" He directs this last bit to his wife, who nods.

"Cole and Anna will drive me home," Leandra says. "I need to start packing the boys' things."

"And yours," Harrison says firmly.

Leandra gives him a wicked smile and I know she isn't going anywhere no matter what he says.

Calypso droops dejectedly as she realizes she has been left out of the plans, but I resist inviting her along. I sense that Leandra doesn't like her.

We drop Leandra off and Cole takes me to my hotel. After parking the car, he follows me into the lobby. Even though it's as worn as the rest of the hotel, it's also small and intimate with a deep sofa; a dusty rubber plant in the corner; and a tall, rather hideous lamp that glows dimly through a red-beaded shade. Men are not allowed in women's rooms, so we take a seat on the couch and are promptly enveloped by the velvet cushions.

Cole scoots over until he is seated closer to me. "Be careful, you could get lost in there." His eyes crinkle up in a smile and I notice his dark circles underneath. I struggle briefly between concern and irritation. Concern wins.

"You need to rest," I tell him.

He shakes his head. "How can I rest after what happened to Pratik? For all we know, Jonathon could be hurt, or worse."

I am silent for a moment and then ask hesitantly, "Harrison said that the authorities had discovered certain things . . ."

Cole is quiet, and I can tell he's struggling because he really doesn't want to tell me. Exasperation ripples up and down my spine. Of all the useless, old-world . . .

He looks down at me and I know he feels my impatience. "Pratik died of exsanguination."

I shiver, even though I have no idea what he's talking about. "What does that mean in English, please?"

"Bloodletting. It means he bled to death. His wrists were cut."

I press my lips together to hold back a moan.

"Other things were done." He swallows and looks away. "Things that no one would have done to themselves."

I shudder, remembering the sunken, sallow tone of Pratik's skin.

Pressing my face against the wool lapels of Cole's peacoat, I take in the warm, piney clean scent of him. I close my eyes, wishing that we were someplace far away where no trouble could find us. He kisses the top of my head and I know he wishes the same thing. It's the closest I've felt to him since he kissed me in the motorcar. My stomach churns. After we dropped off Pratik.

Sighing, I tilt my head back. "Were you and Jonathon friends?"

"Yes. We weren't really close, though. He was in his late twenties, and like many Sensitives found later in life, he was very private. But he was a nice enough fellow." He leans his head back against the seat. "He wandered a lot. When he disappeared, no one thought anything about it. But now . . ."

My mind races. "You don't think he's been held prisoner all this time, do you?"

"I don't know. I hope not."

Neither one of us say it but we are both thinking of Pratik.

He picks up my hand and the warm connection we've always had is made. My chest pangs as I realize that I've felt our bond far too seldom since I arrived in England. Through his fingertips I sense the worry that consumes him. We sit in silence until he turns, his body angled away from mine.

"What's going on?" he asks quietly. "You seem different."

I seem different? Irritation brushes across my skin like stinging nettles and I snatch my hand away. "Why don't we go over recent events to see why I might seem a bit different?" I try to keep my voice mild, but the edginess I feel emerges. "The Society I came here to join is in shambles because of bickering and infighting. A fellow Sensitive disappears and another one is found brutally murdered. I'm working the kinks out in a new routine and going on tour by myself for the very first time. And my boyfriend doesn't even notice when I collapse in front of him!"

"What do you mean, I didn't notice? I caught you before you fell."

"It took you long enough." I don't want to mention that he didn't notice because he was too busy talking to Calypso because I don't want to alert him that he may be attracted to her. Or that I'm being petty and jealous of someone I genuinely like because she happens to be beautiful.

Cole's jaw tightens. "In case you hadn't noticed, we were in the middle of a rather important meeting, discussing the safety of people I care about. I'm sorry I wasn't completely focusing on you."

Stung by the harshness of his tone, I stand. "I didn't expect you to focus on me, but you could have at least noticed I was ill."

He stands as well, and faces me. The air between us snaps with hostility and exhaustion. "How was I supposed to know? You didn't say anything!"

When did this get so out of hand? I should stop this; I know I should. We're both too tired to be having this conversation, but I can't seem to stop the words issuing from my mouth. "You *used* to know when something was wrong with me. Maybe you should stop getting distracted by other . . . things."

His mouth drops. "I'm sorry I was distracted by someone's death. What is going on, Anna? This isn't like you at all."

Everything tangles up inside me. I want him to tell me how he feels about me. I want to be sure of his feelings for me. And I'm angry at my selfishness that I'm even thinking about this right now.

The woman at the front desk clears her throat and I know we have an audience. I close my eyes for a moment. "I don't know."

"If you don't know, perhaps you should have waited to say something until you did." He nods stiffly and moves to walk out the door.

I catch his sleeve. "Don't go like this," I tell him. "I'm leaving in the morning. I'm sorry. I'm just . . ." I pause trying to find a way to tell him that I'm confused, scared, miserable, but nothing comes to me. "I'm just tired," I finish.

My lame excuse sits there for a moment and he chooses to accept it. "I am, too. And with everything that has happened—it's no wonder we're both on edge." He holds out his arms and I move into them, not caring if the clerk is watching the whole scene.

This is Cole, I remind myself. My Cole. I slip my hands beneath his peacoat and feel the warmth and strength of his body. He rests his cheek against the top of my head and I feel my confusion and anger slipping away. This. This is what I needed. When he holds me like this, I know how he feels about me.

But I need to hear it too. Why can't he say it?

I close my eyes and luxuriate in our closeness for a moment before he moves to lift my chin.

My eyes meet his. They're dark and velvety and oh, so warm, but traces of regret linger in their depths. "I'm sorry we fought on your last night here. You'll be with the troupe, I know, but please don't go off by yourself, all right? We don't know who's behind the murder and Jonathon's disappearance and if it is Dr. Boyle . . . well, you've already been at his mercy once. Just be careful."

I nod. I know exactly how dangerous Dr. Boyle can be. "You too. Watch your back. Do you carry a weapon?"

He shakes his head.

"You should at least carry a knife."

He smiles. "I would have no idea how to use it. That's what I have you for."

"But we won't be together."

His smile fades. "No." His arms tightens around me and he suddenly reaches down and kisses me hard on the mouth. After a split second of surprise, I kiss him back, trying to let him know how I feel. Cole isn't demonstrative, he's far too reserved for that, but sometimes it's as if the dam breaks and he can't help himself. He pulls me up off my feet against the length of his body so we are more on level. The feel of his lips against mine makes my head spin and it's so warm and thrilling that I almost cry out when he breaks away.

We stare at one another while my elevated pulse slows. He places me gently on my feet and then bends down, his mouth against my ear. I wait trembling, for him to tell me that he loves me.

"*Au revoir*, Anna. Please take care."

My heart dips in disappointment. "You, too," I manage.

And then he's gone, leaving my heart in turmoil.

EIGHT

The troupe leaves London early the next morning in a fog that makes it impossible to see more than a few feet outside the train window. The plan is to go from London to Dover by train, cross the English Channel to Calais by ferry, and then start the long train ride through Germany and Austria and into Hungary and Budapest. The management of the show, in all their penny-pinching wisdom, didn't provide private sleeping cars for us, so we'll be sitting upright for over eight hundred miles.

As the ferry makes its painstaking way out of the harbor, we head inside to sit in the relative warmth of the observation salon. Sally and Sandy lean against one another and close their eyes, the veterans of countless European tours. The three Woodruff brothers carry their instruments with them at all times, preferring inconvenience over risking their livelihood. Billy sits with Jeanne, Louie, and several of the others.

He's been avoiding me since the party. Well, not avoiding

me exactly. He's been friendly when we run into one another, but he hasn't sought me out. Which is good, I tell myself firmly, ignoring the fluttering disappointment around my heart whenever he's nearby.

The flags outside whip in the wind as we hit open water and the rocking sends more than one troupe member scurrying to the bathroom. I sit at a table and take out a pencil and my stationery, planning to catch up on my correspondence.

The first letter is to my mother, who will be leaving on her own travels in the next couple of weeks. I want my note to reach her before she departs so she won't feel it necessary to track me down right away when she arrives in Europe.

Dear Mother,

I'm sitting on the observation deck of the ferry, but the fog is too thick to see the famed White Cliffs of Dover. Perhaps I shall view them on our return trip. We should be in Budapest within three days as long as everything goes according to schedule. How strange that I'll be traveling through the country you left so many years ago. Do you think we still have family in Hungary? Not that I'll have time for anything but the show. After a week in Budapest, we head to Prague for five shows and then on to Warsaw for several more. I think Louie has a few other stops in the works, but I haven't looked at the final schedule yet.

Rehearsals have gone well.

I chew on my pencil wondering what else I can write that will keep her at bay for as long as possible.

We have another trip sometime after this one to Paris and then we play London in the spring. It's going to be frantically busy, I'm sure.

Hope you and Jacques are doing well and business is thriving. Cole sends his regards.

Love,

Anna

There. That should do it. I put the letter in the envelope and address it.

Cynthia's letter is much more fun to write.

Dear Cyn,

I'm on my way to Calais and thinking of your love for French pastries and French accents. It's hard to believe that in three days I'll be performing in my own show! Have I told you about the other performers? You would simply love Bronco Billy . . .

I write three more pages and then sign off with an entreaty for her to come visit and see the show personally. I wonder what Cynthia would make of Calypso. Probably mincemeat if Calypso so much as looked at her husband. With her mobster background, Cyn doesn't mess around much.

My note to Cole is short and to the point.

Dear Cole,
I miss you.
Stay safe.
Love, Anna.

There's not much else to say. My own feelings are so entangled, I can hardly sort them out myself, let alone explain them to him. Perhaps it's for the best that I'm getting away right now. This way Cole can concentrate on solving Pratik's murder and finding Jonathon without worrying about my safety, and I can focus on the show instead of wondering about Cole's feelings.

"May I join you?"

I glance up to see Jeanne Hart's lovely green eyes smiling down at me. I nod and pack my stationery back in the box.

The older woman sits down and turns to me, her face alight with curiosity. "Are you writing to that nice young man who comes to the theater to watch you?"

"Yes. I owed my mother a letter too."

"Oh yes, don't forget your mother. Especially if she's anything like mine." Jeanne smiles. "Is this your first tour?"

I nod. "It's my first solo show, but I've been performing since I was little."

"That explains a lot. You're very polished for someone so young." Jeanne glances around as if to make sure no one is listening. "Don't repeat this, but Louie is very impressed with you. If I do decide to quit, you'll get top billing."

I sit back on the bench, flabbergasted. Why would anyone want to quit a tour as well run as this one? And expect me to take over at the top of the bill? "But the others are so much more experienced."

Jeanne shakes her head. "Not really and, yes, we have some talented people on the tour, but the acts aren't as fresh as yours. You have a quality about you. If you can relate to an audience as well as Louie thinks you'll be able to, you're in. Just make sure this is what you want."

"What do you mean?"

Jeanne lifts a shoulder. "Take me, for example. I spent the last twenty years fighting and clawing my way to the top of the game only to fall in love with a two-bit manager. Oh, Louie is wonderful and talented, but there's no place left to go. No matter what Louie says, picture shows aren't just a fad, and they're cutting into our business. Pretty soon there won't be a circuit left to perform on."

I straighten, thinking of all the people I know who depend on vaudeville for a living.

"Oh, don't worry, honey. It has a few good years left, and someone with your talent is always going to be able to find jobs, but make sure it's what you want."

"It is," I tell her, ignoring the little seed of doubt inside me. I spent my early years moving from one bad hotel to another at the mercy of poor managers, erratic schedules, and bad food. Do I really want to spend my adulthood doing the same thing?

This is different, I assure myself. This time, I'm in charge and I don't have to worry about my mother being carted off to jail. I don't have to worry about her unpredictable moods either.

Jeanne smiles as if she can read the struggle in my mind. "I was the same way. No more, though. I sang at the New York Metropolitan Opera House and Carnegie Hall. Now I'm headlining at the Polish Theater, which is very nice, I hear, but it's no Carnegie Hall. Besides, I want to settle down and have babies before it's too late. Don't tell anyone, but this is Louie's last tour and I don't even know if I'm going to stay for the whole thing. I have a hankering to head home to Scranton to set up house and wait for my man. Being on the road all the time is tough on a marriage. Not many relationships are as strong as the road is hard."

She stands and pats my hand before leaving to join her secret husband, who is talking to the Woodruffs. My stomach churns as her words reverberate in my mind.

Not many relationships are as strong as the road is hard.

Sally and Sandy rush past me as they make their way offstage. "Tough audience," Sally mutters as he passes me.

I'm not worried. It's much more difficult in a foreign country to sell an act that depends on language than it is an act that's mostly visual, like mine. Even in a cosmopolitan city such as Budapest, where the number of English-speaking attendees is high, subtle double meanings are often lost.

Louie is acting as MC tonight, introducing each act. My assistant for this leg of the tour, Jan, an aspiring magician who needed a gig, is standing next to me, trembling. I hope it's excitement and not nerves. We were only able to run through the routine twice and I pray he remembers everything. I wish my regular assistant could have come but understand her reluctance to leave her baby for so long. For luck, I'm wearing the same black velvet dress with the white pearls that I wore for my last performance in New York.

The theater is more opulent than any I have ever performed in, with frescos on the ceiling, gold leaf on the pillars, and plush carpet in the aisles. I peeked out at the audience earlier and even my exposure to New York aristocracy couldn't have prepared me for the old-world glitter represented this evening.

My stomach twists up inside itself, and for the first time,

I desperately miss my mother. What was I thinking, imagining I could do this by myself? Who am I kidding? Who wants to see a magician as young as I am—and a girl?

I hear my name announced as if through a tunnel and walk out onstage to polite clapping. As I face the audience, panic empties my mind. My heart thuds. What am I supposed to be doing? Out of the corner of my eye, I see my assistant with a deck of cards and everything snaps into focus.

I give the audience a curtsy, take the deck of cards, and begin to do a series of card flourishes designed for both eye appeal and wonderment. I perform wide arcs and dazzling fans, making cards appear and disappear at will. The audience responds well, if not wildly, as I move on to the rest of the show. I note my assistant's whereabouts with my eyes, appreciating his economy of movement. He's basically a prop for me, and many a show has been ruined by a scene-stealing assistant.

As always, I keep in mind how my body is angled with the audience's line of sight. Though the auditorium isn't large, there are three balcony levels and the line of vision of the people above me is different from those seated behind the orchestra, which makes my job that much more challenging.

By the time I get to the escape-gone-wrong trick, I'm warmed up and my body is humming. The audience is appreciative, and the connection between the entertainer and the entertained is firmly established. They aren't going crazy for me but they like me, and for a first show that's pretty darn good.

When the iron maiden is wheeled out, the audience gasps. My assistant and I turn the box around, showing all sides before opening it up to allow them to see the cruel-looking spikes. My pulse races as it always does before doing this trick. There's just so much that can go wrong.

"I need a member of the audience to come up and inspect the box for me. Can I get a volunteer?" Hands wave wildly in the air and I choose a young woman about my age. I rarely choose older men, who are usually so hell-bent on tripping me up they take forever to inspect the box.

The woman hurries up onstage, smiling broadly. "Have we ever met before?" The woman shakes her head. I nod at the audience. "Go ahead and inspect the iron maiden." I wave my hand toward the box and turn back toward the audience.

"The iron maiden was a torture device used during the Dark Ages. Spies, criminals, and even unlucky lovers were placed in the box and tortured. Today, I am going to attempt to escape from the box, fully handcuffed."

The volunteer nods at the audience and then sits in the chair my assistant placed next to the box. This way she can keep an eye on things and it increases my believability to the spectators.

The tension of the audience as my assistant handcuffs my hands behind my back is palpable. I allow the volunteer to check my cuffs and she nods again at the audience. My lips tremble in a suppressed smile at how seriously she's taking her job. I back into the iron maiden, careful not to hit any of the spikes. As I back in, my assistant surreptitiously places a small bag of blood in my hands, secured just that morning from a nearby butcher shop. We've practiced this particular move over and over to make sure the volunteer in the chair can't spot it.

Once I'm inside, my assistant cuffs my ankles, shuts the door, and then secures the box with metal bands placed through the hinges. I wait for a breathless moment until I hear the sound of the red velvet curtain encircling the box. The volunteer is sitting to the side of the curtain so she can see both in front of and behind it. By the time the draperies are completely closed, I've already pulled out the picklock from the sash of my dress where I'd secreted it. I drop the bag of blood to the floor and pick the lock of the handcuffs. My movements are quick but careful as I loosen the pins and remove my cuffs. Within minutes, the box is secure and ready for an audience member to inspect.

Once free, I carefully smear some of the blood on my arm, and then some on my cheek. Shuddering, I pull up the sleeve of my dress and press the bag into my armpit. Every time I squeeze it, more blood will run down my arm and wrist. Uncomfortable, but it does the trick. My stomach churns thinking of Pratik, but I shake the thought out of my head. I have a job to do.

"Jan," I call, my voice weak. "Jan!" This time I project so it can be heard. I know that Jan's exaggerated facial expression is showing the audience his alarm so that they know something went wrong.

He flings open the curtain and the audience gasps when they see me leaning against the iron maiden. Of course, I'm not really leaning against it; it's on wheels after all and would go shooting across the stage if I did. I jump when the woman from the audience screams as she spots the blood trickling down my arm.

A panic-stricken Louie rushes out on the stage and calls into the audience for a doctor. A man with a black doctor's bag rushes up onstage. It's one of the Woodruff brothers in disguise. Jan leads the volunteer to one side as I take the seat. The "doctor" works over me feverishly with bandages as the audience holds their collective breath. While this is happening Jan opens the door of the iron maiden so everyone can see the inside. The volunteer has one hand over her mouth as she looks at the spikes.

When the doctor turns to the auditorium and nods, Jan pulls up my "good" arm in triumph. The restrained, well-bred audience goes crazy, clapping, hooting, and stamping. I give a pathetic smile and am led off the stage. I flush in triumph as the audience screams for a second bow.

"Go out!" Jeanne pushes me toward the stage again.

"Should I?" I ask.

She nods. "This is your moment, darling, take it." Louie, standing next to her, nods in agreement.

Jan and a stagehand wheel the iron maiden and the curtain off as the audience chants my name. I take a deep breath and then reenter the spotlight. Mindful of my arm, I walk to center stage and give the audience a curtsy. The audience screams their approval and I leave the stage, waving my good arm.

This time, Jeanne gives me a one-armed hug, careful not to get any blood on her yellow silk dress. "I'm supposed to follow that?" she asks Louie.

I shrug and smile, knowing she's only teasing. No one alive can sing like that woman.

"We're not going to be able to do that every night." Louie chuckles. "I have a feeling we're going to have more than a few repeaters to see how you're doing. So tomorrow you should have a bandage wrapped around your arm, and skip the blood bit. Damn, but that went over well!"

I agree. "So only once in every city?"

He nods and then shushes me. Jeanne has started to sing, a bawdy little song to warm up, and Louie's eyes close as he hums along. I think about what Jeanne told me about relationships on the road and I think of all the strikes against Cole and me. My magic, his reluctance to tell me how he feels, his grandmother, not to mention we don't even live on the same continent. The happiness of my triumph disappears with a whoosh. I know it's after-performance letdown, but it still leaves me feeling flat and washed out.

Jan rushes up to me after helping the stagehands put our props away. A wide grin lights up his broad face. "We did good, yes?"

I clasp the hand he extends to me. "Yes! We did grand."

"You will take me to America with you?"

I blink. "Oh. Um, I can ask the manager. But I don't know . . ."

"Yes. You ask the manager. I am a good assistant."

"Yes, you are."

He gives another friendly nod for good measure, and as he walks away I hear a low chuckle behind me. Billy is leaning against the wall, laughing. "You're going to have a hard time getting rid of that one."

I smile. "He's a good assistant."

"Are you ready to head back to the hotel? The boss asked me to walk you back. He doesn't like any of his performers out on the street alone."

"Just let me grab my things." With an undercurrent of excitement, I rush back to the dressing room and pack up my things in my valise. I learned a long time ago: Never leave personal things in your dressing room if you want to keep them. When I enter the cramped room, I'm surprised to find a veritable bower of flowers on the vanity. They must have been delivered while I was performing.

Smiling, I sniff the sweet scent of the bouquet. Spying a small box wrapped in purple foil alongside the vase, I pick it up and open the attached card.

I saw these and thought of you.
I hope your performance was a hit. I miss you.
Cole

I rip off the paper, then frown in confusion as I see the box of waffle-shaped cookies. He thought of me? Then it hits me. The first time we went anywhere together he took me out for waffles at Child's. My heart bruises with tenderness. He does love me. I know he does.

Whistling, happier than I ever thought I could be, I wipe away the blood from my arm and run a brush through my hair. I leave the flowers on the vanity to bring me luck for tomorrow's performance and tuck the cookies in my pocketbook before meeting Bronco Billy at the exit.

His blue, blue eyes crinkle up as he gives me that slow smile that starts at the corner of his mouth and spreads across his face like the sun. He holds his arm out and I tuck mine through his. Gasping at Hungary's bitter winter wind, I hurry my steps. Downtown Budapest is bustling, in spite of the late hour, with couples wrapped up against the chill, scurrying from dance hall to dance hall.

"Would you like to stop somewhere for coffee and pastry?"

I hesitate, not sure how Cole would feel. On the other hand, Billy's at least four years older than I am, so it's not as if I'm interested in him romantically. I shrug and he leads me across the street to an all-night restaurant.

The fragrant warmth is welcoming, and I remove my coat as we find a table. The restaurant is packed with gaily dressed revelers intent on enjoying their Saturday night. Cigarette smoke lies heavy in the air and the room is a sea of sequins, feathers, and cloches. It could be any café on any street corner in New York City except for the sound of Hungarian tickling my ears.

I tilt my head, listening. It's tantalizingly familiar and every once in a while I fancy I hear a word I should know.

I order coffee and a *palacsinta*. Billy raises an eyebrow. "It's rather like a sweet crepe filled with walnuts," I tell him as he orders the same.

"*Köszönöm*," I tell her.

Even though her hair is more gray than brown, she gives Bronco Billy a long, lingering look. He smiles at her easily before she moves on. He just has that kind of impact on women.

"You want a cigarette?" Bronco Billy asks after she leaves.

I pass.

He lights his cigarette and blows the smoke out in a huff. "Where did you learn Hungarian?"

"My mother comes from Hungary, but she moved to the States just before I was born. She spoke both Hungarian and English to me as a child, but as she learned more and more English she stopped speaking the old language altogether. Eventually, I forgot I ever learned it. I only remember the odd word or two, but I do remember how delicious *palacsinta* are."

"Where do you come from?"

What is this? Twenty questions? My suspicion of people is as natural to me as my blue eyes, but I suppress it. *He's just being friendly*, I tell myself. "All over, really. My mother was a mentalist and a performer. We moved around a lot. What about you?" I say, before he can ask another question. "You told me about how boring cowboy work was, but how did you actually get into vaudeville?"

He smiles and, in spite of the fact that we're just colleagues, my pulse speeds up. He's just that beautiful.

"I told you how I used to practice my lariat work and gun tricks out of lack of anything else to do, right?" I nod and he continues. "One time the boss gave us younger cowboys the night off to go into town and see a traveling circus. It was one of those poor, tired circuses, but it certainly looked like more fun than what I was doing, so when I was offered a job as a hand, I jumped on it. Once the manager saw my repertoire of tricks, I was promoted to performer. I never looked back."

My eyes widen. "Really? I worked in a circus, too. I was a knife girl!"

He chuckles and shakes his head. "It's quite a life, isn't it? I only traveled with them for six months, but what a cast of characters! There was this old guy, a sword swallower who could swallow three swords at one time."

Excitement causes me to sit upright. "Swineguard?"

His eyebrows shoot up. "How did you know?"

I start laughing. "Swineguard taught me everything I know about handling a knife."

The corner of his mouth quirks up and he raises an eyebrow. "You carry a knife?"

I laugh harder and barely get the words out. "Of course. What self-respecting knife girl doesn't?"

He joins me and the last vestiges of my shyness disappear.

"I can't believe you worked for the same circus I did!" he finally says.

I wipe my eyes, my laughter abating. The waitress comes back and drops off our food and coffee, and for a few moments we're silent as we taste the *palacsinta*, which are every bit as wonderful as I remember.

"These are good," he says, and promptly waves down the waitress to order another.

I nod, my mouth too full to reply, and take a sip of my coffee. "You know, it's really not that surprising that we worked in the same circus. Just how many circuses could there be roaming small towns in the West? The bigger, well-known circuses only hit the big cities."

He nods. "That's true. Did you know Hairy Harold? I would have never believed anyone could have that much hair without seeing it for myself."

I laugh and we talk for the next hour, discussing the people we both knew and the places we've both been. I find myself relaxing and tell him far more about my life than I would just anyone. I even tell him about my mother and the séances.

I finally look at him with a bit of surprise. "It's nice to talk to someone who understands without explaining why you feel certain ways about things or having to censor yourself because your words are too shocking."

He nods. "Most people don't understand that you can do

things you're not proud of to survive and still be a good person at heart."

I feel the sadness of regret coming from him and can detect from his voice that there's something he's not telling me. I don't pry, though. I understand the need to hide things.

In spite of my success and the entertaining night out, a fine layer of melancholy settles over me after I reach my room. I think again of Jeanne's eagerness to leave the kind of life I desired. For so long I thought I wanted the life of a normal girl, and it took a crisis to make me realize just how important my magic is to me. Now that I have that, I'm strangely dissatisfied. Isn't this what I wanted?

Restlessly, I ready myself for bed and turn down the gas lamp. The hotel the company put us up in is shabby, but at least the heat works and the bed looks comfortable. I pull the heavy quilts up to my chin but am too keyed up to sleep. I wonder what Cole is doing and if he's thinking about me. I hate feeling so insecure about him, but he either doesn't understand that I need occasional reassurance or he's so sure of our relationship that he doesn't feel the necessity. But there is a need. How could I possibly fit into Cole's tidy English life? I remember all the times I've shocked him without meaning to, like when he discovered I'd been with a circus or that I carried a knife. I can't help but wonder how many times he's hidden his shock over something I've said or done.

My fingertips go numb and I roll over onto my side,

hoping the change in position will help. It doesn't, and the pins and needles feeling travels up my hands into my elbows. At the same time, the same feeling attacks my feet and slowly inches up my legs.

My breath quickens. What's happening to me? Something heavy and solid pushes me down into my bed like a weight has been dropped on top of my body. I want to struggle against it, but it's so heavy I can't. I lie on the bed, trying to focus my scattered thoughts. Suddenly, something shatters and my heart slams against my chest. My eyes stare at the mirror above the bureau as little flashes of light emit from the glass. That's when I know:

The lights are coming from the mirror.

Fear, sour and metallic, coats my mouth and my heart feels as if it's going to beat out of my chest. I wiggle underneath the weight of the invisible heavy thing, but it's as if a giant fist is holding me against the bed. I open my mouth to scream, and suddenly my body is released.

I remain motionless, terror pulsing through my veins with my blood. My heartbeat is so loud it's a wonder it isn't heard in the next room. As soon as I'm able to move, I crawl out of bed and light the gas lamp. The glow reaches every corner of the room, chasing away the shadows. I look throughout the small room and bathroom but can't find any broken glass.

My feet ache from the cold floor and my legs tremble as I crawl back to bed. I'm going crazy, imagining things that aren't there. Even as I tell myself that, I know it isn't true.

No matter how implausible it seems, it was real. The only explanation I can think of is that it's a dead person having a joke on me. It's never happened before, but that's not to say it can't. My closeness to Cole has made my abilities sharper and stronger.

I suck in my breath and pull the covers around me tighter. Why have I never thought about that before? What happens if I spend the rest of my life with Cole? Will my abilities continue to change and grow as long as I'm with him? What does that mean? Will I soon be seeing dead people everywhere? Having nightly visions? Feeling everyone's emotions? My chest tightens. What if my ability to control my talents doesn't keep pace with their growth?

Am I willing to risk my own sanity to be with Cole?

NINE

The train broke down. Again.

This is the third time our train has had unexplained mechanical problems. Louie's starting to mutter about a curse and the rest of the troupe agrees that they've never had such bad luck. At least this time the train broke before we left the station and we can wait in relative comfort.

I take advantage of the lull and hurry to a public telephone. Even more unsure of Polish money than I am of British pounds, I reverse the charge and hope that the butler, or whoever answers the phone, will accept.

To my relief it's Cole.

"Anna!"

My heart leaps at the sound of his voice. "Cole!"

"How are you?" we ask at the same time and then we laugh.

"You first. How is the tour going?"

"Fantastic. We played our final show last night and I

should be home in a few days, barring any more train troubles."

"Train troubles?"

"I'll tell you when I get back. How is everything with you? Have you started school yet?"

"No. I'm going to wait until the fall. With everything going on . . ."

I hear the concern in his voice. "Has anything else happened?"

He lowers his voice. "Not exactly. We do have more information about Pratik's death, though. That stone he had in his hand? It had markings on it. Harrison used his contacts to get it checked out. We already knew that it was cult related, but now believe that it was some sort of black magic. Whoever did it needed Pratik's blood for a spell."

My stomach turns as I think of that handsome, sad young man. Who could do something like that? "Do you have any idea who might have done it?"

I could hear his sigh. "No, but the Yard is doing a search on anyone in the country who is an expert in the occult or black magic. Of course, that also includes university professors, et cetera. Once we have the list, we can check it against people who might have knowledge of our existence."

I shut my eyes for a moment. I've been so busy performing I almost forgot about the horror waiting for me back in London. Plus, I have my own horror to contend with here. The strange nocturnal occurrence hasn't happened again, but I have shared a room with Sandy for most of the trip since Budapest. I have, however, had two of those strange buzzing headaches as if a hive of honeybees has been loosed in my head. I decide against telling Cole over the phone. Though no one is paying much attention to me, people are milling about rather close. "I should be able to help once I return," I tell him. "I'll have several days off." I don't say maybe we can do something fun, because it seems so petty considering everything, but I do need it. I need to spend time with Cole alone doing something other than talking about cults and murders. The tour has drained me and I long with all my heart to do something lighthearted and crazy and fun.

Just then Billy strolls past, his handsome features alight with interest as he views the world around him. A slight smile curves his lips as if he finds life endlessly wonderful. He spots me and his smile deepens. A slow blush travels up my body and I smile and duck my head before he can spot the redness in my cheeks. Cole's saying something but I miss it. "Excuse me? I'm sorry. I was distracted."

"I just wanted to let you know that I'll meet you at the station. Perhaps we can go get something to eat? I won't have a lot of time if the investigation heats up, but I'm sure we can figure out something."

I swallow. I can hear the worry in his voice and know his quick mind has already leaped to something else. I confirm the date and time of my arrival and pause, waiting for him to say something personal. He pauses too, and for a moment neither of us says anything.

"I guess I'll see you then?"

A lump rises in my throat and I nod before realizing he can't see me. "Yes."

"All right. And, Anna?"

"Yes?"

"I miss you."

I squeeze my eyes shut. It wasn't much but it was better than nothing at all. "I miss you, too."

I hang up, my heart swelling with disappointment. Seeing Louie waving at me from across the station, I quietly gather my things and join the rest of the troupe. They're chatting excitedly about the new luxury train that had been brought in to take us stranded passengers to our new destination. Billy is by my side in a heartbeat. "Do you need any help?"

I shake my head.

"You just ask if you need anything, you hear? I'll be right there." His blue eyes smile at me and my pulse races.

I could be in trouble.

My excitement mounts as the train lurches into London. The journey from Calais to London had seemed interminable, but now that it's over, it feels as if the entire trip sped by. The troupe fell into an easy routine of traveling and performing and, after some tweaking here and there, we had really come together. Of course, being stuck together during the great train debacles helped. Nothing like being thrown together for hours to forge the bonds and friendships necessary to create a group of people eager for the success of a show. The larger changes, such as reordering acts, will be done over the next few weeks.

"Are you excited to be back in London?" Billy sits in the seat next to me that Jeanne had just vacated.

"Being in the same circus makes us practically kissing cousins," he'd drawled the second night we went out to eat after a performance. I'd blushed, but he gave me such a devilish grin that I ended up laughing.

"Actually I am," I told him. "It will be nice to have a few days off."

"Do you have any plans?"

I chew on my lip. As excited as I am to see Cole, it also means dealing with all the trouble with the Society and a murder investigation. It's not like I'm returning to a happy homecoming. "Visit with friends, I suppose," I say.

"No sightseeing? That's no fun. You should get out and see more of jolly old England. Don't you want to see Big Ben or London Bridge or the National Gallery?"

I roll my eyes. "Don't tell me you're going to an art museum while you're here?"

He shifts in his seat. "Well, no," he admits. "But I would like to see Madame Tussauds wax museum."

"I'd like to see that too, actually."

He nods. "Let's do it, then. Before we go to France, we'll go to Madame Tussauds."

I swallow, thinking of the investigation, the Society, seeing Cole. "I'm not sure I'm going to have time . . ." My voice trails off awkwardly.

For a moment, a shadow crosses his face. "Oh, sure. Well, let me know if you do. If not, I can always go with Sal and Sandy."

My stomach hollows. I'd love to go with him, but is it fair to bring him into the craziness of my life? "I'll let you know. I really would like to go." I give him a smile to illustrate my sincerity and he nods.

"Sounds good."

He returns to his seat just as the train lurches into Charing Cross station. I forget everything as I scan the crowd for Cole's tall form. I don't see him as the train comes to a stop and I drum my fingers on the armrest of my seat, waiting to disembark.

When it's time to get off, I snatch up my valise and handbag and get in the line heading out the door. I step onto the platform, my eyes flicking this way and that, until I finally spot Cole's black Homburg tipped just so. I wave my valise wildly, grinning like a happy monkey. The doubts that have plagued me for the last few weeks vanish like a puff of smoke.

I rush down the steps, my chest pounding. It's not until I'm within several feet of him that I realize he doesn't seem to be nearly as happy to see me as I am him. I falter, wondering if he's going to hug me in greeting or just stand there like a lump of handsome flesh. Discomfort sticks out all over him, from the clenching of his jaw to the tension running across his broad shoulders.

My throat tightens in disappointment. What's wrong?

Has something happened or is this just Cole being Cole and not wanting to show affection in public? And why can't anything just be simple with us anymore? He bends and gives me an awkward kiss on the cheek. "Welcome back. I hope you had a good trip."

It's hard to believe this is the same boy who gave me such a passionate kiss at our good-bye. "Fine, thank you."

Cole reaches out and takes my valise. As his hand brushes mine I try to make a connection but can't.

"Do we need to get your things?" he asks.

Hurt runs through me and tears prick my eyes. I try to tell myself that everything is fine, that this is just the way Cole is, but it doesn't help. "Just the trunk with my clothes in it. All the props are being taken to the theater."

We wait for the porter to unload my case and I try to make an emotional connection with Cole.

Nothing.

My chest constricts. Cole is blocking me. Why? Is he feeling something he doesn't want me to know about?

"Anna!"

My head swivels and Billy gives me a easygoing wave. "I'll see you later?"

His handsome face is so open and friendly that I smile and nod. "Of course!"

His magnetic one-of-a-kind smile lights up his face and he gives me another wave.

Jealousy hits me like a bag of bricks and I turn to Cole in disbelief before the block goes up again. He snatches up my bag. "Are we ready?" he asks. His mouth flattens into a tight line and his back is ramrod straight.

I nod, resentment keeping me mute. How dare he be angry with me because I smiled and waved at someone I work with? How dare he?

Cole clears his throat as we leave the station. "I was a bit worried I'd be late to meet you. Leandra and Calypso held me up at the Society. Calypso wanted to come with me, but Leandra needed to talk to her."

His voice may contain a note of apology, but the words are like darts aimed at my heart. Only Cole would think it all right to tell his girl that he was almost late to get her because of other women.

Once we reach the motorcar, he opens my door and I get in, a mixture of anger, jealousy, and concern swirling in my stomach. I don't even know what to say to him. This is definitely not the welcome I had expected, but considering our argument before I left, perhaps I should have. Maybe I was a fool to think that the kiss had made up for it?

"What's going on?" I ask bluntly after he starts the car.

He glances at me, his brows drawn together. "You're going to have to be more specific. There's so much going on, I don't know what you want to know about first."

Us. I want to know what is going on with us. But all my emotions are tangled inside, so instead I blurt, "What were you doing with Calypso and Leandra?"

He glances over at me, his brows raised. "With everything that's happening, that's what you want to know first?"

Why does he have to make me feel so small? "I was just wondering," I mutter.

"It's like I said. I stopped at the Society this morning and she and Leandra both happened to be there. What is the matter with you? Don't you like them?"

Why does he have to sound so reasonable? "Nothing is the matter. Of course, I like them. I'm just tired. Forget I said anything." I stare out the window, holding back tears of anger and confusion.

Silence falls until Cole clears his throat again. "Now, would you like to hear about the investigation?"

Actually, I'm torn between wanting to hit him and wanting to kiss him, so I just take a deep breath and nod. His face gets serious and I marvel at the way he can separate all his feelings into little boxes. Along with his analytical mind, it's one of the qualities that will make him a good detective.

I don't think I'll ever be that focused and I try to keep my mind on what he's saying.

"We haven't had as many breakthroughs as we'd like, but odd things keep popping up. We did finally find a witness who saw Pratik on the day he disappeared."

"That's good!" I exclaim.

"Yes, except when Harrison and I went to interrogate her, she seemed incredibly confused and had a hard time even recalling the incident."

I frown. "How did you know about her in the first place?"

"We spoke to a shopkeeper near where Mr. Gamel and Pratik live and he pointed us in her direction. Evidently, the woman mentioned the incident to him. She says she thought it odd to see an Indian man being led by a white woman as if he were blind."

I screw up my face, trying to understand. "And now she acts like she doesn't remember?"

Cole nods. "Strange, right? Of course, she complained of having a horrible headache, so we made arrangements to return later that week, but that interview didn't go any better. She said she only vaguely recalls the incident and has no details. She can't remember what the woman looked like at all."

He pulls over in front of my hotel but doesn't get out of the car so I stay put as well.

"Do you have any other leads?"

"Apparently Pratik had been acting strangely the week before his disappearance. Very moody. Well, you met him. But according to Rose and Jenny, he had been really talkative with them. Rose even thought maybe he had fallen in love."

I frown. "That's not the sense I got at all when I met him. Did you notice him acting that way?"

Cole shakes his head. "I didn't notice anything out of the ordinary, but I didn't see much of him in the week before he disappeared. The day we came to get you was the first day I'd seen him in almost two weeks. He seemed preoccupied, but I thought maybe he was really involved in some testing. Sometimes that happens."

"Who was he working with?"

"Mr. Price." Cole chews on his upper lip, his dark eyes brooding. I try to get a sense of what he's feeling, but all I get is his worry. At least he's not blocking me. "What?" I ask, knowing there's more.

"Someone tried to take Leandra. That's one of the reasons I was at the Society this morning."

I straighten. "Is she all right?"

"She's fine. She sent the boys to stay with Harrison's mother in the country but spent the night in the apartment at the Society. Harrison had a late night and didn't want her to be alone so she stayed with the rest of the Sensitives. She was attacked on her way home the next morning. She was walking and someone grabbed her from behind and tried to pull her into an alley. Luckily a Good Samaritan happened by. Harrison is fit to be tied, because very few people knew she wasn't staying in her house."

"Maybe someone is following her?"

"Perhaps." I can tell by his voice that he doesn't believe it.

"What do you think?" I ask.

"Harrison and I believe there's a very good chance that it's someone inside the organization. Or that at the very least someone from the inside is giving out information."

I swallow. "To Dr. Boyle?"

He shrugs. "There's no hard evidence that he's involved, but you and I both know it's a very real possibility."

"Do you have any suspects?"

"No. That's where you come in. You're the only person we know who can sense what other people are feeling. The

Society is trying the business-as-usual approach, so the scientists are running tests. They are all chomping at the bit to test you, so I thought maybe you could check out the scientists first and then make up something to get close to the board of directors. Most of them are scientists too, but not all of them."

I nod. "I'll be happy to help out in any way I can, but as you know, my abilities are still erratic. They're more powerful now, but I can't always pick up someone's emotions by sending out a pulse strand, the way you taught me. Sometimes I need to touch them." When Cole began training me to control my sensitivity to other people's emotions, he told me to envision myself connecting to them with an imaginary ribbon that pulses with their feelings. The description is apt if a bit fanciful, and the name stuck.

"I know." Cole leans back in the seat, thinking.

I bite my lip, knowing what I have to do. "I think I know a way I can touch all of them without anyone being suspicious."

"What's that?"

"I can hold a séance. They're going to want to test me anyway. That would be a perfect way to get a good read off all of them at once."

He turns toward me and takes both of my hands in his. The gesture and the caring I feel from him bring tears of relief to my eyes. I blink them back.

"Are you sure you want to do that?" he asks, his voice soft. "I know how much they upset you."

I shiver, remembering how it felt to be a ghost's mouthpiece. "Maybe I don't have to have a real séance. I can just pretend to have one until I get a solid read on everyone."

"If I remember correctly, the séances you were doing with your mother were fake until suddenly they weren't. We've practiced trying to control how and when you feel someone's emotions, but we haven't played around with your ability to conjure up dead people or your visions of the future."

He has a point. "But Walter is the only spirit I've actually brought up. Perhaps that was just an anomaly?"

"Do you really want to risk it? What if we summon something or someone we can't control?"

I chew on my thumb, wishing I had a deck of cards. Shuffling calms me, and right now my nerves are pinging around my stomach like manic grasshoppers. I think of Jonathon, a young man I didn't even know, and poor Pratik, who I had only met once before he was brutally murdered. I'm connected to both of them in a way that is both baffling and frightening. Then I think about Leandra, Calypso, Jenny, and the other Sensitives who I *do* know and I'm sure of what I need to do. If someone is targeting Sensitives and someone within the Society knows about it, shouldn't I do anything in my power to stop it? Wouldn't that be worth the risk?

I turn to Cole.

"Let's do it."

He nods slowly. "I'll talk to Harrison and Leandra as soon as possible."

We cart my things into the lobby and then he kisses me

on the forehead. "I'll let you unpack and rest. Are we still on for dinner tonight?"

I nod and he's gone, leaving me feeling orphaned and alone. I try to shrug it off, but the feeling clings to me, soft and limp, like a damp blanket.

I check at the desk for messages and mail and receive a handful. Clutching them, I follow the porter who hauls my trunk up three flights of stairs, because the lift is broken again. I wish Louie had at least sprung for a hotel with a lift that didn't threaten to plummet to the ground with every groan.

After putting my trunk in my room, he hovers, waiting for his tip. I cover my sigh with a smile as I hand him a coin. I'll have to get more money from the bank tomorrow. Payday isn't for another week.

Unpacking my clothes, I make a pile to send out to get washed tomorrow. At least the hotel has a laundry service. I rinsed my black beaded dress several times over the three-week tour to get the blood out, but even laundered it will never be the same. Not to mention it smells bad, which made everything else stink, even after Billy found me a cloth bag to wrap it in.

I empty my trunk and am about to close the lid when I notice a lump about two inches long under the lining. Some sort of object is stuck under the silk, but I don't see any loose spots where something could have slipped underneath. The silk lining is pulled tight and sewn under the leather of the trunk. Frowning, I run my finger around the top and find an area that feels different from the rest. I bend for a closer look. The spot is only about an inch long, but it appears as if it's been glued instead of sewn.

Working it with my fingernail, I pull the hole open and then yank on the threads to make it large enough to get my hand in. Tilting the trunk to make it easier, I pull out the object. It's warm to the touch and I drop it the moment I realize what it is.

A poppet.

One of my friends from the circus, Alice Brown, a former maid from Atlanta, also known as Komatchu, the Last of the Zulu Princesses, taught me about poppets, or voodoo dolls. Her mama used to make them on a regular basis to curse people she thought had wronged her. Alice, a devout Baptist, didn't believe in them, exactly, but said she had seen too many strange things happen to people after her mama fashioned one of those dolls.

Gingerly, I pick up the poppet and sit it on the dresser. It's made of wax and molded into the crude figure of a woman. Bright blue beads make up the eyes and a bit of red ribbon is worked into the wax to resemble the mouth. A scrap of cloth is wrapped around it and there are a few human hairs stuck to the head. The hair is dark brown.

Like mine.

My heart vaults up into my throat and my stomach churns. No. It can't be me. Why would anyone want to curse me? Maybe it had been there when Jacques and Mother gave me the trunk? No. It had been brand-new from the shop.

My legs give out and I sit heavily on the bed, staring at the little effigy meant to be me. I think of the lights in the mirror and the mental confusion that has plagued me like it did at Cole's house and at the Society meeting. Cold runs through me as I remember that Pratik had been killed ritualistically. As much as I detest Dr. Boyle, his lust was for money and power. This, this is something else.

One thing is certain. I need to tell Cole right away.

TEN

Cole and I discussed my little stowaway at length during dinner with the Wrights last night. He and Harrison both went on high alert and I could barely get Cole to leave the hotel afterward. His alarm is balm to my bruised heart.

Harrison took the poppet to a friend of his at Scotland Yard to find out more about it, in case there's something that would give us a clue about where it could have come from, though that seems highly unlikely to me.

Because they now believe that I've been targeted, Cole and Harrison tried to insist that I have someone protecting me at all times. Like Leandra, I refused. Neither of us wish to feel like we're prisoners and both of us promised to be careful. While neither man liked it, they are forced to see the logic of it. They can't conduct an investigation while on guard duty.

We did rush the séance along to try to ferret out the mole. I'm standing at one end of the conference room with

Leandra, Jenny, and Cole, keeping a close eye on the door. Everyone, it seems, is eager to see what the new girl can do. Besides the eight board members, four of whom are researchers, three more scientists join us.

Then, because Leandra wanted to be involved, we had to invite the other Sensitives. Including Cole and me, that makes seventeen people at the séance, more than I have ever had. My mother and I never allowed more than seven or eight people and our reasons were simple. The more people there are, the more difficult it is to pull the wool over their eyes. Like the old saying goes, *You can fool some of the people all of the time, all of the people some of the time, but you can't fool all of the people all of the time.*

I'm just elated that I don't have to try to fool anyone this time. These people know abilities are erratic, and though they'll be disappointed if the séance doesn't work the way they hope it will, it won't take anything away from me or my abilities.

According to Leandra and Cole, I have to pass three tests to prove my psychical abilities to the Society and become a member. At this point the jury is still out on whether I actually want to join or not. None of the Sensitives I've met seem terribly happy, and if the only advantage to membership is learning from other Sensitives—well, I can do that without formal membership.

"Are you all right?" Cole asks.

Jenny lays a hand on my arm and my nerves ease a bit at her touch.

I nod. "It's strange to be doing this for so many people whom I haven't even met, and even stranger not to be preparing for it." I glance at Cole, and he understands that I mean it seems odd not to be preparing to cheat people.

Mr. Gamel enters the room and immediately joins me. "Is there anything you need?"

I pull myself up to my full height and look him in the eye. "I don't need any props, Mr. Gamel. I'm not a charlatan trying to swindle money from people."

Cole chuckles next to me, and Mr. Gamel looks confused. "Of course not, I didn't mean to imply anything."

"I'm sure you didn't." Then I raise a finger as if I just remembered something. "Oh, I do need one thing. I need to touch everyone's hand before we get started. It's important that I have a sense of everyone who is in the room so I can recognize any unfamiliar spirits that respond to my presence."

Mr. Gamel tilts his head to the side as if considering my request. I hold my breath.

"You do know that some of the scientists and board members don't like to touch Sensitives? In the past, we've had Sensitives use touch to read minds. It's very disconcerting for the researcher to have his subject know about the argument he had with his wife, for instance."

"I can understand that," I tell him. "But I do not read minds."

Mr. Gamel's thin lips stretch into a smile. "We don't really know what you can or can't do, Miss Van Housen.

Between the incidents here at the Society and your outside activities, we have not had time to test you yet."

"True. But it is my séance. If someone doesn't want me to touch him, he is more than welcome to leave." Remembering the whole point was for me to get a read on everyone's feelings, I put my hand on Mr. Gamel's arm, placating him. "Please inform everyone that I do not read minds."

He nods and joins the others. Calypso sails in the door and gives me a jaunty wave. I haven't seen her since my return, though she did send a welcome note. I've been so busy, we haven't had a chance to talk and I find myself missing her.

"I'm so excited to be a part of this!" Calypso exclaims, kissing my cheek. Her face is flushed and her eyes glitter with anticipation. "Raising the dead, what an incredible ability! I must say I'm jealous."

"I don't actually raise the dead," I tell her, shuddering at the thought. "That would be awful. I merely see and speak to spirits."

Well. One spirit. And only because of Cole's involuntary tendency to make other Sensitives stronger. I look around the room, wondering about everyone else's abilities. I know that Leandra dreams other people's dreams, Jenny makes people feel better through touching them, and Calypso has the power of influence over people. How has Cole's coming back to the Society affected their abilities? I stare at Jared, who is speaking to Mr. Casperson. What are his abilities?

I jump when Mr. Gamel claps his hands. "Anna, would

you like to explain a little about what you are going to do and what we might experience?"

I swallow as everyone looks at me. The thought that one of these people might be practicing black magic or working with someone who does is terrifying. After describing my symptoms to Cole and the Wrights last night, Leandra said it sounded as if I had been psychically attacked.

I didn't ask her how she knew.

People start taking seats and Mr. Gamel waves me to the head of the table.

Cole gives me an encouraging nod and I can feel the connection between us, strong and sure. I smile back at him and face the others. "Thank you for coming today. It's my desire to show the Society one of my gifts—that of talking to spirits. Of course, I didn't know I would be showing the entire society all at once."

I smile and several people chuckle. "As many of you know, there are frauds who claim to talk to the spirit world for money, and, yes, my mother and I made our living for many years with séances. The difference is that I am not a fraud. Colin Archer has witnessed my ability to talk to the dead, not once but twice."

Mr. Casperson raises his hand slightly. I nod at him.

"We've done a bit of investigating, Miss Van Housen, and are not entirely convinced of you and your mother's authenticity. Can you explain your use of such well-known props as the spirit cabinet, the chalkboard, and the laying on of coals?"

I cringe, but Cole and I knew that someone was going to bring my past up, and I'm ready for it. "When I say that my mother and I made our living as mediums, we did commit many acts of fraud."

There's a swift intake of breath and I smile calmly before continuing. "While I have other abilities, this particular one is new and didn't manifest itself until in the presence of Mr. Archer. Also, as you can see, none of the devices my mother and I used during those séances are currently in the room."

Mr. Price nods as if he has just had something confirmed.

"Now I am going to attempt to contact the spirit world." I glance over at Mr. Price, who is running a complicated-looking machine, and he gives a curt nod.

Leandra sets out a half-dozen candles on the battered conference table and lights them. I hadn't thought to do anything like that because in my mind this wasn't a real or even a fake real séance, but Leandra said we should attempt to keep up some kind of appearances. I glance over at Cole, who gives me the go-ahead with a flicker of his eyes.

"Before we turn off the lights, I would very much like to meet all of you formally and shake your hands. Opening myself up to spirits is frightening and it's important that I know who all of you are. Besides, I'm trying to re-create the circumstances that led me to successfully channel the dead in the past."

Some of the researchers look uncomfortable and I hasten to add, "If anyone is uncomfortable shaking my hand, you are more than welcome to leave. I completely understand your reluctance."

I hold my breath but no one moves toward the door and I think I know why. The Society may include all kinds of psychic phenomena now, but it was founded to research the spirit world and communication with the dead. Cole told me that many of these researchers feel I may be the first person they have run across who may actually be able to do it. His testimony and the fact that I have other abilities they don't know about has them intrigued.

I take a deep breath. I hope to God I don't come across any real spirits. All I want to do is find the mole.

Mr. Gamel is directly on my right so I shake his hand. It's thin and clammy and I work at not shuddering. All I feel is curiosity pulsing through him. I shiver and quickly move on.

Mr. Price holds out his hand. "I don't think I had a chance to mention at our last meeting that I am a ghost hunter. It's different from what we do here . . . I don't try to find ways to make the ghosts come to me. I go find them. I'm running the electrograph machine."

I reach out my hand and he clasps it firmly in his large one. The buzz of confidence he emits is tremendous, but I also sense an odd secrecy about him. I look into his eyes and he stares back, a small smile playing about his mouth. Yes, this is a man of many secrets, but are they the ones we're seeking?

Mr. Casperson is next, and to my surprise he looks very

different from the open-faced man I first met for tea. His pale skin is so translucent I can see the blue tracing of veins underneath and the skin under his eyes is bruised from lack of sleep. I sense his tension even before I clasp his hand. As soon as our palms touch, it's accompanied by a familiar spark and my eyes widen.

Mr. Casperson is a Sensitive!

But before I can process that, his fear hits me so hard it takes all my control to keep from crying out. He may be a Sensitive, but he is also very, very afraid of something.

But what?

Of me discovering his secret?

I let go of his hand, relieved, and glance at Cole. He knows something has happened but isn't sure what it is. One by one, I meet the other researchers, briefly shaking hands with each.

My mind races as I turn to the Sensitives lining the walls. The little sparks of recognition I receive as soon as I touch them doesn't surprise me as it did with Mr. Casperson. From Jared I get nervousness and I can feel his shyness with me. Nothing threatening there. Leandra feels tense, and from Jenny I get the sense of calm I always do when she touches me. Cole gives my hand a squeeze and I smile at the slight pressure. Our connection is still strong and true, and I feel his encouragement coming to me on a shining line.

When I feel Calypso's hand, I get nothing. Surprised, I look up into her eyes, but find they are focused on someone behind me. I swivel to see but she gives my hand a warm squeeze. "Good luck," she says, smiling at me.

My legs tremble as I take a seat at the head of the table. What did that mean? The four of us—Cole, Leandra, Harrison, and I—had agreed not to tell anyone what we were doing. I bite my lip, wishing I could just cancel the séance—I did what I came to do, after all—but everyone is expecting more.

"Are you ready?" I ask Mr. Price, who has taken his position behind the machine. He gives me the go-ahead and I nod at Leandra to turn off the lights.

The candles splash shadows against the walls and give the participants a strange cast to their faces. Mr. Casperson's face is almost green. I hope he doesn't get sick in the middle of the séance.

"Everyone hold hands," I tell them even though the last thing I want is to hold Mr. Gamel's creepy skeleton hand. It's probably too soon to tell everyone it didn't work and it's time to go home.

Projecting my voice, I begin chanting the same mantra my mother used at our séances. Might as well go by the script I know until I can call a halt.

"Spirits! Use me as your mouthpiece. I am open, yours!"

The room is silent except for the sound of someone breathing and the nervous shuffling of feet. I pause, my sense of showmanship instinctively drawing out the moment. There is something familiar and almost comforting about the progression. In spite of how much I hated the séances, I spent so many hours doing them with my mother that it almost feels like second nature.

What does that say about my nature?

Then I give an involuntary shiver. Slowly, in that deep, still place that recognizes and fears the unknown, I become aware of something moving that doesn't feel like fidgeting. "I want everyone to place their hands on the table, palms down, and keep perfectly still," I order, hoping that it's just a person.

It's not.

Whatever it is I'm feeling is still on the prowl. I concentrate, sweat beading on my forehead. A pins-and-needles feeling crawls up my legs and a sense of déjà vu sweeps over me.

This is the same being I felt in the hotel in Budapest.

Dread blooms in my chest as the temperature drops. Several people in the room gasp with the shock of the cold washing over them.

A tendril of fog or smoke dances down the table toward me and warning bells go off in my head. It's exactly like the fog I saw before Walter possessed me the first time. I want to scream for Cole but can't open my mouth.

A buzzing starts in my ears and suddenly my mind goes to jelly. Once again, I feel as if I'm trying to think through aspic. Not now!

Suddenly another tendril joins the first one and I moan as they surround me. They merge for a moment and then part, a ghostly dance or fight perhaps. My teeth chatter with cold and my knees buckle.

"Anna!" Cole's voice is far away and I sense him holding me up, but unlike before, the spirits don't dissipate at his touch nor does the confused, fuzzy feeling in my head.

Without warning, it's as if I'm being ripped apart from the inside out like a thousand knives twisting inside my body. The spirits have me. I hear voices in the distance and know that I'm surrounded by people, but can't reach out to them. I feel like I did when I was underwater after being shot when Dr. Boyle tried to kidnap me. Alone. Paralyzed. Trapped. Suddenly, a magnificent gust blows through the room. The candles go out and I hear the clatter of metal falling against the floor. Several people scream, but I'm still frozen. I feel Cole picking me up, cradling me in his arms, calling my name. Leandra and Jenny surround me, speaking quietly, lending Cole strength as he tries to reconnect with me, but the pulse strand he is frantically sending is glancing off me as if there's a shield keeping it out.

I curl against Cole, pain slashing my stomach. Finally I find my voice and I beg them to stop. I try to hold it in, but my core is unraveling and my mind is shattered. I'm completely helpless against the warfare going on inside.

Then as suddenly as it began it's gone. The spirits have vacated and the tumult inside my body is silenced.

The lights flicker on and I sob in relief.

"Anna, are you all right?" Cole's frantic voice finally reaches me. I nod, though nothing inside me feels all right. I've been scared before, but this is pure bone-leeching terror. I draw in long, ragged breaths, trying not to cry.

"Back away," Cole demands as the crowd closes in around me.

His voice is so commanding that everyone does as he says even though he is years younger than they are. The researchers and the board members gather in little knots, chattering in their excitement.

And then I see him. He's standing behind Harry Price, who is desperately trying to make sense of the shattered bits of metal that had been his machine. A young man, the same age as Cole, dressed in an olive-colored uniform.

Walter.

I struggle to sit up, staring so hard my eyes begin to burn. He's looks as if he is frantically trying to get to me, but is being held back by the same shield that resisted Cole's attempt to help me just a few moments before.

"Walter," I whisper, and Cole stiffens. "Something's wrong."

In my peripheral vision, I see Mr. Casperson squinting in Walter's direction. A thin sheen of sweat covers his pale features and tremors are running down his body. Can he see Walter? Does he know something is there?

Then Calypso moves from where she had been standing by the wall. She lays a hand comfortingly on Mr. Casperson's arm. He jumps and then nods at the words she whispers in his ear. Whatever she said calms him down.

Then my attention is diverted again by Walter, who has inexplicably begun to waver and fade. He holds his hand out to me, straining to be heard. His face is knotted in effort and concentration. Desperation fills his eyes as he mouths my name over and over.

Then his mouth twists and I hear a single word.

"Aiwass."

Then he disappears.

Turning my head, I press my face into Cole's jacket, breathing in the good clean scent of him.

"What happened?" he whispers in my ear, but I shake my head, allowing my heartbeat to slow. I don't want to discuss it in front of the others.

What is *Aiwass*? Was he simply trying to say Anna? What was stopping him?

"Anna? May I?"

I turn my head to see Jenny holding up a hand and I nod. She touches my face and this time I feel her cool power wash over me like a spring rain, cleaning away all the confusion, fear, and pain of the last few minutes. I let myself relax and Cole's arms tighten around me. I take a deep, shuddering breath.

"Thank you," I tell her. And then to Cole, "I think I can stand now."

"Let's try sitting first." He helps me to the closest chair.

"Here." Leandra bends over me, concern on her pretty face. She hands me a glass of water and I sip gingerly, remembering how torn up I felt inside. The water is good and I drink deeply.

Mr. Gamel claps his hands. "Ladies and gentlemen. Please, if I may have your attention?"

He waits a moment for order to be restored. "It is extremely important that we interview everyone to get their impressions of the psychical event we just witnessed. If the Sensitives could please form a line, you will each be interviewed by a researcher, then the researchers will interview one another."

Leandra sighs and I sense her frustration just above the darkness she seems to carry around in her like a curse. "I'm going to go make a pot of tea first," she announces. "I think we could all use some. Someone can interview me while I make it, if they like."

Mr. Gamel looks nonplussed at her rebellion, but Harrison nods. "Thank you, Leandra, that's very wise. I'm sure everyone would like a cup of tea. I know I would."

Calypso bends over me. "Do you need anything?"

I shake my head and she lays a hand on my shoulder. I feel a buzz of emotions coming off her and remember her comforting Mr. Casperson. Does she know that Mr. Casperson is a Sensitive? Does anyone else?

She ducks her head closer to me, her dark eyes worried. "Just let me know if you do, all right?" She joins Mr. Gamel and the others.

"We need to talk," I whisper to Cole, and he nods.

"As soon as the interviews are done and everything has been processed, we'll get out of here. I would just take you back to the hotel now, but there's no way they are going to let you leave that easily." He tilts his head toward the researchers, most of whom are talking and staring at me.

Some have fear in their eyes, others are alight with interest and excitement.

I'll be lucky if they don't want to do some bizarre experiment on me, à la Frankenstein. I'm so weak, I just want to go back to the hotel and go to bed.

A hand comes down on my shoulder and I jump.

"My apologies, Miss Van Housen. Are you ready for your debriefing?"

Swallowing, I stare into Harry Price's eyes. He's the one interviewing me?

Uneasiness shivers down my spinal cord. Why do I feel like my day has just gone from bad to worse?

ELEVEN

I enter Harry Price's office with reluctance.

The room is small, about eight by ten feet, and one wall has a long metal table against it, covered with different types of gadgets and machinery. A comfortable-looking leather chair and a small black desk sit in the middle of the room.

Mr. Price indicates that I should take a seat, but I'm too keyed up. Instead, I go to a bookshelf and scan the titles. I've read some of them and found the content to be dubious. But some excite my curiosity, such as an ancient French grimoire and *Corpus Alchemicum Arabicum*, a book on Arab alchemy. Of course, the reason I've always been interested in magic and the occult is because I was looking for answers to my own strange abilities.

Mr. Price has taken a seat at the desk and is watching me, his eyes alert. I know he is eager to grill me concerning my experience but I have questions of my own. Unfortunately, the people with the answers don't want to share them. They only want to poke and prod and ask more questions.

I run my fingers along the spines of many leather-bound books on alchemy, witch-hunting, and demonology. I hide a shiver and turn toward Mr. Price. "For a scientist, you have a lot of books on the occult."

"I research the occult, Miss Van Housen. Why wouldn't I have books on my subject of study? I have one of the foremost libraries on the topic, with many rare first editions. It is my hope to put together a research library someday."

His words are measured, exact. His eyes are almost as dark as Cole's.

Mr. Price pulls out a worn leather book and a heavy looking pen. "Shall we get started?"

Reluctantly, I sit on the chair in front of him. It's as uncomfortable as a park bench.

He stares at me, pen in hand. "You're very young. When did you first realize you could channel the dead?"

"Several months ago. And can we please limit the questions to this evening's experience? I'm exhausted and only wish to go home." I also know that Cole and I are going to the Wrights' after this and I'm already reeling.

Mr. Price's eyebrows rise. "I'm just trying to establish a bit of background."

"I understand, but considering everything, I think we can go over my background at a later date."

"Very well. Please describe to me exactly what you saw."

I hesitate. Being forthright isn't one of my strong suits,

especially when it comes to my abilities and even more so with someone I don't trust. But then again, Cole told me that Harry Price has one of the best minds in the Society. That doesn't make me trust him any more, but it does make me curious. I tell him what I saw and felt, and he frowns.

"You have met this young man twice before?" I nod and he continues. "And last time he warned you of some danger you and your mother were in?"

I shift in my seat. I hadn't really meant to tell him that, but finally I nod again.

"It sounds as if you have a spirit stalker, Miss Van Housen."

I frown. "I don't understand."

"You haven't had experiences with any other spirits except this young man. Yet somehow he has managed to communicate with you, whereas other spirits have either tried and failed or did not recognize you as a medium. Until today, that is."

My stomach clenches. "What do you mean?"

He rises and browses through the extensive books on his shelves. Finally, he pulls a russet-colored volume with a tattered cover. "This is an old book on spiritual possession I found in Constantinople. It describes a scene very much like the one you described. Let me see if I can find it."

He puts on a pair of glasses and thumbs through the pages. In spite of the fact that I don't really trust this man, I am curious.

"Here it is." He looks at me over his glasses. "Now, I am translating, so it will be slow."

"'"When two of the *ruh*, or spirits, wish to *tutmak*, or possess, a single human, the spirits may fight outside or within the human.'" He glances up from the book. "It describes them as foglike beings. Does that sound familiar?"

This time I don't bother hiding my revulsion at being possessed. I nod, shivering.

"Now, considering your history with this young man, it is entirely possible he was trying to protect you from a spirit with menacing intentions."

I think back, remembering how urgently Walter was trying to talk to me. "That's possible. He was trying to call my name, but I couldn't hear him."

Mr. Price taps his fingers on the desk. "Hmm. The question is who, or what, was the other spirit? Did your spirit stalker feel the other spirit was a threat, or was it just jealousy, his way of keeping you as his own mouthpiece? It's difficult to tell without knowing more."

I digest that. "He was trying to talk to me, but something was stopping him. Just like something was stopping Cole from connecting with me to stop the spirits."

"Has Cole been able to do that before?"

I hesitate. I don't know why I am being so open with this man, but I've never met anyone as knowledgeable as Mr. Price and for the first time in a long time, someone seems open to my questions. Finally I nod. "Yes, he's forced Walter out of me before through touching my hand."

"Walter?" His voice is amused and I smile in spite of myself.

"I channeled him for his mother the first time. He died of dysentery in the war. Cole was with me. We think it's because of his presence that my abilities are changing."

Mr. Price leans forward, excited. "Cole has had that effect on other Sensitives. We believe he is some kind of conductor. His brain gives off a higher charge of electricity than other people's do."

I consider that before he asks, "What other abilities do you have, Miss Van Housen?"

"I have visions of the future." I keep my ability to sense emotions to myself. I'm not formally a member of the Society and owe them nothing. "Now may I ask you a question?"

He nods.

"This thing with Cole." I hesitate, unsure if I even want to know the answer. "His ability to increase the talents of Sensitives, does it stop? I mean, I know his presence in my life makes my own abilities grow and become different, but when does it stop?"

Mr. Price closes his book. "As far as we know, it doesn't. This is one of the reasons Cole leaves the Society every few months."

My stomach drops. "He what?"

"Leaves the Society. Too many of the Sensitives we study are high-strung or vulnerable. It's difficult enough for them to control their abilities. Cole's presence makes it harder, even for those like Leandra who have had years of experience at control."

A knock sounds at the door.

Mr. Price puts his book and pen away and opens the door. Cole is standing just outside. "Are you finished?"

I stand. I'm tired and achy and I have had just one too many shocks tonight. I want to hash things over with Cole and the Wrights and then go back to the hotel to sleep for a week. I don't know how much more I can take.

"Thank you for your insights, Miss Van Housen. I've exposed many celebrated mediums for fraud and I've seen many things in different parts of the world that I can't explain, but tonight was a revelation."

I'm not sure what to say to that, so I just nod. "Thank you for your honesty and for answering my questions."

As if sensing my distress, Cole hustles me down the stairs without going back to the conference room. Within minutes we are in his car on our way to meet up with Leandra and Harrison at their house. My mind is so full of things to tell him that I can't decide which one to bring up first. So I start with the one that affects us most personally.

"Why didn't you tell me that you have to leave the Society every few months because of the effect you have on Sensitives' abilities?"

He's quiet for a few minutes before he answers me, his voice tight. "It just never came up."

I stare at him hard in the darkness but can't see his eyes. "I knew you had an effect on other Sensitives, but I didn't know how drastic that effect would be. You should have told me."

"I didn't think it would be an issue, not with you running

off on your tours. We were separated for quite some time when I came home to England and then again for several weeks. I didn't know my effect on your abilities would be so very drastic."

He sounds defensive, and as much as I want to backpedal, I can't help but feel he should have given me more warning. "You still should have told me," I repeat.

He pulls in front of the Wrights' house and cuts the engine. "What would you have done differently, Anna?" he asks quietly, and I want to bite my tongue off because the only thing I could have done differently was refuse to see him again.

"Nothing." I yank open the door of the motorcar and climb out without waiting for an answer. With everything that is going on, why is it that Cole and I can't seem to spend time together without having some kind of argument?

Leandra is busy giving orders when we enter the drawing room. Within moments there's a fire in the small white marble fireplace, the men have drinks in their hands, and the iron-haired housekeeper is bringing in a pot of tea and a plate full of hearty sandwiches.

We keep the conversation light until the food is gone. Then Leandra fixes her sparkling green eyes at me over her teacup. "What did you learn?"

I shake my head. "More than I thought I would and less than we'd hoped. Mr. Price is a man of many secrets, but I don't know if they have anything to do with Pratik or Jonathon. I feel nothing particularly menacing from him."

I pause to take a breath. How could I explain the depth of dark knowledge that Mr. Price contains that leads to him feeling like no one else? I move on. "Did any of you know that Mr. Casperson is a Sensitive?"

Cole's forehead wrinkles. "He can't be. If he were a Sensitive, I would have known."

That stops me in my tracks. Of course. Why hadn't I thought of that? I shake my head slowly. "I'm almost positive that he is. He feels like a Sensitive." I turn to Cole. "You know how we felt a spark when you and I first touched?"

Harrison turns a laugh into a cough and Cole's cheeks redden, but he nods.

"It turns out I feel that with all Sensitives, not just you. I felt it with Pratik and Leandra the first time we met and have felt it with every Sensitive since. When I shook his hand today, I felt the same thing."

Cole shakes his head. "I've never been wrong. It's one of the reasons Dr. Boyle and the others feel I'm so valuable. I have never felt anything even close to that around him."

"Then what could it be? And did you see how bad he looked?"

Leandra nods. "I noticed. I thought he was getting sick."

"Maybe he was," Harrison says.

Leandra refills my teacup. "So what happened during the séance? It looked like you were going to faint."

I shiver. "Walter made a reappearance." At the blank look on their faces, I realize they don't know who Walter is. "Walter is the ghost of a soldier who died in the Great War.

He's the only ghost I have ever been in contact with." I turn to Cole. "Mr. Price thinks he's a spirit stalker."

Cole frowns. "So the mist we saw was Walter? Is he haunting you?"

"Sort of. Let's just say he's attracted to me. Maybe I'm the only person he can speak to. At any rate, he warned me once when I was in danger and Mr. Price thinks he may have been doing so again. Unfortunately, he wasn't the only spirit there, and what you saw was two spirits fighting for possession of me."

"Do you know who the other spirit was?"

I shake my head. "No, but I felt the spirit before in Budapest, only I didn't know that's what it was. I was going to sleep in my hotel room and felt something pressing against me. After I found the poppet, I just assumed that explained it. Apparently not. I don't know why it didn't possess me then. Perhaps it was toying with me. Mr. Price thinks there's a chance Walter may have been trying to protect me tonight."

The room is quiet for a moment as everyone digests that. "But he didn't tell you anything?"

I shake my head. "It was as if there was a shield stopping him. The only thing I did hear was a word that sounded like *Aiwass*, but he may have just been trying to say my name."

Leandra frowns. "Harrison, did you find anything out about the poppet?"

"Only that it's commonly used to hex someone. There's no way to trace its origins because it's made of common candle wax."

"So we can assume that someone familiar with black magic is trying to curse Anna," Cole says.

My skin crawls. "Why would someone want to curse me?"

Leandra shakes her head. "Why would someone want to abduct Jonathon, murder Pratik, or try to abduct me? Have you had any other strange experiences beside headaches and your ears buzzing?"

I want to laugh—my life has been one long strange experience—but instead I nod. "From almost the moment I arrived. When my ears buzz, I feel the oddest sense of mental confusion and my abilities are blunted—not as sharp."

Cole holds up a finger, frowning. He has on his professor face. "Didn't you mention how your trains kept breaking down?"

My eyes widen and I nod. "Yes, they did. Do you think it could be related?"

Harrison nods. "It's a very real possibility. I am checking into how to get rid of the poppet without hurting you. It's too dangerous to just destroy it."

"I don't want you to go back to the Society," Cole says, his voice hard. "It's too risky. I think it's safe for us to assume that the events of the past weeks are all connected."

Harrison agrees. "And whoever is doing it clearly feels that Anna is a threat. I agree with Cole. Anna should make herself scarce and Leandra should join the boys in the country. It's too dangerous."

A sudden swell of rage emits from Leandra like a black cloud and I gasp. She shuts her eyes for a moment and takes a deep breath. The anger and the darkness dissipate as quickly as they arose.

When her eyes open, she is staring straight at me and her lips curl in a rueful smile. My heart pounds. Whatever it is, Leandra is fully aware of it and works to control it.

"We've already discussed this," she says. "The children are safe. My place is with you. I can help. You know I can."

"I'm worried about my mother and grandmother," Cole says, his eyes darker than usual. "Do you think they're in any danger?"

"It's hard to tell," Harrison says. "Probably not, but we don't know what or who we're dealing with. If you're truly worried, you might suggest they take some sort of holiday."

Cole snorts. "I can try but I can't make either of them do anything." He turns to Leandra. "Have you had any nightmares?"

She hesitates. "Nothing clear. I've stopped trying to control it, but the habit of years seems to be hard to break."

I wonder how she controls her nightmares, but don't ask. For once, I just wish I could have a vision or two that might give a clue as to the identity of the murderer, but I haven't had one since Cynthia's scavenger hunt last New Year's Eve. Just when a good vision would come in handy, that particular ability has remained frustratingly silent.

"I think you both are forgetting something," I tell the two men. "I'm the best person to find out who the mole is."

Cole shakes his head. "No. I don't want you putting yourself in danger."

"I'm already in danger," I counter.

His mouth flattens and I know he's dug his heels in. He can be so intractable.

Too bad. I can be just as stubborn.

"I hardly think it's fair that the both of you expect Leandra and me to stand passively by when we have both been attacked—me psychically and Leandra physically. Not when both of us may be able to help put a stop to it. It's not only unfair, it's practically criminal. What if someone else is taken or Jonathon is found dead? And we could have stopped it?"

Leandra claps her hands. "Hear, hear!"

"I'll be careful, but I *will* help." I cross my arms and dare anyone to disagree with me.

Leandra comes over and kisses me on the cheek. "I was worried that you wouldn't be good enough for Cole. Now I'm more worried that he isn't good enough for you."

I give her a smile. I want to trust her, I really do. I know that Cole trusts her and Harrison implicitly. Perhaps if I knew what dark tumult it is that lies just beneath Leandra's pretty blond exterior, I wouldn't be so suspicious.

Cole comes to take my arm. "I should get Anna back to the hotel. She has an early morning call."

He is silent on the way home and I can feel his disapproval, but I ignore it. Surely after all we have been through together, he knows me better than to think I would hide in a room somewhere all safe and sound while people I care about may be in danger. I don't think so.

Instead of dropping me off, Cole parks the motorcar. "I'm going to check out your room before leaving you."

I want to argue with him but am eager to ease some of the tension between us. "All right," I say in a small voice.

He takes my hand as we walk to the hotel and the gesture comforts me. Maybe he is as upset about the distance coming between us as I am.

Because it's so late, the lobby is quiet when we enter and we're just about to go up the stairs when a voice shatters the silence.

"Just where do you two think you're going?"

I whirl around, my eyes wide.

Mother.

TWELVE

A plush silver fur is draped over her arm and she's wearing a black brimless cloche. A rhinestone and ivory Bakelite ornament is pinned to its side, matching her ivory brocade dress and multistrand necklace of graduated pearls. Her creamy complexion contrasts with her dark eyes and the hair curling softly around her delicate jawline.

Mother has always dressed well, and during the lean years became an expert at creating expensive looks out of secondhand clothes. Jacques's money has added a chic sophisticated sheen.

"Where have you been, darling?" she demands, her hands on her hips. "I've been waiting forever. Jacques is going to start to worry about me. He's waiting at our hotel because I wanted to have a little chat with you alone. Now don't just stand there with your mouth hanging open. It's not at all attractive. Come and give me a kiss."

She offers me a cheek, and on legs numb with shock, I walk over and kiss her. She wraps her arms around me for a brief hug. Then she offers a cheek to Cole, who reddens and follows my example. As always, he is struck dumb by her polished, superior presence. His grandmother, for all her snobbery and pretensions, has nothing on my mother when it comes to making someone feel uncomfortable.

I finally find my voice. "What are you doing here?"

"I've come to see you, of course. As soon as I heard you were going to be playing in proper cities, I told Jacques we needed to close up the New York flat and move to Paris early."

Now that my mother is rich, she's decided she must have homes in both New York and Paris, where Jacques comes from.

"What? Prague and Warsaw aren't real cities? Surely you want to visit Budapest again." I say this with tongue in cheek, knowing how much she hates admitting that she is Hungarian. Because she's linguistically gifted, learning English was no problem for her and her accent is very slight. Nonexistent when she puts her mind to it.

She reaches up and pulls a lock of my hair just hard enough to ouch. "Don't be saucy, darling. Now, are you going to show me your room?"

She stares at Cole, her meaning clear. His presence is no longer needed.

He clears his throat. "Will I see you tomorrow?"

I nod decisively. "Of course."

"Why don't you join us for lunch?" My mother gives him a gracious smile and I want to groan. She's taking charge, as usual.

"That sounds nice," Cole says, and makes a hasty retreat.

Lucky.

Mother and I head upstairs and I scan the room quickly to make sure nothing is amiss before moving aside to let her in.

She looks over the room and sniffs. "You would think that the management would spring for a better room, considering your experience."

"Mother," I warn.

She says nothing, staring out my window. It's too dark to see anything, but I can tell she wishes I had a view. I know she just wants the best for me. Well, maybe the second best. She wants the very best for herself.

She sits and pats the bed.

I gingerly sit next to her as if she might explode at any moment. Given my experience with my mother, that isn't out of the realm of possibility.

"So, tell me darling, just how close have you and Cole become? Why was he going up to your room with you? I'm sure that isn't allowed on tour."

Her voice is leading and I sigh. "He just wanted to check the room to make sure it was safe, Mama. We aren't lovers."

"I should hope not—you're far too young for that sort of thing."

I don't remind her that she was exactly my age when she became pregnant with me. My mother is a master of selective memory, and this, like Hungarian, is something she chooses to forget.

Then she frowns. "Why does he have to check your room to make sure it's safe?"

Pressing my lips together, I stifle a groan. I must be out of practice. I'm usually much more careful when speaking to my mother. "He's just overprotective. Like you, he doesn't consider this a respectable place for a young woman." I mentally apologize to Cole for lying about him.

"Well, at least we agree on something," she says.

I frown. "I thought you liked Cole."

"I do, darling. I just don't want you to get too involved too quickly. I want you to have fun first. He's far too serious. You're serious enough all on your own. I'm not saying you don't want someone serious enough to take care of you, but that can come later. Really, how much fun do you have with Mr. Frowny Face?"

"Mother!"

She shrugs an elegant shoulder.

But her surprising insight makes me squirm. Cole and I haven't had very much fun lately. Of course, there are reasons for that—reasons I won't be sharing with my mother.

Sweeping one hand around my room she asks, "Is this what you really want, darling? Bad hotels, bad food, and constant work? I know you love magic, but is it really worth it?"

I don't even hesitate. "Right now, it's what I want to do."

All drama and performance, she heaves an exaggerated sigh. "I can't say I'm surprised. It's all you've ever known and God knows you've wanted your own show long enough. Well, go ahead and try it. Right now every city you travel to will be a revelation but that's only because you're in Europe. Remember, while it may seem exciting to travel from city to city, you really won't see that much because you're working. And once you go back to the States it will become mundane very fast. Nothing in the States can rival the grandeur of Europe's cities. You should know, you've already seen most of it."

She has a point, but I don't tell her that. "It is going to be fine," I tell her firmly.

"I won't bring it up again, but remember that Jacques and I are getting a lovely little flat in Paris and you will always have a room there. Just think, darling, you could go to school in Paris, learn to paint, or write, or just soak up the atmosphere for as long as you like. We'll only be there for part of the year, so the rest of the time it would be like your very own apartment."

I start to speak, but she puts a finger to my lips. "No, no reason to say yes or no right now. The offer is always open."

She reaches over and kisses my cheek before standing. "Now I suppose you should get some sleep. Do you have an early call?"

I nod. "Eight in the morning."

"I'll be there," she says, and is gone before I can protest.

I don't sleep well. Every time I set my book down and try to sleep, my mind spins. Walter. The poppet. Pratik. Witchcraft. Jonathon. Cole. Billy. Mr. Casperson. Mr. Price. And finally, to add to the kaleidoscope of craziness, my mother.

Sleeping with the light on doesn't help and, even though I hate to admit it, I'm just too spooked to sleep in the dark.

So after tossing and turning and barely dozing, I finally give it up at six and get dressed. I head out in search of coffee and sustenance, a dull throbbing in my temples. It's pouring outside, sheets of water cascading down off the hotel awning.

I stare out at the world with distaste. The small café most of the troupe frequents is only a block or so down the street. Hunger wars with my dislike of monsoons and I twirl my open umbrella in my hand, considering. The door behind me opens and I turn to find Billy looking at the rain with equal aversion.

"Are you going?" he asks.

"I think so."

"I'm wondering just how hungry you would have to be to brave drowning."

I wrinkle my nose. "I'm pretty hungry."

"Me too. We should just do it."

I nod and before I can react he snatches up my hand and pulls me out into the storm. Gasping as the cold water drenches me, I quickly position my umbrella over my head. We run wildly, the wind and rain forcing me to keep my umbrella low. My visibility is limited to my T-strap shoes as they splash through puddles.

"This is crazy!" I yell.

He laughs in response and we duck under the awning covering the entrance to the café. I shake my umbrella at him, but it can't make him any wetter than he already is. Water drips down off the brim of his bowler and he grins at me like a loon.

"You're crazy," I insist and then realize he's still holding my hand. My face reddens and he must realize it too because he drops it before opening the door to the café.

"Morning, Mary!" he says as the red-haired waitress sets two cups on a table and pours us coffee from a tin pot. She knows us as those crazy American stage people and has the coffeepot percolating for us in the morning. I smile my thanks as I shrug out of my wool coat. Billy takes off his trench coat and Mary snaps her fingers.

"Give those to me, both of you, before you make puddles on the floor."

Meekly, we obey. She has been serving breakfast to most of us in the troupe ever since we came to London. I'm not sure she approves of us and she nags us in a motherly sort of way.

The café is rather a hole in the wall. It's small, with nicked-up tables and chairs that don't match and an uneven wooden floor. On the upside, everything is kept scrupulously clean and the food is always good, hot, and plentiful. And cheap, which is important as most of us are living off the skimpy wages we get from the company each month.

After ordering scrambled eggs and toast, I sip my coffee, hoping the hot liquid will melt the icy coldness that has taken residence in center of me since the séance. Billy usually has me laughing straightaway with his positive outlook on life, but this morning he regards me gravely over the rim of his coffee cup.

"What?" I finally ask.

"You look tired. And tense."

I shrug, developing a curious lump in my throat.

"You're supposed to only look that way after days on the road, not when we've had time off. Is everything all right?"

Mary brings our plates and I smile up at her, grateful for the interruption. What am I supposed to say? Nothing I could tell him would possibly make sense to this open, self-made cowboy from Philadelphia. Sometimes I feel as if I am leading two different lives—my life as a magician and my life as a Sensitive.

And I used to think being a girl magician was odd.

We eat in silence for a few minutes before he finally asks, "Well?"

I sigh and put down my toast. For some reason I am curiously loath to lie to him, so I tell him the partial truth. "My mother showed up unexpectedly last night. We stayed up late talking."

He smiles, causing Mary, who is refilling our coffee cups, to stare unashamedly. "Thanks, Mary," he says easily.

She startles and stomps off, muttering under her breath about life being unfair to allow a man to look like that.

I understand the sentiment.

His focus returns to me. "So your mother makes you tense and tired?"

I laugh. "You have no idea."

He raises an eyebrow but doesn't question me further, and I don't offer more information. The relationship I have with my mother is fraught with pits of quicksand—just when you think you're on solid ground, everything shifts and you're sinking again.

Wisely he changes the subject. "What time do you have to head to the theater this morning?"

I glance at the silver and enamel wristwatch Jacques and Mother bought me as a going-away gift. "In about thirty minutes."

"We had best get going, then. I'll walk you over."

It's on the tip of my tongue to tell him not to worry about it, but that seems impossibly rude. Hopefully, we'll beat my mother there. The last thing I need is for Mother to meet Bronco Billy and get ideas.

I resist his urgings to run back to the hotel to change. I'm already wet and there's no reason to change just to get wet again.

Mother isn't backstage when we arrive. Perhaps the trip tired her more than she realized and I'll be spared her critique of my rehearsal.

Before I can go to the dressing room, Billy catches my arm. "I know you weren't sure if you would have time for touring, and that things are more up in the air because of your mother, but I'd love it if you could do a little sightseeing with me tomorrow."

His voice is casual, and looking into his handsome friendly face, I weaken at the thought of doing something just for fun. Billy is so easy to be with. "That sounds wonderful," I tell him.

His smile lights up the dull hallway. "That's just fine,

then! See you around lunchtime?"

I nod, thinking this would make the perfect excuse to get out of doing anything with my mother.

After saying a hurried good-bye to Billy, I race to where Mollie is positioning my props onstage. Mother is talking to Louie, while Jeanne glowers next to him. As lovely as Jeanne is, she's no match for the polished flirtations of my mother.

Marguerite Estella Van Housen has inspired romantic fantasies in almost every man who has ever met her. She's wearing fur today and her delicate heart-shaped face rises out of the softness like an exotic flower. Her lustrous dark eyes are lined with kohl, giving her the look of a glamorous Cleopatra. Even up close it's hard to tell she's the mother of a grown daughter except that she exudes a ripe quality no ingenue could possess. Louie is enchanted. His wife is less so.

I wave from the stage to get my boss's attention. He doesn't see me. "Good morning!" I call.

Louie jumps, but Mother merely smiles. "Good morning, darling. Do you always come to work looking like a drowned rat?"

I put my hand on my hip, unwilling to let her intimidate me. "I love you too, Mother."

Her brows arch as she acknowledges my cheekiness.

Louie clears his throat. "Go ahead and get started, Anna. Your mother would like to take you shopping this afternoon, so let's just run through the iron maiden trick."

I nod, though inside I'm burning. How dare she come in and sweet-talk the manager into giving me a day off. This is my job, not hers. She can't just manipulate things to get what she wants. Then I watch Louie, who's completely under her spell.

Well, maybe she can.

I run through the sequence twice, and even though Louie isn't watching, I know my mother is and will give me feedback on my performance later.

When I finish, I thank my assistant and hurry backstage to get my coat. By the time I return, Jacques has joined the group and Louie is looking far less starstruck. Jeanne, on the other hand, is relieved.

Jacques and I embrace awkwardly. We've spent most of our relationship suspicious of one another. Now I'm suspicious that he may be too good for my mother. Neither state of affairs is conducive to me being very comfortable around him.

"It's too early for lunch," I tell them.

"We're going shopping," Mother says climbing into the car that Jacques has procured for their stay in London. "Jacques promised we would go to Harrods, as well as the shops on Bond Street, no matter what the weather is like. Should we let Cole know where to meet us at Harrods?"

I nod. "That's a good idea. If we stop at my hotel, I can write a note and have it sent over to his house."

While at the hotel I change into dry clothes, careful to look fashionable enough for my mother. I hesitate over my hats, wondering if I should go conservative and opt for my black cloche or go fancy with my colorful knockabout.

Grinning, I snatch up the knockabout and settle it on my head. If mother doesn't like my color choices, she can live with it. Back in the car, my lips curl as I watch my mother leaning forward in her seat, her entire being absorbed in the enjoyment to come. Shopping has never held as much appeal for me as it does for her. Food and housing insecurities made me frugal and now I have a hard time buying anything other than necessities. Once in a while I'll splurge, like I did for my hat, but seldom.

Thinking about my hat reminds me of Calypso. Why hadn't I felt anything when I touched her hand at the séance? Usually she's crackling with emotions, but the other night I got nothing. Perhaps like me, gaining control over her abilities also means gaining more control over her emotions and thoughts? I puzzle over that until we arrive at our first destination and I get to see Mother-with-money in action.

I think Harrods completely shatters her preconceived notions, and she claps when she realizes just how immense it is. "We won't be able to go anywhere else today," she tells Jacques. "Bond Street can wait. I bet I can completely furnish our pied-à-terre without ever going anyplace else."

Jacques smiles at her indulgently. "Don't go overboard, *chérie.* We have to ship everything over to France and you will find plenty of shops in Paris. And keep in mind that we haven't even signed for the apartment yet."

She looks crestfallen for a moment, then brightens. "We'll be signing for the apartment as soon as we get to France and at any rate, I can make a good start. There are things the

English just do better than the French. No offense, darling."

"None taken, my love." They put their heads together in a nuzzling fashion as if I weren't there.

I avert my eyes and give a small cough.

Just as if it were a hotel instead of a department store, someone rushes out in the rain to open the car door and escorts us under an umbrella through the front door.

For the next two hours I watch as my mother shops as excitedly as a child. Observing her makes me appreciate just how hard she must have trained herself to prepare for this kind of life. It couldn't have been easy to keep faith, shuffling from city to city, a young daughter in tow, going from bad manager to bad lover. She had to have wondered at times if she hadn't squandered all her chances.

Gently autocratic, she carefully judges the merits of one kind of china over another, compares linens, and considers different types of furniture. Her knowledge of the finer things in life far surpasses anything I could have ever imagined. I know she couldn't have learned this in the small Hungarian town where she was raised, nor as a magician's assistant. Where had she gleaned this kind of knowledge?

It's one of those mysterious things about my mother that I will probably never know because she hates answering questions about herself. By the time we enter the elegant restaurant on the fourth floor, she has reached a point of contented satisfaction.

Like everything else in England, the interior of the Georgian Restaurant, with its towering pillars, stiff linens, and ornate plasterwork, makes me feel just slightly inferior. My mother, on the other hand, sails through the room as if she were born to it. Other patrons watch her progress with a combination of envy and approval. Mother always has known how to make an entrance.

I'm surprised Cole isn't here yet and inform the waiter that we are expecting a fourth.

"Who is the handsome man who escorted you to the theater this morning?"

I freeze and glance at my mother, who's wearing a smug smile. I decide the best defense is nonchalance. "A friend. He's actually in the troupe." I smile at the waiter pouring our tea before continuing. "He's a cowboy who does rope tricks. He shoots as well, but of course, not in this show. Imagine shooting inside some of those fancy theaters!"

"How close of friends are you?" she asks, her voice carefully casual.

I ignore the innuendo. "Quite. He actually worked for the same circus we did—he knows Swineguard!"

This stops the subject cold as she never, *ever* talks about our time in the circus. Especially not in front of her new husband. The conversation quickly moves on to Mother and Jacques's business and stage gossip. Surreptitiously, I keep checking my watch, wondering where Cole is.

"Should we go ahead and order?" Mother asks, her voice petulant.

I nod reluctantly, worry tightening my stomach. Cole is usually so punctual. It's not like him to miss an appointment.

Excusing myself, I make my way to the foyer. "Pardon me. Do you have a message for Anna Van Housen?"

The maître d' looks down his nose at me. "If we had received a message, we would have done our best to deliver it. We're not in the habit of sitting on messages to our patrons."

"Of course," I assure him, feeling small.

I make my way back to our table and sit, my mind racing. Cole has been so worried about me that it never occurred to me to worry about him. I swallow. Surely Leandra or Harrison would contact me if something were wrong, wouldn't they?

Or maybe he just couldn't face the thought of a meal with my mother. But then, I suffered through a meal with his grandmother. Surely, he owes me one.

The waiter brings our lunch and I wish I could tell Mother and Jacques to hurry. All I want to do is get back to the hotel. Maybe he left me a message there.

"Is your lunch not to your liking? Or is something else worrying you? Your young man perhaps?"

I catch a wicked glint in my mother's eyes before she lowers them. I thought she liked Cole. She certainly seemed to in New York. Perhaps it really is because she doesn't want me to get serious about anyone yet, or maybe it's because he's immune to her charm. She doesn't know of his natural reticence or his shyness around women. I smile back at her. "I was just thinking of how well my performance went over in Budapest. You missed out."

Her smile becomes fixed. So she *does* miss performing.

"Well, I'll get to see it when you perform in Paris. What theater did you say you were going to be at?"

I stare at my plate. "Le Petit Théâtre."

"Pardon?"

"Le Petit Théâtre!"

"That's a little out of the way, isn't it?" Jacques asks, clueless that that was exactly my mother's point.

I shrug, wondering how long I have to sit here before I can politely make an excuse to go back to the hotel. I'm pushing my food around on my plate when I sense Cole's presence. I glance up, my heart leaping when I see him standing in the arched doorway. But moments later my stomach clenches as I feel his discomfort. Something is wrong.

Then I see a small figure standing next to him. She comes up to his shoulder and is wearing a knockabout so similar to the one I bought that I almost reach up to make sure mine is still there.

Jealous pain ricochets around my chest like a bullet when I recognize who it is.

Calypso.

THIRTEEN

Unshed tears sting my eyes and I carefully breathe in and out, trying to hold them back.

Why would he bring Calypso to have lunch with my mother? I can see her finding out his destination and pressing to come, but he couldn't tell her no?

Apparently not.

I glance at Mother, but she's oblivious and chatting with Jacques. I put my head down and stare at my plate so I don't have to watch them approaching the table.

"I'm sorry I'm late." Cole's voice has a pleading note that I know is meant just for me.

I lift my head and give him a wide smile. Not for nothing had I been raised by the finest actress never to be in a play. "I'm just happy you made it," I lie. I turn to Calypso and tilt my head. There is something different about her, but I can't put my finger on it. "How lovely to see you again. Are you joining us?" I kiss her cheek, but my words let her know that she is intruding.

"As soon as Cole said he was coming to see you, I invited myself along."

I frown. She seems agitated and I know there's more to her being here than that. Then it dawns on me what's different about her. "You cut your hair!"

She turns her head this way and that, showing off her stylishly angled bob. "Do you like it? I was getting headaches carrying that load of hair around. And it's so much more fashionable, don't you think?" Without waiting for an answer, she turns to my mother. "You must be Anna's mother. I can see where she gets her beauty. And you must be Jacques? So nice to meet you."

My mother's eyes shoot over to me, no doubt taking in my determinedly cheery smile. For a fraction of a second, she looks unnerved, but regains her composure so quickly that no one but me would even detect that she had been momentarily at a loss.

"Aren't you a dear to compliment me so?" Mother extends her hand as if expecting Calypso to kiss it. Calypso stares blankly for a moment and then gives it a little shake. "And look at you two! Aren't you just like twins with your lovely hats. Did you get them together?"

I shake my head. "No, I actually splurged on mine while Calypso and I were out shopping. You must have gone back and gotten one later?"

Cole sits next to me as the disgruntled waiter brings another chair for Calypso. After she sits, she gives me a smile. "I loved the hat so much I had to go back and get it. I knew you wouldn't mind."

I bare my teeth in a smile. "Why would I mind? After all, it's just a hat. And it goes so well with your new haircut."

Calypso hesitates only for a moment. "Thank you."

My stomach hurts. Is Calypso playing a game with me? She genuinely seems to like me, but she also seems to have a special fondness for Cole. Is she just using me to get to him or using him to get to me? Or am I being absurd?

I glance sideways at Cole and find him regarding me steadily. I feel his discomfort, but detect no regret. More is going on here than meets the eye. I know I should reserve judgment until I know more, but the jealousy swirling in my stomach is hard to combat.

The waiter takes Cole's and Calypso's orders and we're left to make awkward conversation as we try to finish our meals and they wait for theirs. I shift in my seat, the plush padding suddenly uncomfortable. I wish I could just leave. Then I wonder what Cole would do if I did. Would he follow me?

It takes Mother's keen intelligence only moments to grasp the situation. I know how her mind works. The only person ever allowed to belittle or otherwise threaten me in any way is her. Everyone else is mincemeat.

With a gleaming glance at me, she turns her formidable attention to Calypso. "I love your name, darling. Calypso. It's so exotic and Gypsylike. I use to know of a pack of Gypsies in the old country. They were so . . . rustic. I wonder if any of them survived the war," she muses.

Calypso's friendly smile falters. "My mother is Spanish, though she was born in Trinidad. My father is English. No Gypsy blood here."

"Really? You have the look of a wild Gypsy girl. And Trinidad? How . . . *peculiar*."

The waiter serves Cole's and Calypso's lunches. I look at my own plate, wondering how long it will take them to finish so I can make my escape.

Having made her point, Mother turns to Cole. Surreptitiously, I make a fist with my thumb between the middle fingers—the signal we used for *no* back when we were performing together.

She ignores it.

"Anna's last letter told me she was going to meet your mother and grandmother. Did you have a good time?" Mother is letting Calypso know of my special status in Cole's life.

My cheeks heat and I cringe.

Cole glances at me and I know Mother saw and interpreted the look. "We had a very nice time. My grandmother is a bit old-fashioned, but I think she liked Anna very much."

I nearly snort at that, but don't. My mother is intuitive enough as it is. She already knows, even without being told, that the meeting wasn't a complete success.

"Wonderful. So you still live at home, then? What about when you go to the university?"

I've had enough. "What is this, Mother, twenty questions?

Let Cole eat." I keep my voice light, but my mother hears the warning.

"It's all right, Anna, I don't mind answering your mother's questions. Yes, I live at home and will continue to do so throughout university. There's no reason for me to move as the school is so close and I'm all that my mother and my grandmother have."

My mother levels a look at him that on the surface seems to say *Aren't you the sweet boy*, but underneath she means How can you be man enough for my daughter living with mummy and grandmummy?

"And you, Calypso, do you live with your parents?"

Calypso, intent on her plate, startles. Did she think my mother was done with her?

"Oh. No."

She doesn't offer any more information and my mother raises an eyebrow. "You're awfully young to be living on your own . . ." My mother's tone is leading.

"I'm not much younger than Anna, and like her, I'm very independent. I live in a boardinghouse," Calypso finally says, realizing my mother isn't going to leave her alone. "My father lives outside town and I moved to London to be close to him."

I frown at her and her cheeks redden. She'd told me she and her father were estranged. "It didn't work out the way I thought it would."

My mother gives her an evil grin. "Things rarely do, do they?"

Calypso pushes her plate away and looks at Cole and me. "Are we ready to go?"

I stand, startling Cole, who's just finished his meal. My mother makes no move to leave. "You young people go ahead. I think Jacques and I will linger over our tea a bit. Cole, it was lovely to see you, as always. Perhaps you can find time between your mother and your studies to visit Jacques and me in Paris. Calypso, it's been a pleasure to meet you. I adore meeting outlandish young people. It keeps life interesting, don't you think?" Without waiting for an answer, she turns to me. "Give me a kiss, darling. I'll see you in the morning." When I bend down, she whispers. "Be careful with that one. She has a knife aimed right for your back."

"She's my friend," I whisper back.

"Whatever you say, darling. Women can't be friends."

"Cynthia is my friend," I shoot back.

"Cynthia is an anomaly."

She has a point.

We walk out to the lobby and retrieve our belongings from the coat check. Cole helps me into my coat and makes a point to take my arm. Worry and concern come off him in pulses. I reach for Calypso's emotions and sense envy before I feel the strange nothingness that I had felt before.

Interesting. She not only learned how to block, she knows that she needs to. How? Who told her that I can read emotions?

We walk out onto the street; and after the downpour of this morning, I'm surprised to see the sun shining brightly.

"Let's walk," Cole orders. I glance at him in surprise. He returns the look. "I'm parked a couple of blocks away. I didn't want anyone to know where Calypso and I were going."

I'm still confused and tell him so.

He looks at Calypso and I get a sense of genuine worry and concern from both of them.

"I was attacked today," Calypso says. "Just before I met Cole. He told me your suspicions that there's someone within the Society working with whoever killed Pratik and possibly Jonathon."

I shoot a questioning glance at Cole. I thought we had agreed with Harrison and Leandra that we wouldn't share our theories with anyone.

Cole jumps in. "I thought it best to share this with Calypso so she wouldn't disclose her attack to anyone else. I wanted to discuss it with Harrison first. So I brought her to lunch. I didn't want to leave her alone."

He's apologizing for bringing her, letting me know that he really didn't have a choice.

I look from one to the other, confused. Just moments before, I'd been hurt and angry. I'm having trouble switching gears.

As if sensing my feelings, Calypso pulls up the sleeve of her coat and shows me her wrists. "Look. They're already bruising." There's no mistaking the vividly blue bruises, or the tears softening her eyes into dark fathomless pools.

I take a deep breath, sympathy and uncertainty warring

in my stomach. Sympathy wins. It's not her fault she pushes my insecurity buttons. So what if she's attractive and bought my hat? I give her a quick hug, ignoring the prickly residue of resentment. "You can move in with the other Sensitives."

"Oh, no, I couldn't do that," she exclaims, shaking her head.

We reach Cole's motorcar and he opens the door for us.

"Why not?" I ask once we're settled. "We don't want you in danger."

"I'm perfectly safe at the boardinghouse. The landlady went on high alert after Pratik was found and she hired a brawny kitchen boy just in case something else happens. I just don't want to walk by myself to the Society and back. Mr. Casperson is doing some really important work with me. I don't want to leave the study hanging. If I could get a ride to and from the Society, I am sure I would be perfectly safe."

"I'm sure someone can drive you to and fro. If not, you can always take a cab," I tell her.

Calypso shakes her head, her face miserable. "I don't have any friends there." She whispers so that only I can hear.

I can feel an agonizing pain coming off her in waves and my throat chokes up. I know what that kind of loneliness feels like. I think about how many people I have in my life now that love me and believe in me. Cole. Cynthia. Mr. Darby. Jacques. Even my mother. Calypso has no one. Her mother lives in the States and she came to London in part to be with her father and now they aren't even speaking. Yes, she can be dramatic and annoying, but maybe that's because she's trying too hard. "Why don't you stay the night with me?" I say impulsively. "Just for tonight. You can decide whether you want to stay at the boardinghouse tomorrow."

She opens her mouth, flabbergasted. "Do you mean it?"

I nod.

"I thought we were going to the Wrights'," Cole says. I can tell he's uncomfortable, but then, he's never been good with spur-of-the moment things.

"I don't want to intrude," Calypso says quickly. "I already horned in on your lunch."

"It's fine. Cole can tell the Wrights what happened. Just pick up your things and we'll go back to my hotel for the night."

Her bottom lip trembles as she gives me a smile and gratitude crosses her pretty features. "Thank you, Anna. You're a real friend."

Shame heats my face and I glance away. Why do I always think the worst of people? Why am I so suspicious? Calypso isn't perfect—I'm fairly certain she has a bit of a crush on Cole—but no one is perfect, and I should be confident in Cole's feelings for me.

But I'm not.

The thought depresses me a bit, but I'm determined to be cheerful, even when we park in front of the old house where we found Pratik's body.

"You stay here," Calypso says quickly, seeing the look on my face. "It will only take me a moment."

Cole offers to accompany her but she shakes her head. "The landlady and the cook are both there. I'll be fine."

"Are you all right?" Cole asks after she leaves.

I nod, though I'm not really. I try not to think about Pratik's staring eyes. Cole takes my hand and I can feel his love for me. I look up into his face, wishing he would just say the words.

He clears his throat. "I'm sorry I've been so preoccupied here," he says, his voice contrite. "There are just so many more obligations here than in New York. You're busy and I am busy and this whole thing with the Society and then Pratik . . ." His voice trails off and he stares into the distance a moment before looking down into my eyes. "Sometimes I wish we could go back to New York when it was just you and me."

He twines his fingers around mine and a lump rises in my throat. "And my mother and Jacques and Mr. Darby, not to mention Owen and Dr. Boyle."

He sighs. "I guess it was every bit as chaotic there, wasn't it? Sometimes I just feel so overwhelmed." Self-doubt emanates from him. Cole has always been confident and assured—he rarely shows this uncertain side of himself. I wish he'd let me see it more often. It makes me feel like he needs me.

I squeeze his hand, but before I can comfort him, Calypso is back with a small overnight bag. My heart dips. If we could only spend some time alone, it would be so much better.

I try not to remember that the last few times we'd been

alone, we had either been arguing or talking about the Society or Pratik's death. Cole pulls in front of my hotel, and surprisingly Calypso gives us another moment alone. I want him to say something personal again but he doesn't. He just gives me a warm, brief kiss and says he'll see me for dinner tomorrow night.

I sigh and join Calypso in the lobby. As she chatters nonstop up the stairs, I let her words wash over me.

Setting her bag on the floor she whirls around and grabs my arm. Pulling me to the mirror, she smiles at our reflections. "We could be almost sisters with our matching hats and dark hair. I've always wanted a sister."

"You don't have any siblings?"

She shakes her head. "Well, sort of. I have a half sister who lives in America."

"With your mother?"

"No. We have different mothers. We share a father."

At the mention of her father, Calypso's mouth tightens and she turns away. I feel a throb of pain before anger and resentment come racing in behind it. Why isn't she blocking me now? Perhaps the block had nothing to do with me or maybe she didn't know she was doing it.

"Is there any chance you and your father might reconcile?" I have a weakness for fathers. Growing up without one, I suppose I idealized the father-daughter relationship. For years I tracked Harry Houdini's career and dreamed about a day that he would acknowledge that I was his daughter, if indeed I am. Now I know that he can't really acknowledge me and I accept the relationship we are able to have with gratitude. That doesn't stop me from wishing for more.

I glance over at Calypso, wondering why she hasn't answered me. A sad little smile plays about her lips. "I dream of that," she says as if in a trance. "I dream of my father accepting me for who I am and acknowledging my talents. Finally admitting that I can do some things better than he can. It will happen. Someday."

I frown at the strange mix of determination and dejection in her voice, and slip my arm about her. "Are you all right?"

She takes a deep breath and smiles. "Of course." She picks up a deck of cards off my bedside table. "You want to play?"

Calypso accompanies me to my rehearsal the next morning, though I make it clear that I have other plans for the day. She brings her satchel along with her so she can leave right from the theater. We'd played cards the night before until hunger forced us out looking for food and we ate fish and chips on the street like urchins before hurrying back to the hotel to finish our game. When we finally went to bed I fell into a deep, dreamless sleep. As if by agreement, we didn't talk about the Society or Pratik or the abduction attempt that morning. It was nice and normal. I'm hoping for more normal today with Billy.

To my relief, my mother sent a note, telling me she had to reschedule and would see me tomorrow morning. My day is guaranteed to be far more normal without my mother in it.

I introduce Calypso to Louie, and then we sit and watch

the various acts. It's odd seeing her reaction to things I've seen so often I could probably recite lines and do the pratfalls. She laughs like a child over Sally and Sandy and claps her hands at Bronco Billy's tricks.

Jared shows up just before I go on, and I raise an eyebrow at Calypso.

"You and Cole don't want me to be alone and you said you had plans, so I thought he could escort me home." She smiles. "I rang him up this morning when you were getting ready for rehearsal."

I note that Jared's pale cheeks are stained red as he takes a seat next to Calypso, and I hide a grin at the confusion and excitement I feel from him. I wonder if she knows he has feelings for her.

I leave Calypso sitting forward in her seat, her eyes shining, with Jared sitting proud and upright next to her.

I'm unaccountably nervous to be performing in front of people I actually know, but I run through my tricks easily until I get to the iron maiden. Once inside, my ears start to buzz and my stomach roils. Sweat breaks out on my forehead as I try to concentrate. It takes me far too long to get the cuffs off—something I can usually do in seconds. I stare at the spike I am supposed to lift upward but can't seem to focus. Panic grows in my chest as a familiar tingling rises in my fingers, leaving them numb. There's no way I can work the pin even if I could figure out how to lift the correct spike.

My legs tremble and I know I'm going to have to admit defeat. If I fall against these spikes, I could be seriously injured. I open my mouth to call out and a wave of dizziness sweeps over me. Gritting my teeth, I keep myself upright. I try to call again, but no sound comes out.

Please someone, I plead in my head, *please someone help me.* I can almost feel energy leaching from me as the numbness travels all through my body. Why can't I move?

I hear Billy from far away. He's arguing with my assistant, trying to get her to open the door. How long have I been standing in here? Black spots whirl in front of my eyes. A blast of fresh air hits me in the face and I stagger forward. My legs fail and strong arms catch me.

Gasping for air, I find myself looking into eyes the color of a summer sky over an open prairie.

Billy.

I lose myself in his eyes for a long, breathless moment that feels as refreshing and pure as an ocean breeze. Then I blink and hear voices as the others cluster around me. It takes a moment for me to sort everyone out.

"Get her a glass of water," Louie commands as Billy sits me down on the stage, careful to keep me upright with his arm. Calypso kneels next to me. She brushes my hair out of my eyes, her gaze wide and frightened.

"Are you all right?" Billy asks, and I take a deep breath before answering.

"I think so."

"What happened?" Louie demands around his cigar.

"I don't know. Everything was fine and then I got dizzy all of a sudden. I feel fine now." And I do. The dizziness and tingling are gone as if they had never occurred.

"Has that ever happened before?" Billy asks.

I shake my head. "No. Never," I lie, my eyes sliding over to Calypso, who had witnessed my collapse at the séance. The last thing I want is for my life as a Sensitive to intrude on my life as a magician. Sometimes I think performing my magic is the only sane thing I have left in my life. Calypso's face is carefully blank and I remind myself to thank her later.

"You're going to go see a doctor tomorrow," Louie barks. "The last thing I need is for you to collapse onstage in Paris next week."

I nod as he stalks off the stage. He may sound gruff but I can feel the worry beneath his words. He cares about his performers much more than he lets on.

I feel silly with everyone standing over me and move to get up. Billy gives me a hand and I stand gingerly. Sandy brings out a glass of water and I drink deeply. "I'm fine," I insist, and Louie yells from his seat in the middle of the auditorium.

"Then everyone get off the stage except for the Woodruffs. I'm trying to work here!"

"Are you sure you're up for our outing?" Billy asks as we go backstage.

I glance at Calypso, who is a few feet away, talking to Jared. "Yes. I'm fine. I just have to walk my friends out."

He nods. "I'll meet you in front of the hotel?"

I promise to be there, feeling a twinge of guilt. Should I really be going sightseeing with Billy? Am I being disloyal to Cole? It's not like I'm attracted to Billy. Well, maybe I am. A little. But I love Cole and that's that. Billy and I are just friends.

Calypso leaves after I promise to ring her later to tell her how I'm feeling. She takes a taxicab home for safety and for the first time I wonder where she's getting her money. I'll have to remember to ask Cole if the Society is supporting her or the other Sensitives. No one seems to have any jobs beyond letting scientists do experiments. But then again, maybe that is how the Society likes it. Why would they want their subjects to be independent?

I push the thoughts out of my head and hurry upstairs to freshen up and change. I am far too excited to be spending the afternoon with a man who is not my boyfriend, but chalk it up to my excitement about an afternoon free of care.

As if to prove to myself that the afternoon means little to me, I change into a plain blue dress and my blue wraparound coat. Nothing special, I tell myself, before taking special care with my hair and lipstick. I pull a straw hat down over my ears before opening the door to head downstairs.

My eye catches something lying on the carpet just outside my hotel door. I frown, bending for a closer look. Lying just inches from my toes is a medallion with some sort of strange symbol on the front. I glance around to make sure I'm alone before cautiously picking it up. The medallion is about three inches in diameter and made of some sort of heavy metal. Perhaps iron or lead. Etched into the metal are a crescent moon and two crossed arrows. I turn it over and try to read the writing on the back but don't recognize the language.

It lies heavy against the palm of my hand and I turn it over and over, considering. Remembering the poppet, I hate the idea of carrying the medallion on my person, but I don't want to leave it in my room unprotected either. It could be a clue to whatever it is that's going on. Who could have left it and when? Did I miss it coming into the room or did someone leave it while I was getting ready? I swallow hard and glance down the hall, feeling vulnerable.

Knowing Billy is waiting for me and not wanting to stand in the hallway any longer, I shove it into my purse. I'll show it to Cole later.

But I forget everything as Billy comes down the street to meet me, wearing his cowboy hat. He rarely wears it beyond performing, more's the pity because it suits him so well. Like Cole, Billy seems to emanate light, but whereas Cole glows warm and dark, Billy is all bright sunshine.

I chide myself for my fanciful thoughts. Enough lights and sunshine and other notions. Cole is my boyfriend. Billy is just a friend.

Isn't he?

FOURTEEN

So far, March in London has been more like a lion than a lamb, but today, the clouds are scattered in a sky so cerulean it almost hurts to look at it.

Billy whistles when he approaches, admiration in his blue eyes.

"Why, you're as pretty as a new saddle," he drawls, and I laugh.

"Oh, please. You really expect me to believe that cowboy talk?"

He grins and offers me his arm.

"What a difference a day makes!" he exclaims. "It's hard to believe this is the same city."

I agree. "Where to?" I ask.

First on our list of things to see is the Victoria Embankment. There we see the Thames and Cleopatra's Needle.

Billy cocks his head to the side. "I bet you I could shoot an apple right off the top of that thing."

I laugh. "Good thing you don't have your guns. I bet the British would frown on that."

"Probably, but think of what an amazing bit that would be."

I grin, relishing the lighthearted banter. No occult, no murders or abductions, and no worrying about my abilities transforming into something unrecognizable. Just a breathtakingly handsome young man and normal, carefree fun.

We stroll the streets of London, delighted by everything from Big Ben to Tower Bridge. Turning a corner, we run smack into a castle and laugh and laugh because we have no idea which castle it is and because castles are so common in this fairy-tale city that you can mix them up.

"Windsor!" I say.

"Buckingham! No, Balmoral," he answers.

"Balmoral's in Scotland. We should have picked up a tourist guide."

He tucks my arm into his. "No. This is much more fun, isn't it? Just two friends moseying around the city?"

We saunter back toward the river and find ourselves in a public garden where winter-pale young children are being minded by proper well-bred nannies, businessmen are sunning themselves on park benches in lieu of lunch, and a puppet show has sprung up as if out of the still sodden grass. A juggler tosses his clubs nearby, and like moths to a talented flame, we head right toward him.

"Were you in the circus when the ball master was there?" Billy asks, and I shake my head. "He was something else. He could juggle so many balls they looked like a solid circle when he had them all going round."

I slip my silver bracelets from my wrists, juggling them in the air. Billy smiles and the juggler moves toward us. I see the juggler raise an eyebrow and I grin and toss my bracelets one at a time to Billy, who catches them effortlessly and to my surprise juggles them as easily as an expert. "Oh ho!" I say, laughing.

The juggler tosses his clubs in a smooth arc toward me, and I start my own circle. He's obviously a showman because he quickly snatches more up from a bag near his feet.

He begins his own circle near me and then with a nod tosses me another pin. I catch his meaning and we begin doing a two-person juggle with Billy in his cowboy hat still juggling my bracelets next to us. A crowd begins forming and children start drifting toward us from the puppet theater. My pulse quickens and I see Billy grinning like a loon. He whisks his hat off his head and catches my bracelets in it as they come down, and then moves into a three-person nine-club-juggling pattern. The juggler sees this too and reaches down, kicking the bag toward Billy. Billy pulls three clubs out of it, and for a moment all three of us are suspended in a time out of time as we prep to bring Billy in and add three more clubs to the mix. I catch the juggler's eyes.

"One. Two. Three."

Billy tosses the clubs in one at a time and the pattern is set. Applause erupts all around us, and the three of us share a complicit smile. We're standing in a triangle and I am the point man or girl, as the case may be, and can watch both the juggler and Billy. Concentrating fully on the smooth transition of clubs, I separate my mind enough to watch Billy's face as we perform together. He enjoys it as much as I do, I realize, surprised.

We stand juggling like that for two more minutes before the juggler senses the restlessness of the crowd surrounding us. He gives me a little nod and drops the extra clubs at his feet, before moving on to another trick.

Billy and I step out of the circle of people and he takes off his hat and hands me my bracelets.

"That was wonderful!" I tell him, laughing breathlessly.

He grins in agreement. "Let's go someplace fun for supper."

I snort. "Is there such a place in London? I haven't been to any, if there are."

Billy throws back his head and laughs. Nannies, in their starched winter suits, stare after him longingly. "Then maybe you're not going around with the right people!" he says.

His words wash over me with cold reality. The afternoon has been so relaxed that I've forgotten that I'm meeting Cole tonight for dinner.

"I think I'm going to have to pass. I guess this morning took more out of me than I realized." The lie is out of my mouth before I even thought about it. Why don't I want him to know I'm going somewhere with my boyfriend? This is the second lie I've told today and the realization takes the top off my happiness.

Whatever is going on with me, I need to get a grip on it and soon, otherwise I am going to end up being as duplicitous as my mother.

Cole and I aren't in his motorcar for more than five minutes before we're arguing.

"You still should have told me," he reiterates. "Where did you say you were all day?"

Irritation crawls across my skin. "With a friend. Sightseeing. Which I wouldn't have to do if you had thought to take me yourself." I'm being beastly, but can't seem to help myself. It's certainly not his fault that I'm feeling guilty enough about spending a very enjoyable day with another young man. And in a way it is his fault. It's not like he's been attentive.

"We did go sightseeing when you first arrived before all hell broke loose," he says, his voice tight. "And what does sightseeing have to do with the fact that you collapsed during rehearsal and didn't bother to tell me about it? Didn't it occur to you that I might worry?"

I cross my arms over my chest. "I was perfectly fine. How was I supposed to know that Calypso was going to run off and tell you straightaway?"

"I won't even dignify the Calypso statement with an answer. The point is, you should have told me." His jaw clenches.

"No. The point is you are making a mountain out of a molehill, like always!"

He pulls in front of the Wrights' trim little brick house and I hop out, giving the door a satisfying slam. He follows me more sedately as if aggrieved by my childish behavior.

Leandra greets me at the door. "What's wrong?"

"Can you tell by my face? Or could you sense it?" I ask, handing my coat to her housekeeper.

"Your face. And women's intuition. And Cole looks terrible, so I know something happened."

We follow her into the sitting room and she asks me if I want any refreshments. "Actually, I could use a brandy if you have it."

Cole stiffens next to me, disapproval turning his mouth downward. I don't care.

Arching a brow, Leandra brings me a drink and I sip it, allowing the warmth to fill my chest. I take a deep breath. "Did Cole tell you about Calypso getting attacked yesterday?"

Leandra listens intently as I tell her about Calypso staying with me and about my near collapse. When I finish, she pours another brandy and moves to stand in front of the fire.

Harrison comes into the room and gives Leandra a kiss on the cheek, his love for her evident in his eyes. My stomach knots. I wish Cole and I could be that easily affectionate.

Leandra pours another drink and hands it to Harrison.

"Do I look like an orphan?" Cole asks. "I've had a terrible day and need something to wash it down with."

"I thought you disapproved of drinking," I flash.

He looks down at the glass Leandra poured him. "Good

God, where would you get that idea?"

From the look on your face when I asked for a drink, I want to tell him, but I hold my tongue. Tonight his disapproval is just universal.

Leandra fills Harrison in while Cole and I sip our drinks. I'm very aware of the fact that we're standing across the room from one another and I regret it, but I'm still too angry to make an overture of reconciliation and he either doesn't want to or doesn't know that he's supposed to.

"Speaking of information, did you get the list of people who are experts in the occult?" Cole asks. I drag my attention back to the conversation.

Harrison nods. "As we suspected, there were the usual—university professors, spiritualists, et cetera—but several are very interesting."

"Let me guess. Harry Price is one of them," Leandra says.

"Of course. Mr. Casperson is on it, as well."

"Really?" Cole's voice goes up in surprise. "I wouldn't have thought he was interested in that sort of thing."

"Why not?" I ask. "Anyone interested in talking to the dead and other psychical phenomena would probably have at least a passing interest."

Harrison's snorts. "Well, his is more than a passing interest. He has studied extensively with one of the top occultists of our time—who, incidentally, is back in the country."

"Who's that?'

"Aleister Crowley."

A chill prickles the hair on my arms. Mr. Casperson

studied with the man the newspapers call the wickedest man in the world? I thought about how Casperson looked the last time I saw him at the séance. Sick. Nervous. Scared. Could he be the mole? Could he have killed Pratik?

I look at Cole and see he's thinking along these same lines.

"Do you think Mr. Casperson could have had something to do with Pratik's death?" he asks Harrison.

"It's difficult to tell, but we need to keep a closer eye on him. I know Scotland Yard will be questioning most of the people on this list. I'll make sure I am there when they get to Mr. Casperson." He glances over at me. "My friend also told me how to destroy the poppet without hurting Anna. He's going to help me do it tomorrow."

"How?" I ask. The whole idea of someone creating a likeness of me to inflict harm terrifies me.

"We have to slowly warm it with our hands until the features become unrecognizable. Apparently, my friend is going to be casting some sort of protective spell over you, as well."

My heart stutters. "I don't have to be there, do I?"

Harrison shakes his head.

"Good, because I'm leaving for France the day after tomorrow." I don't say it out loud, but considering that I am still having episodes, it's a very real possibility that whoever made the poppet has made another one, or worse.

Cole moves over to where I'm standing and takes my hand. His regret and love come through loud and clear and it occurs to me how lucky I am to have him in my life. In spite of the arguments we seem to keep having, our connection is still so strong. I wonder if I could fall in love with someone I didn't have a psychic connection with.

Leandra pours another round of brandy for everyone. "You're doing the Paris shows, right?"

"Just three days."

She nods. "Good luck."

I wince. The words seem inane after the topic we were just discussing and once again, I feel a strange disconnect between my life as a Sensitive and my life as a magician.

Is a normal life even possible? And more important, is it possible with Cole?

The question haunts me until it's time for the troupe to leave for Paris. As I had expected, the doctor found nothing wrong with me, my mother found everything wrong with me, and Cole stuck close by. It was a relief to see my mother go so I could spend the afternoon with Cole. She seemed oddly reluctant to leave me and was only partly mollified that I would be seeing her shortly. As if in accord, Cole and I spoke of nothing negative and, as if sorry he hadn't taken me anywhere for the past few weeks, he showed me the National Gallery then we found an old bookstore where we poked around for hours. It was probably the best time we've had together since I came to London. The thought saddens me even though I'm relieved we were able to reconnect before my trip to France.

The weather holds bright and clear as the troupe once

again crosses the Channel to Calais but instead of heading east this time, we climb aboard a train headed south toward Paris. It's funny to think that Mother and Jacques made this same journey yesterday. Of course, they were in the first-class carriage, while we're riding in second class, but they too must have seen the countryside gripped in that magical moment between winter and spring. It's the kind of weather that makes you think of bicycles and picnics that start out under soft blue skies and end in downpours.

Those of us in the troupe who've never been to France are riveted to the windows as our train meanders past medieval castles, soaring cathedrals, and charming stone cottages. It's about four hours to Paris by train, and they slip by slowly as we travel through the small cities and towns with delectable names that roll off the tongue like Auchel, Amiens, and Beauvais. I'm so mesmerized by the passing scenery that I don't notice that Billy has taken the seat next to me until he asks, "Are you feeling better today?"

I do, however, notice his voice, stiff and somewhat cold. I raise an eyebrow. "I feel much better, thank you."

"Did you get some rest the other night after I left you at the hotel?"

His tone is leading and I nod again, puzzled by his behavior. "Actually, I packed first, but then I lay down. I'm fine now."

There's a moment of silence before he huffs, clearly irritated.

"What?" I ask, exasperated.

"I saw you going out with your friend after you told me you were too tired to go to supper with me."

My face flames as the memory comes rushing back. I had lied to him and now I was caught in it.

"Are you his girlfriend? Is that why you gave me the gate, claiming to be exhausted, and then ran out with him?"

A thought pops into my head so forcefully it almost hurts. He's jealous. He saw me with Cole and he's jealous.

A little seed of pleasure sprouts in my chest.

What kind of person am I? What kind of girl moons over one fellow and then is almost giddy when she discovers another one is jealous over her?

The kind of girl who doesn't know what she wants, clearly.

I realize he's waiting for an answer, but I'm not sure what to say.

"I'm sorry. I forgot I had an appointment with him," is all I can think of.

"An appointment or a date?"

"We were meeting friends for supper."

Billy is silent for a moment, then says, "Anna . . . don't you know . . ." His voice is low, urgent, and I brace myself. Longing is coming off him in waves.

"Anna, Louie wants me to tell you he needs to talk to you before we check into the hotel."

I glance up at Jeanne, grateful for the interruption. Whatever Billy had to say, it was sure to muddle things even further.

I turn back to the window. "Oh, look! Paris!"

Everyone is distracted as we chug into the City of Light. Whatever it was Billy wanted to tell me, the moment has passed.

As excited as I am to see Paris, I'm relieved when the train rolls into Gare du Nord. There's the usual flurry of activity as we disembark, but we're getting better at it now. I immediately head back to the baggage car to watch my magic props being unloaded. The last thing I want is my iron maiden to be shattered because of some careless railway worker. I extract a franc from my pocketbook and tip the porter, indicating my things. He nods, a wide smile on his face. Some call it bribery; I prefer to think of it as insurance money well spent.

As I place my pocketbook into my handbag, my hand brushes against something cold and I pull out the medallion. It had completely slipped my mind and I resolve to try to steal some time in Paris to find out what the symbols on the back mean.

I spot Louie, yelling orders and waving his arms around, his ever-present cigar bobbing in his mouth. Once I collect my suitcases, I lug them over to him and wait for him to finish yelling at one of the stagehands.

"You wanted to talk to me?" I ask once I can get a word in.

He nods. "Yeah, doll. I wanted to let you know I changed the lineup. You've got the top spot. Don't let me down."

I stand on the platform, with all the noise of one of the busiest train stations in the world, and everything fades as

Louie's words sink in. "But why? How?" I know my shows have been successful, but I'm green compared to some of the other members.

He shrugs. "I admit, I was pretty skeptical when Martin Beck insisted I take you on. But then I watched you perform and thought to myself, Self, she's a pretty good little magician and she has that magic—no pun intended—thing that top performers have. And she's pretty to boot. So I took you on. You've been nothing but professional and haven't given me a moment's worry, unlike some of them." He glares over at Jeanne, who is collecting her things, then continues. "Turns out, Mr. Beck and one of his friends were at the Budapest show and were quite impressed with you. They met me in London and while I was discussing the Jeanne situation with them, his friend suggested I put you in the top spot. Seemed real interested in your career. Now don't get me wrong, I'm in charge of the show, but I was thinking about giving you top billing anyway. Now guess who that friend was?"

I shake my head, baffled. Why would a friend of Mr. Beck be so interested in me?

"None other than Harry Houdini himself, missy. You could have knocked me over with a feather when he showed up."

My skin goes cold and hot all at the same time. Harry Houdini was in London? He came to Budapest to watch my first performance? Louie's shrewd eyes are watching me closely, so I swallow and give him a wan smile. "I'm incredibly flattered and honored. I won't let you down."

I don't mention Houdini because I don't know what to say. That he may or may not be my father? Either Louie has heard the rumors or not. I learned a long time ago that mentioning the gossip simply lends it validity.

"See that you don't." He turns away, his quick mind already leaping to one of the many problems he faces every time the troupe travels.

Jeanne saunters up to me, her movements languid and somehow triumphant. She's looking especially beautiful today, her white skin glowing almost translucent and her short red hair a sleek punctuation mark. "Did Louie share the good news?"

I nodded. "I can't believe he's giving me top billing."

Her laugh rings out, pure and vivacious, and people stop what they're doing to watch her for a moment. "Not that good news, silly. Our good news!"

I must look confused because she laughs again. "We're going to have a baby!" Her eyes gleam with happiness and for a moment I'm envious. What must it be like to be so sure of something? I'm hopelessly in love with one young man and attracted to another one.

"Congratulations," I tell her. She looks like a woman who has everything she has ever wanted.

The entertainers take cars to the hotel while the stagehands will follow our props to the theater before getting to do anything else. We'll have a dress rehearsal this evening and will open tomorrow night. Even though our schedule for the next four days is grueling—we'll be doing three shows a day—I'm determined to sneak off to a library at some point to find out what the symbols on the medallion are. If only to make up for the fact that I may have had an important clue sitting in my purse for the last couple of days and neglected to tell anyone about it.

But I also have to be in good form for my performances. I'll be the top bill unless I can't cut it. Louie would have no qualms about bumping me back down the roster—Houdini or no Houdini.

My mother and Jacques are waiting for me when we get to the hotel even though it's several hours before the dress rehearsal. "I hope you're not angry that I came so early, darling," she says after kissing me on the cheek. "I wanted to show you the apartment. It's just off the Champs-Élysées. I'm sure Louie won't mind." She glances up at my boss, who came up behind me with Jeanne.

He waves his hand. "Go ahead. Just be back in time for a quick run-through."

Mother helps me unpack and freshen up while Jacques stays downstairs and talks business with Louie. "You're going to love the apartment, darling. It's quite large, with floor-to-ceiling windows, parquet floors, and quite the modern kitchen."

I smile, wondering why Mother would need a modern kitchen. She rarely stepped foot in any kitchens we ever had.

Jacques kisses my cheeks, very European, and calls for a taxicab in front of the hotel. He speaks to the driver in rapid French and soon we are on our way. It's strange seeing him in his own country. His accent always made him a bit too much of a dandy for my taste, but he seems almost masterful here.

I stare out the window, my eyes wide as Paris unfolds around me. Both brash and bossy New York and staid and self-important London are overtly masculine in how they feel. Paris, on the other hand, is blatantly feminine. Everything, from the soft gray of the buildings to the ornate architecture to the blooming daffodils and the budding trees gives the impression of a young girl in love with herself.

"Isn't the building beautiful?" Mother asks, excitement lacing her voice. I don't think I've ever heard her sound so girlish and lighthearted. I get out of the car and gaze upward, my heart giving a little leap. The building stands about seven stories tall and the facade is made of white stone. Each tall, slender window has a Juliet balcony of curling black wrought iron.

"It's lovely," I breathe.

"Come see!" She snatches up my hand and races into the building while Jacques pays the driver. A doorman opens the door for us and tips his hat. "Can you imagine?" she whispers. "A doorman!"

Her dark eyes are shining and for the second time in a day, I find myself envious of someone's happiness. I tamp it down as Jacques joins us in the foyer and we climb the stairs to the fourth floor.

When we arrive at the door, my mother, always a performer, makes me close my eyes. I smile at her enthusiasm.

There's nothing of the sophisticate about her today. This is a woman whose dreams have come true. She leads me in. "You can open your eyes now!"

I open my eyes and gasp. There are six windows along a narrow living area that look out on Paris and the river. The shining wood floors are dotted with white sheepskin rugs, matching the white furniture that seems to be all ovals and cubes. Plain black tables finish out the room and the only decorations on the wall are three large oval mirrors that reflect the Paris light from the windows.

The apartment is delightfully fresh and modern and the sky is so blue with the clouds scudding across it that I get the illusion that I'm floating above the city. "It's beautiful," I tell my mother and Jacques. "Absolutely extraordinary."

Jacques rocks back and forth on his feet, pleased with himself. "I had my solicitor looking for us and though he found several, I knew immediately, this was the apartment for my new family."

I raise my eyes to his, a lump forming in my throat. Even after our rocky start, he considers me family. Overcome, I hug him and then my mother. Mother shows me the rest of the apartment, pride of ownership apparent in her every movement. From the black-and-white tiles in the kitchen and the bathroom to the crystal chandelier in the small dining area, the apartment is a home that finally fits my mother's perception of herself. Though I will probably always love our New York apartment best, as it was my first real home, I can see my mother being very happy here. The small empty corner bedroom is mine, I'm told, to do with what I will.

"I was hoping you could come and decorate it," my mother says. "Once the tour has ended," she adds hastily, seeing my face.

"That would be nice." It's the truth. The temptation of what mother told me in England hits for the first time. To live in this apartment, to be taken care of instead of taking care of Mother and myself, is alluring.

But didn't I already make that decision? I wonder as we head back to the hotel. In New York, I decided that I wanted to perform my magic more than anything else in the world. I glance at my mother and see the changes Jacques has brought her. There are the obvious physical changes of a spoiled and pampered woman, but there are less obvious changes as well. A fullness about the lips, a softness in her eyes, and a relaxation of her erect carriage, changes brought about by someone who is in love and loved in return. Living with this new mother might not be so bad. But then I remember how she handled Cole and Calypso at lunch. She's not so different. Almost eighteen years with my mother has taught me she has as many colors as a chameleon. I would love to trust this kinder, gentler mother, but I know better and I'm not sure I want to give up my independence to be taken care of, no matter how tempting it might be. I glance at my wristwatch.

"Do you know where a library or a bookstore is?" I ask.

My mother's painted eyebrows shoot up on her forehead.

"You always were a reader. Do you need a book for the train back to London?"

I shake my head. She and Jacques wait, and reluctantly, I show them the medallion. "A friend gave this to me," I lie. "I want to find out what it means."

My mother turns it over in her hand, frowning. "It looks very old."

Jacques peers at it. "*Oui.* I know just the place. The Sainte-Geneviève Library inherited the entire collection of one of the oldest abbeys in Paris. Some of the documents date from the sixth century. The librarians there are some of the most learned men in France. I'm sure that you will be able to find one who is bilingual who would be able to point you in the right direction." He sniffs in subtle disapproval that neither my mother nor I speak French, though I know it won't take my mother long to pick it up. "I can arrange for the motorcar to pick you up in the morning before your first show. Would that be acceptable?"

"That would be perfect, thank you." I try not to get my hopes up. For all I know, someone accidentally dropped it outside my door and it has absolutely nothing to do with Pratik's murder or the poppet.

But I don't really believe that.

We drop Jacques off at his solicitor's office so he can fill out some paperwork on the apartment before heading back to the theater. When my mother stops the car to walk the last few blocks to my hotel, I think she is going to scold me for something. I'm always suspicious when she makes a point to speak to me alone. Instead, she once again surprises me.

"Are you happy?"

Startled, I glance sideways at her but she isn't looking at me. Am I happy? I think of the Society that I thought would bring me a sense of peace about my abilities but instead has only created havoc in my life. I think of Cole, who I love so much, but who struggles to express his feelings in return, and I wonder if I can live with the changes his presence might make to my abilities. I think of the tour, which is exhausting but ultimately satisfying, and which brought me Billy, who has turned into such a wonderful friend and whose presence brings me a levity my life has always lacked. My mother is waiting for an answer, but I am not even sure what to tell her, because I don't know. Finally I say, "I think I am. What is happiness anyway?"

She is silent for a moment, then says, "I used to wonder the same thing. Oh, I had moments of happiness, especially with you."

My eyes widen. It's the closest to an admission of love that I've ever heard from her.

"Oh, you didn't think me capable?" She laughs. "Trust me, I doubted it myself. But Jacques has brought me happiness, which for me will always mean security. I have the security of a good man who loves me, work I find interesting, and enough money that I don't have to worry about my daughter or myself ever going without again."

I'm speechless. My mother has never been one for

introspection, nor has she ever been so forthright.

She continues, "You know what I want. I want you to stop touring and live with Jacques and me until you find what happiness means to you." I try to speak, but she raises a hand. "I know, I know, you think you're doing what makes you happy, but I'm having a difficult time believing that the girl who always begged me to stay in one place will be truly happy being on the road nine to ten months out of the year."

As much as I hate to admit it, she has a point. "I'll think about it," I promise. "I can't leave the tour midway, but I will think about what you said and let you know before it's time to return to the States."

Her mouth purses and I know I haven't heard the end of it, but all she does is nod. I change the subject. "Are you coming to the show tonight?"

"I wouldn't miss it. Don't forget dinner after."

Her driver, who followed us as we walked, pulls up just as we reach the entrance to the hotel. She embraces me and for a moment holds me close before turning away. Another lump forms in my throat at the gesture, but she says nothing and I have to wonder why the people in my life always seem to have such a hard time saying I love you.

The library, now a part of the University of Paris, is the largest building I've ever been in and I'm filled with awe as I tiptoe past the iron columns and the long gleaming wood reading tables. Giant arched windows reach to the ceiling, which must be at least two stories tall. Never have I felt my knowledge to be so incredibly small and insignificant as I feel in that beautiful building full of ancient texts. I spot a thin young man sitting at an official-looking desk and head toward him. I don't have much time before I have to be back at the theater.

He raises an eyebrow at me and I clear my throat. "I'm sorry to bother you, but I am looking for someone to tell me where I can find out about an artifact." I'm not sure it's actually an artifact, but I don't know what else to call it.

Without a word, he scoots off his stool and saunters across the room. He disappears behind a closed door and is gone so long I begin to fidget, wondering if he's coming back. When he reemerges, he's followed by an elderly man whose round balding head has tufts of wispy gray hair sticking out over his ears.

"*Que voulez-vous?*" he asks in a thin querulous voice.

"I'm sorry. I don't speak French," I'm forced to admit.

The man heaves an impatient sigh. "What can I do for you? There is some question about an artifact?"

The man's English is as flawless as Jacques's.

"Yes." I take out the medallion in a hurry before he changes his mind. "This is it."

I drop it into his outstretched hand and he frowns. "*Merde*," he says under his breath, looking at it closely. Pulling out a desk drawer, he rummages about until he finds a magnifying glass. He peers through the glass, turning the medallion over and over. The young man watches the proceedings from behind his book.

"Where did you get this?" the old man finally demands.

I swallow at the threatening look on his face. "A friend gave it to me."

"You need some new friends, young lady."

I knew it was something bad. "What is it? What does it say?"

The man shakes his head. "I can't tell you what it says, but I know what it means."

I'm baffled. "Excuse me?"

He shoves a finger at the crescent moon and arrows on the front. "This is an ancient occult symbol for death or, more precisely, a blood death."

My whole body goes cold at his words. He flips the medallion over. "This side is written in an alphabet called Enochian. It's most often used to transcribe spells. Like Hebrew it is written right to left. I recognize the symbols, but not enough to translate. If you would like to leave it here . . ."

I shake my head and hold out my hand. "No. I'm sorry, I can't do that."

He reluctantly gives the medallion back to me. "I wouldn't hold on to that for too long, young lady," he warns. "Nothing good can come from keeping it."

I agree wholeheartedly and, after thanking him, take my leave.

Suddenly I can't wait to get back to London to turn the medallion over to Harrison and the others. I don't want it in my possession any longer than necessary.

FIFTEEN

Our four days in Paris are a triumph for me and for the troupe. We're now working together like a perfectly oiled machine—all the cogs are performing their best as everyone knows that anyone not doing so will be cut at the end of this leg of the tour. And I've decided top billing suits me. The iron maiden bit is such a success that reporters are starting to flock to the dressing rooms after the show to try to get an interview or a look at my arm. Billy has taken to heading them off in the hallway, the tension of our last conversation apparently forgotten. His protectiveness gives me a warm cozy feeling. Mother made me wash the blood off after the first night to make sure I really wasn't hurt. I could have no better compliment, and I leave Paris with the sense that I'm actually going to miss my mother.

Her words haunt me. A home in Paris is a tremendous temptation, but what would I do? Go to school? I've always loved books and loved to learn, but wouldn't I miss performing? Why do having a stable home and performing seem to be mutually exclusive?

The French countryside passes by, but only part of my mind notices. The other part has moved on to the next question. The medallion. Why would someone leave a clue to their murderous handiwork at my doorstep? Is it a threat? I am hoping that the list of people who study the occult is complete by the time I return to London. I've had no more episodes, but the threat of one has me jumpy and ill at ease in my own skin.

I can't help but feel that all this somehow leads back to Dr. Boyle. I remember his single-mindedness in putting together a stable of Sensitives for his own gain. I can't believe he would give up so easily. Harrison said his contacts had yet to come up with any information on his location . . . I just wish there was some way I could check on his whereabouts . . . My heart stops beating in my chest. Of course! Why hadn't I thought of that before?

Cynthia.

Well, not Cynthia exactly, but her uncle, the infamous Uncle Arnie, also known as Arnold Rothstein, the man rumored to be behind the 1919 World Series cheating scandal. He'd helped me when my mother had been kidnapped because apparently any friend of his niece was a friend of his. I was able to return the favor the night of the scavenger hunt and he told me to call him if I needed anything, but does his network of influence extend to England? My shoulders slump. Not likely.

But it's worth a shot.

Of course, writing a letter is out of the question and would take too long. I decide to send a cable. Whoever is behind

Pratik's murder and Jonathon's disappearance isn't playing around. Both Leandra and Calypso have been physically attacked and I have been under almost constant psychic assault since I arrived. Who knows what could happen next. I've never met Jonathon, but I don't want him to come to the same fate as Pratik. My stomach twists again as the image of Pratik's body flickers in my mind.

"Can we switch places for a few minutes?"

I startle as Billy addresses these words to Jeanne, who's sitting next to me. With a knowing glance, Jeanne nods and rises from the seat. Billy sits with a bashful smile. He's only spoken to me when he's had to the last few days, and I miss his lighthearted banter even though I've told myself that it is probably for the best.

I swallow hard and return his smile.

"So it occurred to me the last few days that I was angry with you for all the wrong reasons."

His voice is relaxed, conversational, but I can feel his nervousness.

"You have every right to see whoever you like. I wasn't angry with you for the lie, I was angry because you were with another man." He takes a deep breath. "I like you, Anna. I like you a lot. I've never met a girl I like even half so much as I like you."

My pulse racing, I glance up to find his eyes, as blue as the sky above Paris, staring straight into mine. Their determination shows me he won't be put off. He wants to have this conversation now. And why shouldn't he? He deserves to know how I feel about him. "I like you, too," I tell him, hoping that will suffice.

It doesn't.

He shakes his head. "No, I mean I care about you deeply. There's just something about you that I've never felt with anyone else. There's a depth to you, like there is so much more that you're not showing me. I guess I'm saying that I'd like to be your steady beau."

My head jerks up. "No! I mean, this is sudden."

He smiles easily, unfazed by my reaction. "I just wanted you to know my intentions. There's no pressure. We've got a long tour ahead of us. But is this what you want to do for the rest of your life?"

"I don't know," I say, turning to look out the window. "I don't know what I want to do or who I want to do it with. And I wish everyone would quit asking me that."

He puts a finger up to his hat and stands. "Maybe everyone who cares about you wants you to be happy. I just wanted you to know that I'm on that list." He ambles off and I watch him go. Why is everything so confusing?

I didn't have enough time to cable Cole and let him know what time I would be arriving home, so I ride back to the hotel in a taxi with the crew. I'm eager to talk to Cole, but right now I'm more eager to send the cable to Cynthia. I have it all composed in my head and don't even unpack before writing it down.

Dear Cynthia. I miss you! Need favor. Can dear uncle ascertain whereabouts of one Dr. Franklin Boyle aka Dr. Finneas Bennett? Urgent. Much love, Anna.

I have the hotel clerk send the cable for me and return to my room. I wonder what Cynthia will think of the message. She knew Dr. Finneas Bennett as her mentor in spiritualism, a man who disappeared with her money under mysterious circumstances without ever building the American version of the Society. I know she'll do what I ask but I'll have a lot to answer for when she sees me.

I'm suddenly filled with longing for my best friend. Cynthia is far more of a mob princess than the socialite she pretends to be for her husband's sake, and is a good person to have by your side in times of trouble.

Restlessly, I unpack a few things and then decide to walk down to the café to get something to eat. Breakfast was a long time ago and I hadn't been hungry at lunch. I'm suddenly famished and snatch up a light tweed jacket. Knowing I shouldn't go out by myself, I consider asking Billy if he'd like to join me, then decide against it. So instead I knock on Sandy's door, hoping she isn't asleep, which is a very real possibility. Most of the crew had expressed their intention to nap for at least two days once back in London.

When she doesn't answer, I decide to go ahead and get dinner alone. It's not yet dark, and if I hurry I'll be able to get there and back before the sun sets.

Even though the sun is shining, I feel a sense of apprehension on my way to the café. It's not really specific—not as if someone is watching me or anything like that, just a vague sense of uneasiness. Perhaps I'm more tired than I thought. I try to shake it off. After all, I'm in public, it's still light, and I have my knife.

But I'm still happy when I reach the safety of the café.

Mary doesn't work in the afternoons and I don't recognize the woman scooting among the tables. It's busier than it usually is during the early mornings and it seems as if the whole neighborhood decided to dine out tonight. I'm searching for a place to sit when my eyes spot a familiar hat at a small table in the back near the kitchen. As if sensing my presence, Billy turns and sends a slow smile across the room. He indicates the chair across from him and I make my way through the tables. To do anything else would be cruel.

"Thanks," I tell him, taking off my jacket and hanging it on the back of the chair. "I was going to try to sleep but then realized how hungry I am. I didn't think there was going to be a place for me. Have you ever been here at night? Is it always this crowded?"

He raises an eyebrow at my babbling. "Not usually," he answers. "But the weather is getting dryer so maybe more people want to go out."

Well, that takes care of the weather and the crowded conditions. What else can we talk about?

I shouldn't have worried.

"You know this place reminds me of a little café in New Mexico . . ."

He puts me immediately at ease with stories of the Old West while we wait for the meat pies we ordered.

It's not until he gets to a story about a friend of his called Francisco that he stops talking.

"Go on," I urge. "Why did Francisco need all that rope?"

Billy hesitates. "Some stories aren't worth repeating."

His jaw tightens and I wonder what he means. I send out a pulse, and to my surprise he feels constricted and, underneath . . . shame?

Oddly, the feelings I am sensing from him only make me like him more. I think of all the things I have done in my life that I'm ashamed of. I bite my lip and offer, "Remember when I told you about how my mother and I cheated people out of money?"

He nods.

"I can't even tell you what a relief it was to share that. Some stories may not bear repeating, but it sure makes you feel better when you share with someone you trust."

The waitress brings us our food and he looks down at the table. "I robbed a bank," he says quietly. "I didn't exactly mean to, but I knew Francisco was up to no good and I just went along with it. Hell, I actually helped. You know how good I am with a gun and a rope. We got away and I joined the circus two days later. I ended up sending the money back. Oh, I know, that part is more unbelievable than me robbing a bank, but I did. I'm not a thief."

My mouth opens. Of all the things Billy could have told me, that hadn't even crossed my mind. His cheeks redden at my expression and he looks away. I need to say something, but what? A Billy-the-Kid comment is dancing on the tip of my tongue and I start to giggle.

After a look of shock, the corners of his mouth start to twitch and I giggle harder.

He finally grins. "Go ahead. I know you want to."

I shake my head and then give into the temptation. "Billy the Kid, you're alive!" I say with a Southern accent.

He shakes his head, smiling, and I try to get myself under control. The other patrons are starting to notice.

"You do know that Billy the Kid operated in New Mexico and the Old West? Not the South?"

I nod and take a drink of my tea. "I'm sorry. I don't know what came over me."

He waggles his eyebrows at me. "It's fine. Being laughed at by a pretty girl is what I dream of. I'll have to trot out the old rob-the-bank story more often."

I wonder how long it's been since I've laughed that hard. Surely Cole and I have laughed that way since I've come to London? But then, we haven't had much to laugh about.

A familiar scent comes to me over the smells of the food wafting through the kitchen door every time it opens and shuts. I frown, sniffing, wondering what it is and where I've smelled it before. The realization hits me just before painful red stars erupt in front of my eyes.

I'm having a vision.

The strong aroma of burned sugar plays around my nostrils and my heart pounds. I want to call out for Billy to help me, but he doesn't know what is happening. I can hear his voice coming as if from a great distance.

"Anna?"

Like Cole once taught me, I try to breathe through the vision and not let it terrify me, whatever it is, but the visions, accompanied by electric flashes of light, are quite simply terrifying. I see Calypso, her mouth open wide in a scream as her dark eyes are turned inward in terror. She looks as if she's being eaten from the inside out. I half expect to see blood erupting from her mouth. Then I see Walter, his face pleading. I can't hear what he's trying to tell me, only that something is very wrong. He's trying to warn me and screams my name over and over.

"Anna! Anna!"

Shuddering, the images and lights fade and Billy is kneeling next to me with one arm about my shoulders. People are looking at us strangely and I shiver, feeling oddly cold.

"I'm so sorry," I tell him. My cheeks burn with embarrassment and I would give anything for the last few minutes not to have happened. I need to talk to Cole. I need to warn Calypso.

"Are you all right? What the hell was that?"

I shake my head. "I haven't had one in so long. I didn't expect . . ."

"What are you talking about? Isn't this the same thing that happened during rehearsal?"

I blink, surprised. "No. This was different, this was—" I stop and he presses on.

"What was it?"

I take a deep breath. "I need to leave. Can we get out of here?"

He nods and pays the bill while I put on my jacket. I hesitate before stepping out onto the sidewalk, making sure to look both ways. It's much darker than I thought it would be, and I imagine danger behind every shadow.

"What's going on, Anna? Are you in some kind of trouble? Are you sick?"

His voice is low and concerned and I can tell my behavior has put him on alert. I try to sort out how much I should tell him. I've lied to him once and can't do it again. Nor do I want to put him in danger. "I have visions of the future sometimes," I finally say.

I don't look at his face. If he doesn't believe me, I don't want to know it. I just can't think of anything else to tell him.

"My aunt used to have visions of the future," he finally says. "Or at least she used to know when something bad was going to happen to one of us kids. We learned to trust her instincts. She didn't act like you did though. She'd get all quiet and stare off into the distance for a few moments. We learned to take her warnings pretty seriously."

I glance over at him in surprise. I had been expecting incredulous denial, or perhaps derision, not calm acceptance. Maybe there are more Sensitives out there than I've ever even dreamed of.

"So what did you see? It looked pretty upsetting."

I laugh, but there is no mirth to it. I can't even explain what it was. I just want to get back to the hotel and telephone Cole. I need to talk with him so badly. I shiver and Billy puts his arm around me.

"Are you sure you're all right?"

We round the corner to the hotel and I see Cole's motorcar out front. I quicken my step. "Cole!" I yell, waving my arm. The figure opening the hotel door turns and I want to sob in relief. He'll know what to do.

His anger hits me before I can even see his features. He's furious. Why? What did I do? Then I feel Billy's arm tighten around my shoulders and I know.

I shrug away from him, ignoring the look of hurt crossing Billy's face. I can't worry about him right now. I have to explain to Cole.

"Where on earth have you been? Did you ever think that people might be worried about you?"

Cole's fury lashes out and I feel Billy stiffen next to me. He and Cole face off, like day and night, staring each other down.

"That's no way to talk to a lady," Billy says.

"No! It's all right. It will be all right. Billy, I have to talk to Cole about what I saw. Please go inside." My voice is pleading and he looks undecided, clearly not wanting to leave. I give him a little push. "Please."

The look on his face is unreadable but he does what I say, though he and Cole bump shoulders as he passes.

"I'm sorry," I tell Cole as soon as Billy was gone. "I was hungry and left without telephoning you first to let you know I got back safely."

His jaw works and I anxiously want to run my fingers along the side of his face to make him feel better, but I can't. "What's going on, Anna?"

I nod toward his motorcar. "Can we get inside there? I need to talk to you."

"Are you afraid of what *he* might see?"

His voice is bitter and my mouth drops open.

"What are you talking about?" I ask.

I understand his jealousy and know how it must have looked to him, my walking up the street with Billy's arm about me. I have felt it plenty of times over Calypso, but as he always tells me, we have more important things to discuss.

"No. Never mind. I had a vision, Cole. We need to talk."

He brings himself under control, though I know I haven't heard the last of it.

"What happened?" he asks once we're inside his motorcar.

"I was eating dinner . . ."

"With him," Cole states flatly.

"Would you stop it? I didn't even go to the café with him. He was already there so I ate with him. Now do you want to hear what I have to say?"

He shuts his mouth.

"I was eating and I smelled burned sugar, then the visions started." I put my hands over my face as if that could block the images I'd seen. "When it was over, I felt so awful that Billy brought me home. That's why I was leaning against him."

I feel a pang of guilt and erect a block so Cole can't feel what I'm feeling. I can tell from the pain in his face that it's too late and I look away.

"What did you see?" he asks.

I glance over at him to find him staring out the front windshield. In a small voice, I tell him exactly what I saw.

"Do you think we should warn Calypso?"

He shakes his head. "I just dropped her off. She was meeting Mr. Casperson to talk over some test he wants to conduct. She's fine."

Jealousy flares and I know Cole feels it because he turns to me with a sardonic eyebrow. This time it's my turn to look away.

"Have you seen Walter since the séance?" he asks.

I shake my head.

"Because it sounds as if he is trying to warn you. Which is pretty much what Mr. Price said." He scrubs a hand over his face and meets my eyes. The midnight velvet of his eyes has never hid his emotions so well.

"There's more," I tell him, taking the medallion out of my purse. "I found this outside my hotel door just before I left for France."

He takes it and frowns. "What is it?"

I shrug. "I'm not sure but I had it looked at while I was there, and the expert told me that the symbol on the front means blood death and the letters are from the Enochian alphabet, which is—"

"I know what it is." His voice sounds like death itself. "This is the same lettering that was on the scarab found in Pratik's hand."

My stomach turns.

Cole continues, "It took the Yard several days to even find out what language the symbols were in. It wasn't until we started checking ancient languages that they finally figured it out." He glances at me. "How did you find someone so quickly?"

"The library I went to in Paris has documents and collections from the Middle Ages. It took the old librarian sixty seconds to know what it was."

Cole snorts. "That figures."

"So if we already knew that Pratik's murder was ritualistic, what does this tell us?"

"Good question." Cole rubs his temples as if the whole situation is giving him a terrible headache. I know the feeling.

"Harrison says there are only a few organizations that actually use the Enochian alphabet. One of them is the Hermetic Order of the Golden Dawn, though there are rumors that one of the adepts is trying to throw it out because he believes it to be demonic rather than angelic."

"How does he know so much?" I ask curiously.

"Harrison was friends with a man in the order when he was younger. They keep in touch and Harrison brought him in as one of the consultants on the case."

I shiver. In all our days as fake mediums, my mother and I never strayed into the occult. I'd touched on it, of course, in my quest to discover the truth about my abilities, but other than saying the odd magic spell during our séances for effect, I had pretty much left the occult alone. We had run across too many mediums who'd played with it and ended up burned.

Now here I am stuck in the middle of it.

Cole continues. "According to his friend, a blood sacrifice

is needed in order to cast spells that take a lot of energy, such as curses."

I can almost feel the blood draining from my face. "So we can expect more horrible things to happen?"

"It's a possibility and I think we should be prepared."

So Pratik's blood had been stolen to do more evil. As if what had been done to him wasn't evil enough. "Why would someone give me a clue linked directly to Pratik?" I ask.

"Maybe they're getting cocky," Cole says slowly. "Or perhaps there is some reason they want us to know that something is coming."

We sit in silence for a moment and I wish more than anything that he would take me in his arms, but I know that isn't going to happen. Underlying his worry and concern, I can still feel his hurt. "Be careful, Anna. I couldn't bear it . . ."

I hold my breath waiting for him to say the words that would make everything seem better, even in the midst of all this chaos, but he doesn't say them.

"I wish I could get my mother and grandmother out of town," he finishes.

My heart feels as if it's being crushed and I'm having a hard time breathing. I nod and climb out of the motorcar. "You'll be back tomorrow?"

He nods and, after I shut the door, pulls away.

SIXTEEN

Cole hasn't been back.

He sent a note yesterday, telling me that he was taking his mother and grandmother to visit relatives in Bath and would be back as soon as he got them settled. I know he has to be relieved that they will be someplace safe, but I can't help but wonder if he isn't thankful to have an excuse to avoid me. At least his mother and grandmother are out of danger. I spent yesterday napping and reading, only going out when I was forced to. Not only was I worried that Cole might get back from Bath but I was afraid of running into Billy.

Not because I didn't want to see him. Because I did.

Now I'm waiting for him to come downstairs because I have the information I need on Dr. Boyle. Not only is he in England, he's currently residing in London. The address is in my coat pocket, as well the number of a man Uncle Arnie gave me just in case I wanted some help. I shuddered to think of what kind of help this man would offer, but I pocketed it anyway.

I have a hard time believing that Dr. Boyle is behind Pratik's murder. Not that I don't think he could kill someone if he felt he or his master plan were threatened, but I can't see him draining someone's blood. He's just too fastidious.

So my plan is to talk Billy into going with me and take Dr. Boyle by surprise. Hopefully, I'll be able to get both information and a clear read on his emotions. In other words, if he is hiding something, I'll be able to tell.

Now I have to talk Billy into helping me without telling him why.

Cole would have kittens if he knew what I'm about to do, but if there's a chance that Dr. Boyle knows who killed Pratik or where Jonathon is, I have to take it. Plus, I think I'm a little annoyed that Cole isn't here when I need him.

As an added measure of safety, I take my balisong out of my handbag and put it in my coat pocket, where I can get at it more easily.

Billy smiles when he sees me. "I thought you'd run off."

He's so handsome in his cowboy hat and his face is so kind that I can hardly even look at him. I clear my throat. "I need a favor and it's a big one."

His smile disappears. "It sounds serious."

"It is. I need you to come with me when I confront someone and keep a lookout for me." It sounds ridiculously silly said out loud and he raises a brow.

"It's not the fellow you're seeing, is it?"

I shake my head.

"Good, because I don't want to get messed up in that. All right, then. I'll do it."

I let my breath out in a rush. "Perfect. Thank you."

"Lead on, Macduff." He tucks my arm into his and I frown at how comfortable I have become with him. It makes me feel twitchy and guilty.

I push the thought out of my head to concentrate on the task before me. My nerves jangle as each step takes me closer to my enemy. We take a taxi, while Billy plays twenty questions, trying to figure out what is going on. Finally he just asks what he wants to know: "Are you in any danger?"

I give him a grim smile. "Not with you around."

I have the driver drop us off a block away from Dr. Boyle's address at the end of a line of smart row houses. I would prefer not to have to go into his home but can only wait so long in this neighborhood before someone sets a bobby after us.

By the time we get out of the taxi, I'm strangling Billy's arm.

"Are you sure you want to do this?" he asks a little anxiously.

I nod. "I don't have a choice."

His jaw tightens and I know how difficult this must be for him. "Are you going to introduce me to your friend?"

"He's not my friend," I say shortly, and then think about it for a minute. Why not? "I actually think that will be a good idea. The idea is to intimidate him enough to not only ensure my safety but to get the information I want."

"Are you blackmailing someone?" he asks, his voice amused.

"Unfortunately not. That would be more fun." My voice is grim and he grows quiet. I feel his jitteriness through his arm, but also his determination. I feel much better knowing how seriously he is taking this. Even though he's several years older than Cole, his playful personality and humorous outlook on life often make him seem younger.

The sunny weather has disappeared and the rains are back. It's as if the sky itself is dripping all around us. Suddenly I see a figure coming toward me. My heart leaps as I recognize him.

I take a deep breath and nod toward the man. Firming my step we walk toward the man who once tried to kidnap me.

"Dr. Boyle!" I call, raising my voice. Watching my mother taught me a lot about gaining and holding the upper hand. Of course, she has years of experience and is naturally more intimidating than I will ever be.

I feel rather than see his surprise. For a moment he seems nonplussed as he recognizes me. "Anna."

Dr. Boyle hasn't changed. He still looks like a jovial English squire. Hard to believe how callous he can be when he wants something.

"Billy, this is Dr. Boyle. Dr. *Franklin* Boyle." I stress the name so Billy knows exactly who I am talking to and Dr. Boyle knows that Billy knows.

Billy acknowledges the introduction with a curt nod.

"Shall we walk, Dr. Boyle?" He nods, his gray eyes

watchful. I take Boyle firmly by the arm, trying not to show my repugnance. I still get a better read on people's emotions if I touch them.

"Whatever you wish, my dear."

Billy falls in behind us.

"I'll be right behind you, if you need anything," Billy calls.

I take my balisong out of my pocket and open it with an expert flick of my wrist. "And just in case my protector doesn't impress you, know that I have a weapon and have no qualms at all about using it." The knife is lying benignly in the palm of my hand, the blade glistening even in the gray light of day. I give him a quick demonstration, the blade and the covers swinging ominously, before I close it up. He watches the knife carefully and knows I didn't put it back in my pocket even though I lowered my hand to my side.

"Your show of force is understandable but quite unnecessary, Anna. I don't mean to harm you. I didn't mean for you to get hurt the last time we met. And, remember, my dear, I didn't put this little surprise visit together."

I keep my voice even. "I know, but whether you meant for me to get hurt or not, that is indeed what happened, so you'll excuse my caution."

He nods. "Fair enough. Just know that the whole ordeal was entirely mishandled."

"It's hard to kidnap someone well," I flare before remembering that only by keeping my composure can I keep the upper hand. "But I didn't come to discuss the past with you."

"Then why did you come?" he asks.

I keep my hand on his arm, trying to sort out the myriad sensations I'm getting from him. He's nervous, that much is coming loud and clear, and also curious. "I've come because I find myself in the odd position of needing your help."

"Indeed?" The inflection in that one word shows the depth of his surprise.

"Yes, unfortunately."

"What on earth would give you the idea that I would help you with anything?" He smiles expansively, reminding me just how charming he actually can be.

"Because, as unconvinced as I am that you have any human compassion whatsoever, I do know you have a great sense of self-preservation."

"I always knew you were a particularly astute young woman. I have very little compassion, nor do I want it. I have found that it only gets in the way of personal ambition. Most of the great men of the world, the ones who have accomplished much, were selfish in their pursuits. But I am not a monster. Contrary to popular belief, I don't experiment on humans."

I snort. "Sensitives desperately need to know how to control their abilities. For you to withhold that information on purpose is no better than performing experiments on them."

He shrugs. "Honestly, what makes me so much worse than the Society's board members or scientists? They don't want the Sensitives to learn control any more than I do—why do you think they have discouraged interaction among the Sensitives? And they do conduct experiments on people.

What makes my methods so different?"

"They are allowed to leave."

"Touché, Anna. The only Sensitive I have ever wanted to have on board without his full cooperation was Cole. You were a by-product of that. But I'm not going to debate my methods. I have places to be. Why are you speaking of self-preservation?"

I feel his irritation and decide to get to the point. "How would you like to go to prison for murder, Dr. Boyle?"

He stops in his tracks but I yank him along beside me and keep talking. "Pratik Dahrma was found brutally murdered and I think you know something about it."

"You can't prove anything." His voice is cold. "Don't make empty threats"

"Oh, they are far from empty. I think you forget just how enterprising I can be. Now don't fret, all I want is information. I know you are putting together a stable of Sensitives. Did you want Pratik for some reason? Did something go wrong?"

He is silent for so long I think he isn't going to answer. His indecision is evident in the emotions coming from him.

Then he tilts his head to one side and considers me for a long moment. Nodding his head as if he just made up his mind about something, he says, "I have a colleague who has proven untrustworthy."

I tense. He *knows*. "Why should I care about your problems with your help?"

"Because my help is insane and murdered Pratik Dahrma."

His blunt response turns my stomach and I stumble. I hate that he got to me and I especially hate that he knows it. Slipping my knife into my pocket, I wipe my hand on my coat. Somehow holding it in my hand doesn't seem right when thinking about what happened to Pratik.

"Why haven't you gone to the authorities?" I ask through clenched teeth. "Only a monster would sit on such knowledge and then pretend to care."

His head jerks back as if he'd been hit. "Don't be ridiculous and don't insult me. My patience is wearing thin. You say you want information and by giving it to you I am ascertaining that you and your self-righteous young man will take care of a problem for me."

"Perhaps. You have yet to tell me anything. It is difficult to know what I can do unless I have more information."

"As you wish. My colleague is not only insane, she's incredibly resourceful. She has certain abilities that make it difficult for me to stop her. She's a loose cannon and, quite frankly, if you don't stop her, I'm afraid someone else will get hurt."

Her. It's a woman.

My mind is spinning and I have a hard time focusing on what he is saying.

"You must go to her father. Only her father has the power to contain her."

"Why? What kind of abilities does she have? Who is it?"

"Come on, Anna. You're a smart girl. Haven't you guessed?"

I know as surely as if he'd said it. I think perhaps part of me has always known. "Calypso," I whisper.

He nods. "I thought her talents would come in handy. After all, her ability to influence people is extremely useful, especially when paired with her obvious charms and her other talents. I knew she was a bit unbalanced, but unfortunately, I underestimated just how demented she actually is."

My stomach churns. "What other talents?"

"Don't you know? She's a witch. A black magic practitioner. Likes to dance with the dark side, does our Calypso."

Panic blooms in my chest, remembering how Pratik had been murdered. My God. She led me to Pratik's body. The poppet. The psychic attacks. God only knows what else she had been planning.

"What do you expect me to do?" I ask, trying hard not to be sick.

"Stop her, of course. I wash my hands of her. All I wanted was someone on the inside to give me information on what the Society was doing and if there were any new recruits. Contrary to what you might think, I don't abduct people."

"What about Pratik?" I ask.

He shakes his head. "I had nothing to do with Pratik. Not really. She persuaded him to join us."

Something isn't adding up. "But Mr. Gamel's home had been broken into."

He shrugs. "Perhaps she wanted everyone to think it was a crime scene. Perhaps she has interesting ways of persuasion. Who knows? I only know that both he and Jonathon came willingly enough to begin with. Whether that's still the case with Jonathon or not, I don't know."

"Wait. If he joined you of his own accord, why don't you know?"

His mouth tightens. "She disappeared from our little hideaway last week and took several of my Sensitives with her."

It dawns on me what he wants in return for his information. "You want me to get them back."

He shrugs.

"You're just as insane as she is if you think I am going to help you in any way." I start to turn away and Dr. Boyle grabs my sleeve. Billy hurries toward us.

"Don't forget, she's the one who killed Pratik. She said she needed the blood for a major incantation. Do you really want to take a chance with the lives of four young men, Anna?"

Billy comes up next to me. "Everything all right here?"

I don't answer. Dr. Boyle is still holding my arm and our eyes lock as if we're frozen in some kind of battle of wills. Neither one of us wants to be the first to look away.

"There's one more thing, Anna." His voice is soft, almost caressing. "You recall I said the only one who could control her is her father. That's because her father is the only person I know even more powerful than she is. Do you want to know who her father is, Anna?" He leans toward me and I will myself to remain motionless.

"Aleister Crowley," he whispers.

I gasp and jerk my arm from his grip. I want to run, but am frozen in place.

"That can't be true. Someone in the Society would know!"

He adjusts his coat, smiling—a smile that doesn't reach his cold eyes. "The Society doesn't care about the Sensitives any more than I do, my dear, so why would anyone check Calypso's background?"

I close my eyes for a moment as I digest this truth. Then I glare at him. "What do you want me to do?" My voice is harsh and I sense Billy's confusion next to me, but I can't think about him right now. I can't care about what he must be thinking. I focus on Dr. Boyle, and his triumph makes me want to hit something. Makes me want to hit *him*.

"Find her. Subdue her. I don't care how. Let me know when it's over so I can see my . . ." He stops, glancing at Billy. "Just let me know when I can see my employees."

"I'm not going to just hand those people over to you," I tell him. My eyes are smarting with unshed tears. I feel as trapped as a bird in a cage.

He shrugs. "So give them a choice. I pay them, Anna. Contrary to what you've been told, they can come and go as they please except when they are needed. I think you will be surprised by their decision."

And just like that he's gone.

I'm shaking like a leaf and Billy puts his arms around me and pulls me close. He's not Cole, but his warmth is comforting and right now I need all the comforting I can get.

"What the hell was that all about?"

The laugh that erupts from my mouth doesn't sound like a laugh at all. "That, my friend, was me being put in a ghastly position."

He pulls away and I miss his warmth. "Is there anything I can do to help?"

I shake my head. "Unfortunately, I think I'm going to have to handle this one all on my own." I pray Cole has returned from Bath so we can warn everyone.

I only hope it's not too late.

SEVENTEEN

"Anna, wait!"

Billy tugs on my arm and I impatiently pull away. I'd been practically running ever since I left Dr. Boyle, while Billy's been chasing me down the street, trying to get my attention. Part of me appreciates how humorous we must look—a cowboy chasing a flapper down the staid streets of London—but the larger part of me is terrified and horrified and desperate to reach Cole.

Billy finally grabs me around the waist and picks me up off my feet.

"What are you doing? Let me go!" I struggle and fall just short of clobbering him on the head with my umbrella.

"Stop it. What the hell are you involved in? Murder? Blackmail? What?"

He holds me easily in his arms and I'm aware that I am being held so that the lines of our bodies are flush against one another. I stop struggling. "Please put me down."

He does what I ask, and I begin walking again. "I can't tell you everything. Suffice it to say that a friend of mine was murdered and that man knows who did it. For reasons I can't explain right now, I can't go to the police. And, no," I say, spotting the look on his face, "it's not because I've done anything wrong. It's actually to protect innocent people."

"I don't understand," he says flatly. "And exactly what are Sensitives?"

I stumble before catching myself and moving on. "Never mind. Just . . . thank you." I stop and look around. "You know, I have no idea where we're going."

He shakes his head. "I was wondering about that. The next street looks busier. We can get you a taxicab."

We walk in silence until he flags a taxicab. "You can trust me, you know," he says, opening the door for me.

I look into his eyes and they are so pure and openhearted that my throat swells and tears rise. "I know."

It feels criminal to leave him there on the street, knowing he would do anything for me. But I don't have room for regret. I have to find Cole as soon as possible. I ask the driver to drop me off at the Wrights'.

"We need to talk," I tell Leandra as soon as she enters the sitting room I'd been escorted into.

Her green eyes widen as she greets me. "Your hands are like ice. What happened?"

"I had a run-in with Dr. Boyle. I know who killed Pratik and I know who Jonathon is with. We need to get Cole and

Harrison here right away." I almost sob with relief as the weight of my knowledge is off my shoulders.

She nods and calls in her housekeeper. "Could you please contact Mr. Wright at work and tell him to come home? It's an emergency. And make tea. Oodles of tea."

She turns back to me. Her concern is so evident that I'm ashamed I ever mistrusted her. I shouldn't have judged her for the darkness that lies just beneath her surface—God only knows what sort of things she has seen in her nightmares.

"Cole telephoned Harrison to tell him he was getting back this morning and they made plans to meet. Hopefully they will both be here soon. Now who killed Pratik?"

"Calypso." I watch her face carefully.

She closes her eyes and takes a deep breath. "That explains my nightmare."

"You had a nightmare?"

Leandra nods and I freeze, my heart pounding. "What was it?"

Her voice is strangely composed as she describes her dream. "I saw Calypso, screaming. She looked like Satan was chewing her up from the inside. Then I saw Pratik, only not the man I remember, but like he was already dead yet still moving and talking." Then she looks at me, frowning. "Then there was a young man in uniform whom I've never seen before."

Walter.

My heart races in my chest and it takes me a moment to

catch my breath. "I had a vision the day before yesterday. It was exactly like you described."

We stare at one another for a moment, the hair on the back of my neck prickling.

"Are you saying instead of seeing your nightmare, I saw your vision? How can that be?"

I shake my head. "How does any of this happen?"

Leandra takes another deep breath. "I think you had better tell me what happened from the beginning."

I tell her everything. When I get to the part about Dr. Boyle, Harrison and Cole come in. Cole pauses upon seeing me, but then concern crosses his face and he hurries to my side. Leandra pours us tea and nods.

Cole stops me. "Wait. You took Billy with you? He doesn't know about the Society, does he?"

I wave my hand impatiently. "Of course not."

"So he went with you even though he had no idea what was going on?"

I can feel my face heating. "I told him I was going to be meeting someone I didn't trust. What was I supposed to do? Go by myself?"

"No. I just don't know why he would do that." Cole's eyes are probing and I swallow.

"Because he's my friend," I finally say. "Can I continue?"

He nods, his mouth tight.

By the time I'm finished, Cole is shaking his head. "This is so hard to believe. Calypso is such a flibbertigibbet . . . Are you sure?"

My head snaps up. I had expected many reactions, but not this. “What do you mean, am I sure? Don’t you think I would know if he were lying?”

“Yes, of course, but have you felt anything sinister about Calypso? If she were capable of Pratik’s murder, don’t you think you would have sensed something?”

“Calypso’s emotions change so quickly it’s difficult for me to feel anything concrete from her. At the séance I felt nothing at all. Cole, what is going on? Why don’t you believe me?”

I feel as though I’ve been kicked in the stomach. Doesn’t he trust my judgment at all? After everything we’ve been though?

“It’s not that I don’t believe you,” he says slowly. “It’s just that I am wondering why you are so quick to believe Dr. Boyle over someone you called a friend.”

For a moment I am tempted to get up and walk out on him, but I know from experience that won’t solve anything and we have to stop Calypso.

I take a deep breath. “Cole, I know what he told me is the truth. I can feel it.”

I turn to Leandra and Harrison. “What do you two think?”

Leandra twitches a shoulder. “I’ve never liked her. Of course, not liking someone is different from suspecting her of murder.”

Harrison reaches up to massage his neck. “The Yard has a dossier on Crowley almost a foot thick. He’s written several books and has apparently created a new religion.”

"Yes, it's called Thelema, and apparently he was given the text by his guardian angel. He was also involved in the Order of the Golden Dawn," I tell them.

"How do you know so much about it?" Leandra asks.

"I read quite a bit on the occult while growing up. I was trying to find clues about my abilities," I explain and she nods.

"Understandable." She turns toward Cole. "I've been to the Society almost every day but haven't seen Calypso in a week. But that isn't unusual. She's always avoided me. When was the last time you saw her?"

Cole shifts in his seat and I raise my eyebrows.

"This morning. She came by the Society while I was talking to Jared."

"What did she want?" Harrison asks.

Cole glances over at me, his eyes unreadable. "She wanted to know when you were coming back. I told her you got in two days ago but that you had been busy."

I look down at the floor. Billy's face leaps to mind and I push it away. Focus. I draw in a deep breath. "So what should we do?"

No one says anything and we all look at one another helplessly. "Well, don't everyone talk at once," I say.

"Can't Scotland Yard do something?" Cole asks Harrison.

"Of course, once we have enough evidence. But we need to find the Sensitives before we do that. If we try to question Calypso now, she'll either clam up or go over the deep end if she really is as demented as Boyle says she is. Neither one would help us. You don't think she's holding four men all by herself, do you?"

I rub my forehead. "I hadn't even thought of that. She has to have help from somewhere."

"What are the chances this is some kind of trap set by Dr. Boyle to get Anna?" Cole asks.

I shake my head. "Slim to none. I've been traveling in foreign countries. If he really wanted me, he could have had me. There were plenty of opportunities."

"All right. Then we go on the assumption that Calypso has squirreled away the Sensitives, is a ritualistic murderer and an occultist. Considering who her father is, that's not difficult to believe. But what is her motive?" asks Harrison.

"Do insane people have to have a motive?" Cole wonders.

Harrison nods. "In this case, yes. Everything she has done has been planned out. She has a reason. The problem is, it may not make sense to anyone but her, but if we are going to find where she has hidden the Sensitives and who is helping her, we need to know what it is."

Leandra stands. "It's almost time for supper. Anna, would you help me? Leave the boys to figure this out?"

We stare at her, puzzled, as the Wrights have a very good and capable cook and she's not the type to leave anything to the "boys." "Check in on Cook," she explains patiently.

I finally get her meaning. "Of course."

Instead of taking me into the kitchen, she pulls me into

a small office near the back of the house and shuts the door behind her.

The room isn't as neat as the rest of the house. In fact, it's a mess, with piles of paper on the desk. The small settee is stacked with books and shelves are leaning precariously under the weight of even more books.

"It's Harrison's office. He won't let the housekeeper near it. Claims she hides things. We almost lost her over it once so we made a deal, he cleans it every spring, whether or not it needs it."

I smile and automatically walk over to the bookshelf. "I take it it's that time of year again?"

Leandra waves a hand. "Oh, no, he just did it."

I laugh. "What did you want to talk to me about?"

"Was I that obvious?" She smiles. "I actually wanted to talk to you about a couple of things. First, I want to know what is wrong with you and Cole. And if it's none of my business, go ahead and tell me."

I bite my lip, torn between very politely telling her it isn't any of her business and confiding in her. Girlish secrets have never been my forte—confiding in my mother was not an option—and though I adore Cynthia, she's currently on another continent, so I can't ask her for advice either. "I don't know," I finally say. "I thought everything was fine. Different, of course, because we're now living in his country instead of mine, but I thought it would all sort itself out. Then Calypso happened. I'm jealous. He's clueless and distant and has a hard time understanding when I need reassurance. And then there's—" I stop suddenly and Leandra gives me a shrewd look.

"It's bound to be different here," she agrees. "It's also difficult when you happen to be smitten with a gentleman who has a difficult time telling you how he feels or showing affection. Harrison and I love the brat, but he spent most of his life among strangers. He isn't overtly affectionate. And his grandmother is a terror."

I snort in agreement.

"I know you will work it out but if you don't . . ." Leandra shrugs and my stomach hollows. "You're young. Cole may not be your one and only. And it's all right if he isn't, you know."

I shake my head, feeling helpless. "The problem is I don't know what I want anymore."

She nods. "Very well, then. You do know that whatever the boys are planning right now, it won't involve you or me, don't you? They're trying to come up with a way to try to catch Calypso without either one of us knowing what they're doing."

"Then why did we leave?" I ask, alarmed. I hurry to the door, but she catches my sleeve.

"They would have done so at their earliest opportunity anyway. This way, we can plan what we're going to do without them knowing."

I relax. "You have a plan?"

"Not a plan, really, more like a thought. What motivates women? I mean really motivates them?"

I frown. "Ambition?"

Her eyebrows shoot up on her forehead at my answer. "No, silly, love! Women are motivated by love."

"You don't know my mother," I mutter.

"Pardon?"

I shake my head, remembering how different Mother is now that she has Jacques. Maybe Leandra's right. Or partly right anyway.

"So you think that's Calypso's motivation?" My stomach clenches. "Do you think she's in love with Cole?"

Leandra's face screws up. "Oh goodness, no. I never got that from her. She's one of those women who flirts with every man around her. It's a game. And combined with her ability to influence people, let's just say I kept Harrison as far from her as I could. I think she wanted to get to you."

"Why would she want to get to me? I didn't even know her."

"I think she was concerned about the power of your abilities," Leandra says. "All the scientists and board members have a great deal of respect for Cole . . . He's male and his abilities are so different. Cole told everyone he thought you were one of the most powerful Sensitives he had ever known."

"So she was threatened by me. Maybe afraid that my abilities would be able to detect her plan, whatever it is. Or maybe she's jealous." I think of her haircut, and how she ran out and bought a cloche just like mine. "But what does that have to do with love? Who could she be in love with?"

"Perhaps it's not the kind of love we think." Leandra's face scrunches up as she thinks. "Did she ever say anything about her father?"

I straighten, remembering. "Yes. They're estranged. When she speaks about him, she sounds rather bitter."

"Perhaps this has something to do with him?"

I close my eyes and take a deep breath, trying to relieve some of the tension. "Maybe, but that doesn't address the original question: What are we going to do?"

Leandra shakes her head and shrugs at the same time. "I just know that we need to come up with something or the men will leave us out completely, and, quite frankly, it's going to take a woman to catch a woman."

She has a point. I chew on my lip for a moment. "I think I have an idea. But it could be dangerous."

"We're talking about a person who murdered a fellow human being in an unspeakable manner. It's bound to be dangerous."

I shake my head. "Even more frightening. We have to get it past her father."

Before Leandra and I formulate a plan, I decide to go visit Harry Price. If anyone knows about Aleister Crowley and how we can protect ourselves, it'll be Mr. Price. Or at least he should, with all his knowledge of the occult.

The next morning I wash and dress quickly, planning to forgo breakfast in order to get to the Society before Cole does. He'd been quiet when he brought me home last night and when I tried to sense what he was feeling, he was so blocked off I felt nothing, not even that warm individual feeling I always get from him. Even though I knew he was doing it just to keep me from knowing he was planning on going after Calypso himself, it still hurt. Or maybe he is still upset over my friendship with Billy and this is going to be the way it is from now on.

It hadn't helped that Billy had been reading a book on the couch when Cole walked me into the hotel. Billy'd stood and stretched, his long lanky frame towering in the lobby.

"I just wanted to make sure everything was all right," he drawled in his best Texan.

Cole had tensed next to me and for a moment they eyed one another like rival bulls over a heifer. Not very flattering to me, but an apt description.

"Everything is fine," Cole said stiffly. "Thank you for assisting Anna."

"Of course. I would pretty much do anything for a friend." He had given me an easy smile and ambled off to his room. Cole had given me a quick kiss, but I could tell he wasn't pleased.

That's all right. I wasn't pleased that he was putting himself in danger and cutting me out of helping him.

The sun is just coming up as I hurry down to the corner to catch the tram that will take me to the tube. Being spoiled by being driven everywhere in Cole's motorcar, I wouldn't have known how to get around in London had Calypso not shown me how to ride the underground wherever I wanted to go.

The thought of Calypso turns my stomach. All along she had been conning me, but for what?

Within half an hour I am ringing the Society's bell. To my surprise, Mr. Casperson opens the door. He's wearing a plaid woolen jacket and a hat, as if he were on his way out.

His eyes widen. "Anna! I am surprised to see you. I thought you were on tour."

He looks much better than he did at the séance, but still rather wan. "I got back several days ago. Is Mr. Price in this morning?"

"Yes, yes. You do know where his office is, don't you?"

He glances at his wristwatch and I narrow my eyes. He's jittery, nervous, and I sense panic coming off him in waves.

"Yes, I can see myself up. Are you all right?" I ask.

He nods. "I'm fine, I just have an early morning appointment. So if you'll excuse me . . ."

He looks meaningfully at the door and I move aside. Waiting for a moment after the door closes before peering out the blinds covering the tall window next to the door, I huff in frustration when he climbs into a motorcar across the street. If he had been walking, I would have followed him. Right now, everyone seems suspicious to me. Pulling off my gloves, I pause before the door, taking in the beautiful wooden marks. I've never asked what the marks mean and suddenly recall how Calypso wouldn't touch it that first night. A connection? Perhaps.

I open the door and move down the hall to Mr. Price's office. The heels of my Mary Janes click-clack across the floor and it sounds so loud to my ears that I'm surprised no one sticks his head out of his office to see what the clatter is. Perhaps no one is here yet. I'm glad when I make it to Mr. Price's office without seeing anyone, though. It'll be easier if I can just slip in and out without getting waylaid. Leandra is picking me up out front in an hour for stage two of our plan.

I rap lightly on the door and take a deep breath before entering. Nerves whirl in my stomach. At this point, I suspect everyone of colluding with Calypso.

Mr. Price has a book on his desk and I note he closes it when I walk in. "Anna! Sit, sit. To what do I owe this pleasure?"

I take off my wraparound coat and then sit, laying it and my gloves across my knees. "I'm hoping you can give me some information."

His lips curve and his dark eyes look pleased. "I can't promise anything, but I will do my best. What sort of information has brought you out so early in the morning?"

"I want to know more about Aleister Crowley and about black magic."

His response is immediate. He stills, his genial smile disappearing and his wide face becoming impassive. "I know of Mr. Crowley, of course, but what makes you think I have any more information than you could get from the newspaper archives?"

I smile and nod toward his massive bookshelf. "Anyone

who has studied the occult knows about Thelema and Aleister Crowley. I know about him and my studies haven't been nearly as extensive as yours." I lean forward, my shoulders tense. "It's incredibly important that I discover as much as I can about him."

He relaxes but his dark eyes are still watchful. He leans back in his chair and knits his fingers across his chest. "So tell me, Miss Van Housen. What do you wish to know?"

EIGHTEEN

"The newspapers have called him the wickedest man in the world. Is he really evil?" I ask.

"The newspapers exaggerate to sell newspapers. Don't get me wrong. I believe Aleister Crowley to be the most powerful occultist and warlock in the world, perhaps of all time. His intentions in the beginning were altruistic. He believes in good and evil and has an intimate knowledge of both forces. Unfortunately, he seems to have chosen one over the other."

"You say in the beginning, what about now?"

Mr. Price shrugs. "Who knows? Time changes a man. Fame changes a man. I can hardly comment on the motivations of a man I haven't spoken to in nearly ten years."

I blink. "So you know him personally, then?"

He nods. "Yes, we both belonged to the Order of the Golden Dawn. We both rose through the ranks, or orders, very quickly but have gone in different directions."

It's on the tip of my tongue to ask him if he is still involved in the Golden Dawn, but on second thought, I don't want to know. The less I know about that secretive organization, the better, and it isn't important for what I need anyway. "How well did you know him? Do you know, for instance, if he has any children?"

"I know he has a daughter named Lola whom I believe lives with her mother. He may have another child now, but you typically don't discuss your family much with Golden Dawn members."

So he doesn't know about Calypso? I study his impassive features for a long moment. Is he telling the truth? I sense no deceit in him at this moment, but the heavy dark power he is infused with makes me doubt what I'm feeling. "So what you're saying is that most people have nothing to fear from him?"

His eyes narrow and I suddenly feel a deep sense of mistrust coming from him. I understand. I don't trust him either.

"Typically no," he says. "I wouldn't cross him. As I said, he is very powerful. But he doesn't go around arbitrarily harming people, contrary to the lurid newspaper descriptions of Thelema. He's been accused of human sacrifice, but I doubt that story. Animal sacrifice, most definitely, but then many of God's chosen people also sacrificed animals at God's behest."

"Are you saying Aleister Crowley is one of God's chosen people?"

At this Mr. Price throws back his head and laughs. "Certainly not. But who's to say who God's chosen people are but God himself? But on the whole, the average person has nothing to fear from Mr. Crowley during a casual meeting. Of course, that said, it must be pointed out that both of his wives went insane and a number of his mistresses have committed suicide."

My blood chills, thinking of Calypso. Perhaps she herself is in some way a victim of this powerful man. I switch directions. "How badly could a poppet hurt someone?"

His brows arch ever so slightly. "The poppet itself is harmless until it's in the hands of a skilled practitioner. Anyone can make a poppet with all sorts of intentions, but unless he knows how to activate and manipulate the poppet, the doll is harmless."

"But in the rights hands it could be . . . ?"

His reply is immediate. "Deadly, if combined with a blood sacrifice."

I swallow. I have no way of knowing if Calypso has made another poppet yet. I haven't felt any psychic attacks lately, but that doesn't mean anything. Maybe she has been distracted by her guests, or maybe she is just gearing up for something really dangerous. "How would one go about protecting herself?"

"She would have to bind the practitioner's powers." He leans forward, warming to his subject. "There are a number of ways to do this. A circle of salt is very effective, though in this day and age, you can't really keep someone locked in a circle of salt forever. There is also a way to bind someone's powers with a blood sacrifice, but the exact ritual is quite vague. It's also said in the ancient texts that witches and warlocks can steal someone's powers or abilities, but again the texts are vague. As you can imagine, many practices have been lost due to people not wanting to write them down. Magic, black or otherwise, is primarily an oral tradition."

"That makes sense," I say. "Rather like a cook not wanting someone to steal her recipes, right?"

He laughs. "Essentially. It was a way of protecting oneself. Bad things generally happened to those women found to be witches. No one wanted to be found with a book of spells. There also are charms and symbols that are protectants."

"Like the symbols on the door below?"

He raises an eyebrow. "Very astute. Yes, they can't be touched by someone who practices black magic. It's not foolproof, of course—there are ways to get around it—but someone would have to know how and even then be very determined. My colleagues are less likely to believe in our need of protection than I am. I feel it prudent to have a protectant wherever I spend a great deal of time."

Speaking of symbols . . . I tilt my head to one side, considering. Then I snap open my pocketbook and hand him the medallion. "Have you ever seen anything like this?"

I watch with interest as his face blanches. "Where did you get this?"

"It was left for me as a gift. Why?"

"You know what it means?"

I nod.

"You have made some interesting enemies since you came here, Miss Van Housen."

I want to ask if he has many enemies, but he rises abruptly and walks over to one of his shelves. Taking down a large wooden box that looked vaguely medieval, he sets it on the desk and opens it. I try to peer over the hinged top but can't see from where I am sitting. He rummages through it, his face intent.

I squirm, my curiosity getting the better of me. "What is that? Pandora's box?"

He regards me over the rim of the cover. "Perhaps." Pulling something out from the inside and palming it, he closes the lid and replaces the box.

"I have a gift for you," he says, holding out his hand.

I eye him before hesitantly sticking my own hand out, palm up.

"You're not a very trusting person, are you, Anna? You're perhaps the only woman I've ever encountered who meets the words 'I have a gift for you' with suspicion." His voice is laced with humor, but his eyes are not. Whatever he is giving me is extremely important, as are the reasons behind the gift.

The object he drops in my hand is heavy and green with age. There's a long, dark silk cord attached to it and I know it's some kind of pendant. It's shaped like a coin and imprinted with the spokes of a wheel. Within each spoke is a symbol, much like the ones present on the door below.

"What is it?" I ask.

"It's an ancient Celtic protection amulet. I've had it for many years and have been waiting for the compulsion to give it to someone. The power in this kind of pendant is increased by giving it away, so you don't give them lightly."

My skin crawls with foreboding. I hold the amulet up and it swings in front of me. "And you were compelled to give it to me?"

"Yes. In exchange for the medallion."

"A trade?"

"Of sorts. Trust me, my dear. You do not want this in your possession."

He has that right.

"Do you have any more questions, Miss Van Housen?" His voice is formal, which I take as a sign that the meeting is over.

I place the cord over my head and slip the amulet down the front of my dress. The pendant lies heavy and warm against my skin and I am certain that I made a good trade. "What are you going to do with the medallion?"

"Destroy it."

I shiver in relief at his words. "Thank you, Mr. Price. And thank you also for the amulet. It's lovely."

He nods his head and I hurry out of the office and down the hall, feeling as though Harry Price knows far more about magic, the real kind, than he lets on.

Leandra is waiting for me in Harrison's neat, unpretentious British Model T.

"What did you find out?" she asks as soon as I hop into the front seat.

"We should be fine going to visit Aleister Crowley. The

newspapers exaggerate, though Mr. Price did warn me that he is a very powerful warlock. He also gave me a protective amulet."

"Only one?" Leandra gives me a grim smile as she pulls the car onto the street.

"Only the one." I pull it out and let her look at it. She does, nearly driving into a pushcart in the process.

"Oopsie," she says, righting the wheel.

I tuck the amulet back under my dress. "Did you get the information we need?"

She nods. "If he's in London, I know where his house is. Unfortunately, he travels quite a bit. I also have some bad news."

I look over at her, my heart sinking. "What's wrong?"

"Today is the last day I'll be able to help you. My husband cornered me last night and told me in no uncertain terms that I am joining our progeny at his mother's." She gives me a pained glance. "How could I say no? He told me that putting myself in harm's way was an act of selfishness. Of course, I didn't mention that as a Scotland Yard detective, he puts himself in harm's way all the time, but somehow it's different for me. At any rate, I will be on the train headed for Manchester this evening."

"It's all right," I say, though I'm sick to lose her. "You need to be with your children."

"As much as I have relished the break, I am missing them dreadfully." She sighs. "But I have the morning and afternoon. What should we do first?"

I rub my temples, doubt assailing me. Do I even have a right to ask her to help at all? Harrison is right: She should be playing in the country with her two little boys whose pictures I've seen on the mantel of her sitting room. On the other hand, I really need her brains. Not to mention her support. If I had Cole's . . . I push the thought out of my mind and make a decision. "Let's go see Aleister Crowley. Maybe he can give us a clue as to Calypso's whereabouts."

"What are we going to tell him?"

I put my hands up in the air. "Your guess is as good as mine."

By the time we arrive at the modest house just off Old Brompton Road, my hands are slick with sweat. Silently, Leandra and I walk down the brick path and up the steps. I can feel Leandra's nerves and that ever-present darkness that lurks just beneath the surface.

"Look," she says, pointing. Someone has painted the words *Do what thou wilt* in rusty red above the door. My stomach churns as I realize that the paint could very well be blood. The line is from *The Book of the Law*, the text Mr. Crowley claims was divinely given to him by his spirit guide.

Perhaps madness runs in his family, but then again, who am I—a girl who has visions, talks to a dead boy, and feels what others are feeling—to throw stones?

Leandra's face is determined as she reaches up to knock on the door, but before she can, a man so ancient he almost looks prematurely mummified opens it.

"Please come in," he says.

Leandra's mouth forms a little *O* before she closes it and drops her hand.

He escorts us into a dusty sitting area that smells strongly of sawdust, old straw, and something dank and growing, like mushrooms sprouting from a rotting log deep in the forest. The shelves on all four walls are so cluttered they make Harrison's office look tidy. Plants sit here and there on stacks of books, which no doubt accounts for the scent of old straw.

At first glance, the room is just the normal messy abode of a bachelor professor, but my stomach churns as I look closer. Hanging on every wall are African masks, some made of wood, others of ivory or ceramic. All have wide-open mouths as if their primary purpose is to scream. The blank eyes look as if they are watching our every move. Suddenly, Leandra clutches my arm and points to a shelf near the front window.

"Are those what I think they are?"

I step forward to get a closer look and realize a moment too late what they are. Heads. Ancient shrunken heads, the kind missionaries used to bring back with warnings of the wicked savages.

"Ah, I see you've found my bonces." The timbre of the voice, slow and deep, sends a chill down my spine and I turn.

The newspaper pictures I remembered seeing of Aleister Crowley had shown a dark, handsome man, with rather florid features and round, intensely dark eyes. The man in front of me is a much heavier caricature of that man. His features have softened like melted wax and he's lost every bit of his dark, luxuriant hair. But the eyes—the eyes are the same, only so much more terrifying in person. Immensely more terrifying. A shot of fear runs through me and I feel Leandra stiffen.

I find my voice. "You are interested in Africa, Mr. Crowley?"

"I am interested in everything," he says. "Now please do me the honor of telling me who has so charmingly invaded my home?"

Leandra steps forward and starts to hold out her hand. I grab it and pull it down next to mine. Mr. Crowley's eyes flick over the movement, but he says nothing.

"My name is Anna, and this is my friend Leandra." My voice is as firm as I can make it, but I get the feeling that Mr. Crowley detects the tremor and enjoys it immensely.

He bows his head slowly. "Leandra, Anna. And what can I do for you? It's not every day I have two such lovely visitors. Would you like to have some tea or other type of refreshment?" His words are polite, but the hair on the back of my neck rises at the way he looks at us, as if he could devour us, even after a jolly big lunch.

I shake my head. "Thank you, Mr. Crowley, but we are in need of some information about your daughter."

He frowns and for the first time looks surprised. "Lola? I just heard from her. What could you possibly want to know about her?" He picks up a pencil from a cluttered side table and works it between his fingers. When I raise my eyes back to his face, his gaze is boring into mine. Classic distraction trick.

"You're an American, aren't you?" he says. "I've lived in the States. In New York, actually. On an island in the Hudson River, but my mind wanders. What do you want?"

"No. Not Lola. Your other daughter, Calypso."

The pencil in his hand snaps and the threat I feel coming from him is instantaneous.

It's followed by a wave of anger that hits me so hard I gasp, doubling over for a moment.

"Anna!" Leandra cries.

She puts her hand on my shoulder and I receive another bone-jarring hit of rage so deep and menacing that I almost cry out. I have never in my life felt anger like that, fury so wild and unleashed, it's like a deadly plague from the heavens.

And it's coming from Leandra.

I stare at her, my eyes wide, but even as it transmits itself from her hand to my shoulder, she reins it in. I straighten. "I'm fine," I tell her.

Mr. Crowley looks from me to Leandra, his eyes alight with interest. "Well, well, well. What have we here? Not just pretty women, but women of power as well. Could it be the reincarnation of Catherine Cadière, or perhaps the original Jezebel, who have come to visit me this day? At any rate, I hate to disappoint my fellow practitioners, but I don't have a daughter named Calypso."

My body trembles from the emotional hits I just took

from both Mr. Crowley and Leandra. I stare at him, uncomprehending. If Dr. Boyle lied about that, what else might he have lied about? But no. I can feel dishonesty oozing from Mr. Crowley like sweat from pores. Whatever he says, Calypso is his daughter.

"Calypso is in over her head," I continue as if he hadn't spoken. "If she isn't detained or subdued, she could go to jail, or worse, end up in an asylum."

He stares at me, his black eyes glowing like dark twin embers. I feel as if he is reading and dismissing my abilities. Leandra is frozen next to me and I can feel her trembling with the effort it's taking to control herself. We're at an impasse, the air around us crackling with power and tension.

"What has Calypso done?" he finally asks.

"Sacrificed a human," I tell him, my entire being focused on him. His jaw tightens and the disgust I feel is immediate. Whatever the rumors are, this is a man who has not sacrificed humans.

His face stills and the clenching of his jaw eases. His control over his emotions is incredible. "Assuming I am the father of a girl named Calypso, what would you have me do? Especially if I haven't seen her for months."

"Tell me where you think she might be hiding."

"Are you her friend?" he asks. I hesitate for a moment too long and comprehension dawns. "You're not. So what is your stake in all this? How do you plan on subduing her?"

"I was hoping you could tell me how to do that."

He turns away and walks to the door. For a moment I think the interview is over, but he gives his man rapid orders in a language I don't understand.

"When you subdue her, bring her to me. Do not give her to anyone else except me. You may not die if you betray me, but you will wish you had." His voice is as cold and commanding as a north wind blowing from Siberia.

Leandra is clutching my hand and I feel her shaking like a leaf. I clutch at a straw. "Why don't you come with us, sir? I am sure she will be more amenable if you are with us."

He chuckles as if we were discussing the weather instead of the life of his daughter. "Because she thinks she hates me right now. She is being quite rebellious. Plus, I am in the middle of a casting a lengthy and rather complicated spell and shouldn't leave the house." He laughs again, and the sound is so disturbing, I almost feel sorry for Calypso. But then I remember what she's capable of. Mr. Crowley can have her. They deserve each other.

The old man comes in and hands me a paper. I glance down and find an address on it. "Is this where she is?"

"That's where she could be," Mr. Crowley corrects. "And may I ask if you are properly protected?"

In answer I pull out the amulet and show it to him. To my discomfort, he steps toward me and narrows his eyes. He's so close I can see his pupils darting around the various symbols as if he's reading them. He probably is.

He licks his lips. "Where did you get that?"

I shudder. "Mr. Harry Price gave it to me."

He nods as if his suspicions were confirmed. "That should protect you fairly well." He looks at me for a moment longer. I resist the urge to step back, even though every instinct I have is screaming for me to run; but logic tells me that running will make me look like prey and Mr. Crowley is definitely predator. "Beware of mirrors. In my world, mirrors can be pathways for all sorts of undesirable visitors from the netherworld. Now, as enjoyable as this has been, ladies, I must get back to my work."

The old man firmly sees us out the door and Leandra and I find ourselves standing on the steps, just that fast.

"Did we really just have a meeting with Aleister Crowley in a room with shrunken heads?" Leandra's voice wavers and she continues without waiting for an answer. "No, don't tell me. I would think that was a nightmare, except that I don't generally have nightmares in the middle of the day."

I snort. "I do."

"Really? You must tell me about it sometime, but right now I say we quit this place."

We hurry down the steps to climb into the car. The sky is dark and ominous and I feel eyes boring into my back. "I think there's going to be a storm," she says after she starts the engine.

I'm silent but finally decide to just ask, "What happened in there? Not with Mr. Crowley but with you?"

For a moment she looks straight ahead and I think she isn't going to answer.

But then she shrugs. "I don't really talk about it. Let's just say that anger is as much a part of who I am as the color of my hair or eyes. I don't have any choice in the matter. I do, however, have a choice about how I let that anger control me. As a mother and human being, I refuse to let it affect my life. But sometimes like today, its gets the better of me. I felt the threat from him toward you. Plus, it almost felt as if he were stripping me of my control." She gives me a rueful smile. "I rarely lose control like that anymore. It nearly ruined my life once. It may have except I met Harrison. He introduced me to the Society and I learned to diffuse it. That's why I get upset at how the Society has changed. We Sensitives *need* that knowledge."

I want to ask more, but sense her reluctance to say anything else.

"You can ask Cole about it. He can give you the rest of the story. I am just not up for it today. Besides, we have more important things to consider, like what our next move should be."

I've made up my mind. I'm not going to put her at any further risk. She deserves to go spend time with her children. "I need to pick up a few supplies to confront Calypso, but after that I want to head back to the hotel, if you don't mind. I think I'll wait for Cole to come with me."

"All right. Where do we need to go?"

I tell her and she takes me to a grocer's. I'm worried she's going to see what I'm planning, but her mind has already leaped ahead to the moment when chubby arms and sticky fingers will be wrapped around her neck.

I hug her hard before she leaves me at my hotel.

"Be careful," she whispers.

"I will. Enjoy your children and stay safe."

I wave as she chugs off and then go upstairs with my bag of supplies. Once in my room, I pull a box out of my wardrobe and take out several pairs of handcuffs before selecting three. I have no idea what I'm walking into and I should be prepared.

I pack them in a small satchel and add a length of clothesline that I picked up at the grocer's. Then I pull out the solid silver knife and leather strap and sheath Cynthia had given me for my going-away present.

I strap it on to my thigh and smooth my slip down over it. I pull down the mirror from over the dresser, shivering when I remember Mr. Crowley's warning about mirrors. I set it against a chair and turn this way and that until I'm satisfied that the knife doesn't show. I haven't put it on until now. Of course, I've never had to until now.

Lastly, I take out the two-pound bag of salt I bought at the grocer's and add it to the satchel.

Taking a deep breath, I look at the materials I've gathered. They seem inadequate against an occultist who practices black magic and commits ritualistic murder to harness more power, but it's all I've got. Besides my ace in the hole.

Walter.

NINETEEN

Of course, I have to contact Walter and enlist his help, and I'm pretty hazy on how I'm going to do that. I'll think about that later. First, I have to write a note to Cole.

I'm taking a risk by not going over the plan with him beforehand, but if he knew what I'm about to do, he'd try to stop me. I'm not going to put more lives at risk because he wants to keep me safe.

Maybe Calypso does practice witchcraft, but I don't for a second believe she can wave a wand and make things happen like in a fairy tale. Spells, at least how I understand them, take time to prepare and execute. In the end, Calypso is just a girl and she's younger than I am.

Cole,

I'm going to confront Calypso. I've spoken to her father and he wants me to take her to him. I believe he will help us. Please meet me at the following address as soon as you get this note.

I jot down the address and chew on the end of the pen, wondering if I should add something personal. If something bad were to happen to me tonight, wouldn't I want him to know how I feel? Cole's sensitive, handsome face comes to mind and the image bruises my heart with tenderness.

So I simply finish with *Love*, *Anna*.

It's my plan to send the note to him and go directly to the address Mr. Crowley gave me. No matter how strained things have been between us, I know Cole and he'll be there within minutes.

As added insurance, I also send a note to Harrison. I may be foolhardy, but I'm not completely stupid. Though I suppose my intelligence or lack thereof is completely dependent on how tonight turns out.

I write another note to Louie, apologizing for missing rehearsal tonight. I hope he doesn't think I'm taking liberties because I'm top billing now.

My final note is to Mr. Gamel and the Society, declining their invitation to join. It turns into a two-page letter, telling them why I won't be involved and giving them tips on making the Society a place that I might like to be a part of someday. I finish up with:

In closing, I guess I'm just too American to accept "taxation without representation," so to speak.
Anna

That done, I lie on my bed and wait. It's important that it's almost dark when I get to where Calypso is so she won't see Cole or Harrison coming.

Unrelated thoughts float through my mind. I wonder if Harry Houdini is still in Europe and why he made it a point to come to my debut. I wonder if my mother really wants me to stay with them and if I could ever be happy not performing my magic. Then I wonder if I will be happy being on the road all the time. I wonder if Jeanne and Louie are going to have a boy or girl and what Louie will do if he quits vaudeville. I think of Cole, not the disapproving Cole, but the Cole with the wonderful laugh and the dark, velvety eyes that always have a special warmth just for me. Then Billy pops into my head, smiling as if he were channeling sunshine. And I stare at the cracks in the ceiling and face the truth. Billy's friendship, the relationship we have, is very special, but it's not the same as how I feel about Cole. My heart pounds as the truth settles over me. I love being around Billy but he's not Cole. Cole feels as necessary to me as breathing.

Restless, I check my watch and then sit up. Maybe I should try to call Walter or something, but then I shudder and decide against it. In reality, I don't know whether Walter is friend or foe. Instinctively, I feel as if he might be a friend, but what if he just wants to inhabit my body and doesn't care about Calypso or the other Sensitives or anything else that I care about? No, I can't risk it. I'll have to wait to call him . . . and hope he shows up.

It's still a bit early in the afternoon, but I'm too twitchy with nerves to rest. I put on my coat, slip my balisong into the pocket, and gather up my things. Stopping in the lobby, I hand the clerk my notes with a coin. He will give them to a messenger boy to deliver. That done, I hurry out into the wind and rain, clutching the address in one hand and my satchel in the other. The storm has arrived.

I duck my head against the rain and run right into Billy.

He puts his hands on my shoulders to steady me. "Whoa. Slow down there, Nellie." He turns on the twang, which usually makes me laugh, but I'm not in a laughing mood.

He takes one look at my face and grows immediately serious. "What's wrong?" He looks down at my satchel. "Where you going?"

Caught unaware, I'm too startled to make something up and his eyes narrow. "This has something to do with that man, doesn't it? Wherever you're going, I'm going too."

"No, you don't have to," I protest. "It's fine, I'm just going to . . . dinner."

But it's too late and we both know it. The taxicab I had the clerk call pulls up to the curb, and Billy reaches for the door. "If you want me to remain scarce, I will, but I *am* going with you."

I hesitate. I suppose I could try to make him stay, but the truth is, having Billy watch my back is tempting. Who knows when Cole will get there, and Harrison is probably taking Leandra to the train station. If neither one of them receives the notes in a timely manner, I'll be on my own. Reluctantly, I nod. "But you have to stay outside, all right?"

He nods and waves a hand toward the cab. I crawl in and scoot across the seat. The driver opens the small sliding window between the front and the back seat and I hand him the address.

"Do you trust me enough to tell me what's going on yet?" Billy's voice is quiet.

I shut my eyes for a minute as the taxi rattles and shakes down the street. "It's not a question of trust," I finally tell him. "It's not really my secret. So, no, I can't let you know what is going on."

The sun is just starting to go down, but I can still see the look in Billy's eyes. My heart wrenches at the disappointment on his face. "People are in danger," I say, unable to stand it. "It's complicated, but I have to go confront the person responsible and see if I can't keep anyone else from being hurt. I really can't tell you more, but thank you for wanting to come."

Tears clog my throat as I see his face soften. "Anna, I will always be here if you need me."

Letting myself fall in love with Billy would be so very, very tempting, but I feel the wrongness of it in my gut. Even if Billy fits perfectly into the part of my life that is performing and magic, could he ever understand the part of me that is a psychic?

I give myself a mental shake. There will be plenty of time for pondering my love life after the Sensitives are safe and Calypso has been taken out of the equation.

I look out the window, my heart sinking. Wherever Calypso is holding the Sensitives, it's not in an upper-crust neighborhood. In fact, it's as seedy a part of London as I have yet seen. There are fewer streetlamps and many of those don't work. Those that do, illuminate shuttered buildings and people huddled in doorways.

The driver pulls up in front of a dilapidated apartment building several stories high. My heart races and I take a deep breath. This is not good. Had it been a house, I would have felt more comfortable leaving Billy to guard the front. As it is, I'm not sure what to do. The driver passes me back the paper with the address on it. My heart sinks further when I see the apartment number 13 on it. Had that been there before? I rub my eyes. I hear a faint buzzing in my ears but when it doesn't grow any louder, I ignore it. Apparently the pendant is already working and blocking the mental confusion.

"What now?" Billy asks after we exit the taxi. "I'm not letting you go in there alone."

I shake my head and pull my coat tighter around me against the wind. "I have to go in. Someone inside one of the flats may need my help. Can you watch the door for me from the hall? If I don't come out in, I don't know, thirty minutes or so, you can bust in after me. Isn't that what you cowboys do?"

I'm babbling and he knows it. I can feel his apprehension through his hand on my arm, but I also feel his determination. He won't let anything happen to me if he can help it.

We enter the building. Most of the electric lightbulbs in the hallway are broken and the plaster is falling off the walls in places. I shiver as a sense of foreboding fills me. The building itself heaves with the anguish of centuries, and my skin crawls with the eerie sense that the halls have seen unimagined horrors—murders, ghosts, and intrigue of the most despicable sort.

Calypso is not the first person to commit murder here. I feel spirits all around me, touching me with their long bony fingers, whispering in my ears with their foul breath.

Maybe it's my imagination.

"If I'd had some warning, I would have brought my guns," Billy whispers next to me. "This is not a good place."

Or maybe it's not my imagination.

In my experience, apartment buildings like this are loud, but no noise issues from behind the doors we pass. Perhaps the occupants know to keep quiet and let the ghosts reign. Or perhaps there are no occupants.

We arrive at number thirteen and I twitch my head. As if he's done this type of thing before, Billy melts back into the shadows. He probably would have made a good bank robber had he wanted to, I think inanely. Of course, any women present would have been able to give a detailed description of him, so maybe not. I place my hand on the doorknob and then jerk it back. My heart pulses in my ears.

It's warm.

Maybe from her black magic?

It's locked. Taking out my picklock, I silently make short work of the lock. Then I clutch at the amulet at my throat, say a quick prayer, and make the sign of the cross over my chest even though I'm not Catholic. In spite of all that, fear slices through my body. Nothing in my life could have prepared me for this kind of terror.

Heart in my throat, I open the door as quietly as I can. It takes a moment for my eyes to adjust to the dim light, but when I do, I gasp. Red silk hangs from the walls like I've entered the apartment of a sultan. Cushions and low tables line the walls. My eyes take in a window on one side and a hallway on the other. A giant mirror in an ornate wooden frame hangs on one wall. I shudder, remembering Mr. Crowley's warning. For a moment I think I'm alone, but then I spot a young man propped upright in the corner. He's bound and gagged and his eyes are closed. His skin is ashen and he's so thin, his cheekbones jut out of his face like knives. I pray that whoever it is is still alive. Then I hear a low moan coming from down the hall and gay laughter that is so out of place that a shiver runs down my spine.

Calypso.

Moving silently, I first check on the man. His eyes fly open in terror at my touch and I put my finger to my lips. He nods. I take the gag out of his mouth. He licks his lips.

"Is she alone?" I whisper. Unable to speak, he nods.

I want to cut him loose, but first things first. I need to make a circle of salt on the floor to bind her with and then get her to step into it. The odds are slim, but if I can't subdue her, I won't have a chance. Who knows what kind of evil she's capable of? Pulling the bag of salt out of my satchel, I quickly make a large circle in the middle of the room. It's not straight—my hands are shaking too badly to pour a perfect circle, but I think it will work.

The silver knife is sharper and sturdier than my balisong, so I reach under my skirt and pull it out of its sheath. I'm about halfway through the young man's bindings when the hair on the back of my neck tingles and his eyes widen.

I know Calypso's behind me before I even turn around.

Her short hair is mussed as if she just crawled out of bed, and she's wearing a long, peacock-blue dress with kimono sleeves. She claps delightedly, causing the sleeves to float like bat's wings. "Oh! You came! I was so worried you wouldn't!" Then she eyes the knife in my hand. "Oh, you won't need that."

Suddenly something begins squeezing my hand, and within seconds the pressure increases so much that I drop the knife in pain. It falls to the floor with a clatter.

How did she do that?

My stomach knots as I search for a probable explanation. Psychokinesis, as far as I know, is just a parlor trick done by fake mediums. The only person near me is the young man, whose arms are still bound. Which leaves spiritual interference. Considering what I now know concerning her father, that's a very real possibility. I glance at the floor. She's about three feet from stepping into the circle.

"Why?"

"Why won't you be needing your knife? Or why all of this?" She waves her hands around the room.

"Why all of this? Why didn't you just send me an invitation?" I speak casually, but my heart is pounding so loudly that I'm surprised she can't hear it. Or maybe she can, it's difficult to tell. I can feel something hovering nearby, but no matter how often I turn my head I can't catch it. I can almost see it, but not quite. It's like a dark shadow, or a puff of smoke in the corner of my eye, that disappears when looked at directly.

Calypso tilts her head to the side in a strange birdlike gesture as if listening for something. Or perhaps she's listening *to* something.

Then she straightens and smiles, her black eyes flat. "This way was so much more fun! Plus, I needed time to gather everything together. According to Aiwass, everything comes together in good time."

The name jolts me. That's what Walter said during the séance. "Who is Aiwass?" Suddenly, the thing out of my line of vision is swirling around me. I swallow convulsively.

"My father's spirit guide. Aiwass left him long ago and came to me, because he knows I have far more potential than even the great Aleister Crowley."

Her voice is petulant, like a spoiled child's, and I shudder.

Everything, all of this, is because she wanted to show up her father?

My God.

But Aiwass, the spirit guide, is not the figment of a deranged mind. The scent of evil, like rotting meat, assaults my nostrils. My stomach roils and I cling to my composure by the thinnest thread. Why did I come in here alone? *Why did I come here at all?*

Behind me, the young man whimpers and I remember. There's more at stake here than just me and my fear.

I keep my eyes on Calypso. Somehow I have to keep her from looking down. Three more steps. With more self-control than I knew I possessed, I focus on Calypso and not on the vaporous evil weaving around me like a snake dancing around a mouse. I need to force her to make a mistake—to look away, step into the circle, anything. Frantically I use the only thing I know that really upsets her. "Maybe Aiwass is using you to get to your father."

Calypso frowns. "No. You don't know anything. You think you do, but you don't. For instance, you don't know why I chose you in particular."

Her gaze is unfocused as if she's been smoking hashish. I move forward, willing her to do the same. She takes a step and my pulse speeds up. Just a bit more . . . "You chose me for my good taste in hats, didn't you?" I say.

Calypso stops and laughs, a lilting girlish sound that sounds freakishly innocent. "No, silly. I was going to use Cole until I met you. But you had such interesting abilities and so much power. I felt it the moment I met you. Everyone was talking about it. So I chose you!"

I take another step toward her, but my toes are at the salt and I don't want to get into the circle with her. "You chose me for what?"

The spirit being is still undulating around me as if sniffing for a way in. I shiver as the coldness brushes my skin.

"I chose you because I want your abilities. I discovered an incantation, you see. One that will allow me to claim your powers for my own."

I have one hand on my balisong in my pocket, but I don't want to pull it. For some reason giving Calypso a knife seems like a bad idea. "That's why you killed Pratik?"

She nods. "I needed the blood. Dr. Boyle was angry because he wanted Pratik alive. Pratik's ability to see people's auras would have come in very handy in Dr. Boyle's quest for fortune. He would have been able to tell Dr. Boyle exactly who was corruptible and who was not. But I decided I didn't need Dr. Boyle's money anymore. If I could combine my abilities and your abilities, I could make all the money I needed."

She moves to a table and picks up a small urn. My heart sinks as she steps farther from the circle. Dipping her fingers into the urn, she touches her forehead and her nose and chin. I gag when I realize what it is.

Blood.

Aiwass leaves my side as if attracted to the scent of blood. Again, Calypso tilts her head to one side as if listening, and then her eyes turn to me. "What do you have? What are you wearing?"

I glance down at myself before I realize what she means.

The pendant.

"Take it off!" she commands.

I cover it with one hand, protecting it. "No, thank you. I think I'll keep it." I must get her to step forward. "How did you use Cole to get to me? I thought you couldn't influence Sensitives?"

She smiles and I shiver at the craftiness that comes over her face. "I can if they wish to be influenced. Pratik wanted to believe that I was in love with him. Cole was more difficult because he's in love with you, but even he was flattered by my attentions. Men are so very, very easy."

"If men are so easy, why can't you influence your father?" I taunt, trying to push her over the edge. I'll never gain the upper hand as long as she is in control of herself. Not with Aiwass by her side.

Calypso's mouth tightens at my words and she slaps her hand against her thigh repeatedly. "My father is the most powerful man in the world! Don't talk about my father! Your father won't even acknowledge your existence."

My stomach knots. In spite of the situation, her words still sting. "How do you know that?" I demand, even though I know I shouldn't let her sidetrack me.

A triumphant smile curves her lips as if she knows that she got to me. "Aiwass told me. He tells me everything."

I shake off her words and focus. "My father cares about

me in his way. Does yours? I'm not so sure. He and I had a long visit today, you know."

"You're lying!" she says through gritted teeth, but I sense her uncertainty.

I feel Aiwass whipping back to me as if frustrated. Bless Harry Price, I think reverently. The tension in the room presses in on me from all sides, making it difficult to breathe. "No, I'm not. He wants you to come see him. He sent me to bring you home."

Her face contorts. "Liar!"

The door opens with a bang and both Calypso and I jump.

It's Billy, holding Mr. Casperson around the neck with one arm.

"You didn't tell me what to do if someone was going in, so I improvised."

Billy takes in the situation with a glance but doesn't comprehend what's going on or where the danger is. All he sees is two young women arguing.

Mr. Casperson slumps, and Billy is momentarily thrown off balance. He regains it quickly, but doesn't loosen his hold. Then he moves to my side, dragging the now inert man with him.

Out of the corner of my eye, I see Calypso's lips curving up into a smile. "Let the man fall to the ground," she says.

Her intent hits me as Billy's eyes glaze over.

What have I done?

TWENTY

"Billy, run!" I scream.

But it's too late.

"Let the man drop!" Calypso commands.

As if puzzled by his own behavior, Billy lets Mr. Casperson go. The man drops to the floor, apparently unconscious. Calypso turns to me, triumph written on her face. *"Get Anna's necklace."*

I whisk my balisong out of my pocket and flick it open, but Billy is too fast for me and the chain is broken off my neck before I can get my knife up to his arm. The pendant clatters to the floor and I hear a hiss as the spirit makes a beeline for me. I shove Billy out of the way and bend to try to grab the necklace.

"No," Calypso cries before running toward me. I glance up when she screams out in frustration.

She's in the salt circle.

The spirit hits me and I can feel an excruciatingly cold

mist penetrating my chest. I want to cry out, to scream for help, but there is no one here who can help me. My ribs feel as if they are being pried apart as the spirit forces its way inside me. I drop to my knees as my body convulses in protest. Instinctively, I know that if this spirit possesses me, I will never be the same. Even now I feel the insanity eating away at the edges of my mind. *Cole!* I reach for him with everything I have but feel no answering spark, no warmth of connection. I am alone and for the first time I feel complete and utter despair. Then I remember.

"Walter!" I cry out with every bit of fight I have left.

Suddenly, the spirit is violently torn away from me and I whimper. With effort, I raise my head, blinking as my sight clears.

Calypso is still screaming, charging about the circle like a caged animal. The salt circle worked! I nearly sob in relief until my eyes take in the horror happening in the air over her head.

Two separate entities are clashing in the air so violently that I almost imagine I hear the crashing of thunder, though in reality, their fight is eerily silent and the only sound in the room is Calypso's howling madness.

Billy slumps back against the wall, watching, horror written all over his face, as the mists momentarily become one, part, and then come together again. Slowly, one of them takes on the form of a slightly built young man in uniform.

Walter!

Calypso rushes toward the edge of the salt circle. I snatch

up my pendant and scramble back at the fury on her face. She turns toward Billy. “Break the circle,” she shrieks. “Break it! Break it!”

Billy stands to do her bidding but doesn’t understand the command.

“Billy, don’t listen to her. She’s evil!” I try to reach him, but he just looks confused at my words.

Walter and Aiwass come together, and I feel rather than hear Walter’s soft cry. My heart breaks as I watch him start to crumble. He’s no match for Aiwass’s power. Like Billy, he came to protect me and, like Billy, is in danger for his trouble.

As if sensing her spirit guide’s imminent victory, Calypso regains control of herself. “On the floor, Billy, clean up the salt on the floor.”

Billy looks down, uncomprehending and I hear Walter whimpering.

No. I will not let her win.

In one smooth lightning-fast movement, I bend and grab both my knife and the satchel I’d dropped earlier. I somersault into the circle and am on my feet before Calypso can react. I try to get the rope out of my bag, but as I work to free it, she throws herself at me and I’m knocked to the floor. I slash sideways with my knife and my stomach turns as it glances off something soft.

Calypso pulls back and cries out, grabbing at her arm. The scent of blood draws Aiwass away from Walter and he is on her in a flash. I can’t tell what he’s doing, but her screams fill the apartment. I crawl backward in horror.

Something shatters behind me, and I whirl in time to see flashes of light as the mirror erupts into a thousand shards of glass. Billy hurls himself in front of me, protecting me with his body.

The pathway to the netherworld must be closing.

"Calypso!" A voice thunders and everyone, even the spirits, freezes.

Trembling, I turn. Standing in the doorway like a towering monolith is Aleister Crowley.

With a rush, Walter is by my side. I feel the cold of him but welcome it for the first time.

Mr. Crowley waves his hand and Aiwass dissolves into mist, then vanishes altogether. Some of the heaviness in the room disappears with the spirit. Calypso stares at her father from the floor, her eyes transfixed.

Her father steps toward her and stops at the edge of the salt circle. "Miss Van Housen," he says to me without taking his eyes off Calypso. "I've come to take my daughter home. Please break the salt circle."

He senses my hesitation. "She won't harm anyone. Not ever again." Calypso winces but is perfectly still. His voice is so commanding that I find myself doing what he says and, using my foot, I break the circle. Mr. Crowley holds out his hand and, whimpering like a beaten puppy, Calypso slowly gets up off the floor and steps to his side. I can see the blood dripping from her arm and almost feel sorry for her. Almost.

Mr. Crowley turns toward me. "I strongly suggest you remove everyone from the building as soon as possible. You're protected, but the others are not. There are many malicious spirits here and I have no control over what sort of mischief they might do to your friends." He gives me a formal nod of his head. "It was a pleasure meeting you, Miss Van Housen. Be careful how you handle your abilities. Someone with your special talents will always be at risk. Your spiritual defender won't always be able to protect you."

With another nod, he leads his daughter away by the hand and disappears through the open doorway.

The instant after that I see another form at the entry.

"Anna!"

"Cole!"

He rushes toward me and sweeps me up in his arms. "Why did you come here? Are you insane?" He holds me close, his heart beating beneath my cheek.

"I had to stop her," I tell him simply.

"We can talk about it later. Let's get everyone out of here. Harrison is waiting downstairs. I wouldn't let him come up."

I sense his rebuke and know I deserve it for bringing Billy without taking into account Calypso's special abilities.

Billy picks up my silver knife and finishes cutting through the man's bindings. His mouth is drawn up into a tight line and I know I have a lot of explaining to do.

Cole's eyes widen. "Jonathon!"

The young man nods at Cole but says nothing.

Mr. Casperson wakes up and I toss Cole a pair of handcuffs.

He raises his brows but slips them on Mr. Casperson's wrists. No use taking chances.

"What were you thinking?" Cole asks as he cuffs him.

Mr. Casperson's face falls into the lines of a beaten man. "I wasn't," he says in a weary voice. "I just did what she wanted. She told me to hold Pratik and I did."

My stomach churns.

"I'll check out the rest of the rooms, see if there's anyone else," Billy says, avoiding my eyes. He skirts around me and I wonder what's wrong until I realize he can see Walter, who is still standing by my side.

I face the wan young man who died so young. His cheeks are hollow and his skin has a yellow cast, but I can see where he might have been handsome when he was alive. I can imagine how proud his mother must have been of him.

"Thank you."

He shrugs and his melancholy drenches me like a soft wash of tears. *"There isn't much else for me to do but to look in on you from time to time. You're the only one I can talk to."*

"Isn't there somewhere else you can go?" I ask gently, not caring if the others think I am talking to myself.

"Some kind of white light? A portal? A doorway?" Walter shrugs. *"If there is, I haven't found it."*

"I'm sorry." And I am. It must be horrible to be able to see people but not communicate. No wonder he stuck close to me.

"You don't mind if I talk to you from time to time when I can, do you?" His voice is wistful. *"I can't do it all the time. I think it has to do with place . . ."*

I'm a bit uncomfortable at the thought of having a ghost stalk me, but what can I say? He probably saved my life. "No. That's would be fine. Sometimes."

He nods and then with a sad little salute, disappears.

Billy brings out three other young men. All are rubbing their raw wrists where they'd been bound. One of them is sporting a black eye.

A scant thirty minutes later Billy, Cole, Harrison, and I are sitting in front of my hotel in Cole's motorcar. Cole had telephoned Mr. Gamel before coming and he was waiting for us by the time we came down. He took the other Sensitives, Jonathon, and Mr. Casperson, home with him. I wondered what would happen to Mr. Casperson and then decided I don't want to know.

Billy opens the door. "Thanks for the rescue," he says. "Right in the nick of time and all that."

Cole nods.

Reluctantly I get out of the motorcar. It doesn't make any sense for me to stay with Cole as he has to go drop Jonathon off, but I am hesitant to leave him. There is so much I want to tell him.

"I'll see you tomorrow?" I search the darkness of Cole's eyes. All I am feeling from him is relief and a strange sense of fear.

He nods again and I close the car door, feeling as if I've just lost everything.

Billy and I walk into the lobby of our hotel and I know I need to talk to him, to tell him the truth of how I feel.

If I can find the words.

I place my hands on Billy's shoulders and he turns to me, pain in every line of his body. "I can't thank you enough," I start, and he puts a finger against my lips.

"Don't thank me. I let you down."

"You did not! You probably saved my life."

He shakes his head. "The dead boy did more for you than I did. I don't know what happened there, but I'm sorry for breaking your necklace. Oh hell, I don't even understand half of what went on tonight."

"I wish I could tell you . . ."

He shakes his head. "I don't want to know. Just know that I would do anything for you, Anna. You're special." He gives me a lopsided smile. "I didn't know how special until tonight."

"You're special, too. You saw Walter. The dead soldier."

I glance at the clerk behind the desk and draw Billy farther away.

He shakes his head. "My aunt occasionally saw loved ones who had passed on. I've seen a couple of ghosts in my time, but it's not something I seek out. Don't make more of it than what it is. There are all sorts of things in this world I don't understand and have no wish to. I have no desire to mess with the spirit world. Not like you do."

It's on my tongue to tell him that I don't want to mess with the spirit world either, but I keep my peace. What if Mr. Crowley is right? What if I'll always be a target because of my abilities? So I just give Billy a regretful smile and gaze up into the sunshiny blue of his eyes. "Thank you for everything, Bronco Billy. You are one of the best men I have ever known." There is so much more I want to say, but it's all tangled up inside, so I say nothing about how much I care for him but that my heart belongs to someone else.

I sense from the resignation emanating from him that he already knows.

The corner of his mouth quirks upward into a sad smile. "Aw shucks, miss. Now you should go get some rest. I'll see you at the theater, right?"

I nod.

"Then go on with you." He turns away from me, his shoulders resolute.

In my room, I try to do as he says and even change into my nightclothes, but in spite of my fatigue, I'm oddly fidgety. I sit on my bed, tuck my feet up under my nightgown, and stare out the window at the glittering lights of London. I wonder about Jonathon and the other Sensitives. Would they choose to go to Dr. Boyle, whose greedy ambitions cause him to treat other human beings like cattle? Or would they choose to stay at the Society, where they were only valued for the information they could impart? Why wasn't there another choice? Would Calypso have been different had she had real family or were Sensitives just inherently more susceptible to insanity?

I had thought all of my questions about my life would be answered once I moved to London to perform my magic, but instead I just have more questions. Should I stay on the tour when it goes to the States, or should I move to Paris and let my mother try to be a real parent? Do I want to attend a university somewhere? What do I want to do with my life? The only real answer I have is who I want to do it with.

Cole.

Restlessly, I get off the bed and, with difficulty, open the rain-swollen ancient window. The storm has passed, making the London night look washed clean, and I stare out at the lights, as brilliant as stars. The small side street that the hotel is located on is empty and quiet. I shiver as the chill of the air hits my skin, but it feels so fresh that I lean farther forward into the darkness, waiting, as if I'm on the edge of the cliff that is the rest of my life.

Suddenly the lights of a motorcar turn the corner. My heart leaps up in my throat because I know who it is before it even comes to a stop in front of the hotel.

Without thinking, I turn and race down the stairs and across the lobby past a surprised clerk, my nightgown billowing out behind me. The night air chills my skin but I ignore it.

"Anna!"

I leap into Cole's arms and he catches me up close to him. For a long moment neither one of us speaks as our psychic connection is made. Time slows and is measured only in the strong, beloved heartbeat against my ear.

I'm not sure how long we stay that way before he loosens his grip just a touch so that I slide down his body until my bare feet touch the ground. I know we have to talk, that there are things that must be said, but I also know from the lilting happiness inside me that it will be all right in the end.

"Are you in love with him?" he asks first. The pain in his voice brings tears to my eyes. I know I need to choose my words very carefully. There are disadvantages to having someone you love be able to feel what you feel.

I stare into his eyes, letting him see, as well sense, what I am feeling. "I could love Billy if I let myself. He's a wonderful friend and a wonderful man and he understands things about me that you won't ever understand."

I feel his pulsing misery and I continue. "But I can't love him, because I'm already in love with you. There is no room left for him in my heart because it's already filled with you."

Cole's arms tighten around me convulsively. The relief he feels almost makes me cry out.

"I love you, too," he says, and I hear the catch in his voice.

"Then why don't you ever tell me that?" I ask against his chest.

"It's hard for me. I don't know why. And things have been so crazy since you got back from your trip to France. When I saw you coming down the street with Billy the other night, I just kept thinking that I had lost you and maybe it was for the best."

I tilt my head to see his face in the glow of the streetlamp. "How can you say that?"

"I don't know what my presence in your life is going to do to your abilities. I won't ever let myself hurt you in any way."

"It will hurt me more to lose you than it would to deal with whatever happens."

"I love you, Anna."

"I love you too, Cole," I murmur before his lips meet mine. I'm not alone anymore. I won't ever be alone again.

In that moment, things become clear for me in a way they never have before and I know what I'm going to do. With Cole's help, I'll build a new Society and it'll be a place where Sensitives are valued as human beings. A place where we can learn from one another and no one will have to feel as if he or she is totally alone. Together, we can help others find their way. Then I stop thinking and let myself be swept away by the enchantment of kissing Cole.

I know real magic when I feel it.

ACKNOWLEDGMENTS

I was blessed to have a cadre of the most talented people who supported *Born of Deception* and I thank them from the bottom of my heart. Number one will always be my agent, Mollie Glick, who believes in my writing and my career and whose foresight changed my life. I also have to thank my editor, Kristin Rens, whose brilliance and editing choices consistently make my books better. Big sparkly props also go to my copy editor, Martha Schwartz, who has the thankless job of cleaning up my messes; production editor Kathryn Silsand; publicity guru Caroline Sun; Emilie Polster and Stephanie Hoffman in marketing; and of course, book designer extraordinaire Ray Shappell.

Personally, I need to thank my kid lit author friends, April Henry, Cat Winters, Amber Keyser, Inara Scott, and Miriam Forster, who write with me and listen to me whine. I have to thank my tribe, Anita, Dave, Jasmine, Jeff, Billy, and Vickie, who have been my friends through the good, the bad, and the ugly.

Thanks to my son, Ethan, and his wife, Megan, for being awesome and huge thanks to my daughter, Megan, for being the other girl in my house.

And as always, thanks to my heart, Alan.